MAGIC LOST

MAGIC LOST

THE EVERMORES CHRONICLES™ BOOK 6

MARTHA CARR
MICHAEL ANDERLE

Cover by Fantasy Book Design

A Michael Anderle Production

LMBPN Publishing
PMB 196, 2540 South Maryland Pkwy
Las Vegas, NV 89109

Version 1.00, April 2022
ebook ISBN: 979-8-88541-349-7
Print ISBN: 979-8-88541-350-3

THE MAGIC LOST TEAM

Thanks to our JIT Readers

Diane L. Smith
Dave Hicks
Zacc Pelter
Dorothy Lloyd

Editor

SkyHunter Editing Team

CHAPTER ONE

Fran Berryman roller-skated down the wintry, windswept streets of Mana Valley and up to the door of the Worn Threads carpet shop. She stopped outside long enough to take off her skates and switch into her sequined sneakers, shivering as she did so, then strapped the skates to her backpack and hurried inside.

Gail Ortiz was standing on a stepladder at the far side of the store while her husband Raulo held the ladder steady. Gail looked around as Fran came in, smiling brightly from behind her long blue hair.

"Hey there, Fran!" Gail waved a tinsel-covered cardboard star. "Happy New Year!"

"Happy New Year to you guys too!" Fran peered into the box by Raulo's feet, which was full of a growing heap of tinsel, baubles, and other ornaments from the midwinter festivities. "Do you have to take all of these down?"

"It's another year. That means the season has passed."

"But they're so bright and colorful. It seems a shame to lock them away in the back room."

"I'd lock them away in the basement, but it's full of you guys. If we left them up all year, they'd lose their impact."

"Not for me. I always love bright things."

Gail laughed. "Tell you what, why don't you take one of the baubles? You can hang it over your desk all year to keep things festive."

"Really? That's so generous."

Gail and Raulo exchanged a look, then they both burst out laughing.

"You know that you and your company are worth more than this whole shop and its contents, right?" Raulo waved, then hurriedly clutched the ladder again as that started to wobble. "A bauble doesn't seem so generous by comparison."

"I..." Fran was about to deny his grand statement of her value, but then she remembered the report on Mana Wave Industries that had been on the news stream that morning, and she decided that maybe, just maybe, he had a point. "The bauble's personal, though. That makes it a generous gift."

"Aren't you sweet?" Gail came down the ladder. "Shouldn't you be getting to work?"

"I will, but this is a big choice..."

Fran looked over the selection of baubles in the box, carefully trying to pick out the best one. They were all so splendid. She settled on a large green one, so shiny that she saw her face reflected in its surface, with tinsel around the middle.

"Thank you. And Happy New Year again!"

Clutching her chosen bauble tight, she hurried to the

back of the store and through the door that led into the basement.

She stopped at the top of the stairs, caught off-guard by the sound of voices. She was used to sharing the Mana Wave office with five other magicals, the team she'd founded the company with. The noise that greeted her now was more than they'd ever made together. It was a roaring, rattling tumult of voices that echoed from the concrete ceiling and around the open space, mounting in volume as it went.

With tentative steps, she descended the stairs and looked around. The room that had seemed so excessive before now felt overcrowded. Every spare space was full of desks and computers, except on the far side of the room, where there were workbenches and racks of tools instead. Some sort of magical occupied every seat: gnomes, dwarves, elves, witches, wizards, Arpaks, all jostling for space as they hurried between desks, excitedly talking into phones or tapping away on keyboards.

"What..." she muttered. "How..."

"Fran, you're here!" Bart Trumbling, the white-haired gnome who was Mana Wave's chief financial officer, walked up to her with a smile and a fistful of receipts. "Did you have a good break?"

"Great, thanks." She kept looking around, wide-eyed. "I got to spend loads of time with Cam, which was lovely. Bart, who are all these people?"

"They're the staff we agreed to hire to manage sales and administration and handle all the extra business we've got coming in. That's the sales team themselves..." He pointed at a large bank of desks where everyone seemed to be on the phone. "Over there are our internal administrators, including the purchasing clerk and secretary. Around the central workbench with Singar and Smokey is the expanded technical team. Elethin's assistant is in the corner…"

"Elethin has an assistant now?"

"Oh yes. Do you have any idea how much more communications and PR work we have to do? They're still covering marketing as well, although I've got interviews to fill that niche tomorrow."

"Should I have an assistant?"

"Definitely. If you could talk Gruffbar into taking one on, that would be great. We can't have all our legal affairs relying on one dwarf, not when things are moving so fast."

"They are?"

Bart took her by the arm and led her through the throng to his desk. He opened his laptop and brought up a graph.

"This is a sales record for the Fun Delivery System, week by week."

Fran's jaw dropped. "It keeps going up!"

"It does."

"I thought that once some people had it, sales would fall."

"Eventually, yes, but hopefully, we'll have a Mark Two by then. This spreadsheet lists all the people inquiring about creating licensed software for the system."

"It's a long list."

"It is."

"Hey, I recognize that name. And that one. Wow, they want to work with us?"

"They do. This list is all the law enforcement agencies, on Oriceran and Earth, that want to put in orders for our magical criminal containment unit."

"We need a name for that thing."

"Elethin's working on it."

"Cool." Fran looked around the room at all the people. "I get it now." A grin filled her face. "This is amazing. It's a proper tech company, just like I always dreamed of!"

"We're getting there. Speaking of which, there are some issues we should discuss as soon as you have time, like the IPO and what we make next. But really, we should prioritize recruiting your assistant so they can prioritize these tasks in your calendar."

"I'm going to have my own PA. I can't believe this is real." Fran looked across the room where a large, heavy cloth hung across one wall. A dwarf was moving heavily laden trolleys from the workshop to that side, and there was a *bang* as each one slammed against the wall. "What's that guy doing?"

Bart looked over.

"Ah, yes. We're moving some of the testing and development work to a back room at the new factory site to create a quicker feedback loop. Albed is getting some of the equipment ready for transport."

"He needs to be more careful."

Fran started moving across the office, but it was hard to make headway with so many more desks and people. Bart followed her as she pushed her way past her new and unfamiliar employees.

"It's all right," he said. "Singar oversaw the packing of

the tools and components. They can take some rough handling."

"That's not what I'm worried about. It's the mirror, and who's in it."

"The mirror?" Bart finally realized what was bothering Fran. "Albed! Stop, now!"

The dwarf turned to look at them. As he did so, the secondhand trolley he was pushing turned on its uneven wheels. One corner slammed into the cloth hanging from the wall. A cracking sound made half the people in the room turn to look.

"Oh, no," Fran whispered.

The cloth fell and for a moment, revealed a vast mirror. It reflected the room and the people in it, but there were other people too—a scarred and sneering elf, a gnome with two missing fingers, a witch and a wizard, both dressed in black with silver-blond hair. The attackers who the Mana Wave team had trapped in the mirror back when they were starting up. They all stared out angrily at the company's success.

Then the crack that Albed had made at the bottom corner of the mirror spread and became a web, a wave of them rushing across the surface of the glass. It could almost have been beautiful if it wasn't so ominous.

The mirror collapsed, pieces crashing to the floor, and the prisoners stepped out. The witch pointed straight at Fran.

"It's her fault," the witch hissed. "Get her."

The elf raised his hand and a bolt of magic flew at Fran. She flung herself aside and collided with a desk, knocking over the computer sitting on it. The magic flew past only inches from her shoulder and froze one of the sales team.

Fran pulled out her wand. She didn't need it to cast magic, but she didn't need her employees to know that. She pointed it at the witch and fired off a bright beam of light that hit the witch in the eyes. She screeched and staggered back, temporarily blinded.

"Grab her while you can!" Fran shouted.

Singar, the Willen in charge of the company's hardware, leaped from her workbench onto the witch, and her team followed, overwhelming the target beneath a pile of bodies.

Fran turned, but the wizard was already on her. He punched her and grabbed her arm, twisting it around, trying to drag the wand from her grasp. He fought with skill and determination, shifting his weight as Fran struggled, keeping a tight hold on her. A few months before, that might have defeated Fran, but she was a different person now. Time training with her father, learning the ways of war and hunting had revealed talents she never knew she had. She twisted one way, then back, catching the wizard off-guard. Her elbow slammed into his stomach, he buckled over, and she slid from his grip.

"Got him." Gruffbar, her dwarf head of legal affairs, wrapped a muscled arm around the wizard's neck and pressed him against the desk. "You keep on top of this."

The scarred elf was still standing by the remains of the mirror, flinging out spells at anyone who came close. Elethin, the head of communications, wove her magic as she approached him, deflecting his spells as deftly as she launched hers. He countered those, dispelling their power before they could touch him, and the two elves stood facing each other amid a magical haze, trapped in a stalemate.

Fran strode up to them, taking her pack off her back as she went, so that its whole weight hung from one hand. She swung it back, feeling the weight, judging how it would move and what force it would take to give it a solid swing.

"Hey there!" she called.

The elf turned his head at the sound of Fran's cheery greeting. At the same moment, she swung the bag forward with all her strength. It whipped up, skates swinging from the side, and the skates hit the elf under the chin, snapping his head back. His magic flickered and vanished as one of Elethin's spells hit him in the face, leaving him doubly dazed. Fran hit him once more with the backpack, and he collapsed like a dropped sack.

"Three down," she said. "Where's the last one?"

"Over here," Bart called. He had the gnome from the mirror pinned to the floor with one arm twisted behind her back. Her other hand reached for something on the floor, a piece of wood the size of a domino.

"What's that?" Fran asked.

"I don't know," Bart admitted. "I figure that if she wants it, she shouldn't have it."

"I agree." Fran kicked the wood away. "Now what do we do with this lot?"

She looked around the room. Half of their new employees huddled by the stairs or under their desks, alarmed by the sudden and unexpected outbreak of violence. The other half helped out or stood nearby, looking for a way to be useful. That seemed like a good sign.

"I've got an idea." Singar left her team holding their captive and hurried back to her part of the workshop, whiskers twitching excitedly. She returned to the broken mirror with a black plastic box, magical runes, and digital displays glowing on its sides, wires trailing from openings in the top. "It's a chance to test this."

"What is that?" Fran asked.

"A new, more adaptable model of the containment unit."

"We really need a proper name for that thing."

"You're not wrong." Singar was attaching wires to large pieces of the broken mirror. "Right now, I'm more interested in substance than style."

"Doesn't the containment unit need a frame to cast its field around?"

"Not anymore." Singar tapped the box. "I've refined both the magical and the technological components to detach the physical mechanism powering the containment field from the way it's structured. It relies on energy lattices and runic webs rather than physical markers of a magical effect."

"Could you maybe explain that differently?" Fran looked at the wired-up mirror shards, which were starting to glow. "I mean, I get the principle, but what does it mean in practice?"

"Short version, this box can turn any mirror, or piece of mirror, into a containment unit, as long as it's plugged in. The size of the subject it can hold depends on the size of the mirror. With time, I hope to scale the device down to make it more portable and make the whole containment process more efficient." Singar grinned a wicked grin. "Trust me. Our security clients are going to love this."

Fran still didn't love that they had security clients, but it helped to support the fun side of the business, and she had to admit that the work was doing some good in the world. "All right, then. Let's give it a go."

With some struggle and many curses, they maneuvered the captives onto a piece of mirror each. Singar hit a button on the box, and magic fields shot up from the mirror pieces, trapping each captive behind a flickering haze.

"Great work," Fran said. "That's so cool."

"We've come a long way in less than a year." Singar nodded proudly. "What do you want to do with these jerks?"

"Um…"

"I'll take them to the Silver Griffins," Gruffbar said. "Dealing with criminals is their job."

"Won't that raise some awkward questions?" Fran asked. "Like, why have we had these guys here for so long?"

"Someone sent them to commit criminal acts. They'll get muddled enough trying to come up with alibis, never mind explaining what's happened since. I'll have space to talk our way out of this."

"Okay. I trust you."

It felt good to say that. Fran had built such a great team to run her company. She would trust any of them with her life. They'd come a long way.

The prisoners struggled futilely against the containment fields as Gruffbar and some employees carried them toward the stairs on their mirrors. At that moment, the door at the top opened, and a cat walked in. More accurately, a shifter walked in, in the shape of a cat.

"What's with all the mess?" Smokey asked as he prowled down the stairs. He sniffed the air, and his whiskers twitched. "Why does it smell of spent magic in here?"

"Remember these guys?" Fran pointed at the captives. "They got out."

"Oh." Smokey considered that for a moment, swishing his tail from side to side. Then he came as close as a cat could to shrugging. "If that's all, I've got code to write. This business isn't going to run itself."

He hopped up onto his desk and powered up his computer. Other employees took his lead and returned to their work while Gruffbar wrestled captives up the stairs.

Fran looked around with pride. Nothing could throw the people she worked with.

CHAPTER TWO

Across town, Fran's roommate also felt proud of herself and the people she worked with.

"This way," the restaurant's manager said, leading her past the kitchen to the back room. "Can I say what a pleasure it is to host you ladies again?"

"That's very kind of you," Josie said. "It's always great to come here."

"Tell all your friends." The manager winked. "Even if they can't all join your special club."

A door was pushed open, and Josie stepped into a comfortably appointed back room, with a dozen chairs set around a circular table. A witch occupied all but one of those chairs, and all but one of those witches worked at the same place as Josie—Philgard Technologies, one of Mana Valley's greatest magitech firms.

"Josie, you made it!" Julia Lacy, PA to the CEO, got out of her seat to welcome the late arrival. "We were starting to worry that you'd deserted us."

"Never." Josie laughed. "Not when the food's so good.

Sorry I'm late. I was getting another briefing about plans for the Manaphone upgrade."

"Of course. We put it out, what, a month ago, two? It must be time for a new version already."

The rest of the witches laughed.

"Sorry if I've kept you all from eating." Josie settled into her seat.

"Don't worry. We've had drinks to see us through." Sylvia Dodd, sitting on the other side of Josie, raised her glass in salute.

"Isn't it a little early for that?" Josie asked.

"Doesn't usually stop us."

"We usually meet at lunchtime, not in the morning."

"What's brunch without a little something to cushion the blow of getting out of bed?"

"When you put it that way..." Josie picked up the drink that someone had thoughtfully ordered for her and sipped. The combination of sparkling wine and exotic juices was incredibly refreshing. "I'll have to be careful how many of these I have before going back to work."

"Not a problem I face." Sylvia took another gulp of her drink.

"Sorry." Josie frowned at her own insensitivity. "I didn't mean to rub it in."

Sylvia shook her head and set the glass down. Waiters had come in and were setting out bowls and plates on a rotating disk in the middle of the table. Between more traditional breakfast food like bread, fruit, and pastries, there were dumplings, bowls of steaming noodles, and some flaky parcels that Josie didn't recognize but was determined to try while she was there.

"No need to apologize." Sylvia grabbed a croissant. "I've been enjoying having a little time to myself. Of course, getting fired has given me a new view on the world, and most especially on our glorious leader, Mr. Howard Phillips."

"Have you had any luck finding a new job?"

"Julia suggested that I hold fire on that for a little while." Sylvia raised her eyebrows. "I think our real leader has something planned."

Josie decided not to respond to that comment, in part because she knew almost as little as Sylvia. There was a sense of excitement in the group, with glances shooting Julia's way, an extra tone of expectancy to the conversations. Julia had kept her cards close to her chest, and they were all patient enough to wait for her to reveal her hand.

"This is a lot richer than I'd normally have for breakfast." Josie took one of the pastries and some of the noodles, which turned out to have a sweet sauce. "I'm usually a soaked oats and green tea girl."

"Can't live healthy all the time," Sylvia said. "Where would the fun be in that?"

The clear ringing from a knife tapping against a glass drew everybody's attention. Julia set the knife down and raised her glass. Josie half-expected her to stand and deliver a speech, but she stayed in her seat, on a level with them.

"Ladies," Julia said, "thank you for taking time out from your schedules to meet like this."

"It's our pleasure," someone said.

"Agreed," another replied. "Thank you for arranging this. For everything you do."

"You're too kind." Julia smiled. "I do appreciate it. As you know, I've always valued these little get-togethers. I think it's important to have good support in the workplace, and when that workplace doesn't provide it, you can scream in frustration, or you can find a solution.

"That's why I started this, a little networking, some support and guidance for those coming up through the business. Over time, I like to think that we've become more than that. We're a sort of team within the team. A coven even, as gatherings of witches have so often been called."

"Oh no." Sylvia gave an exaggerated eye roll. "She wants us to dance naked under moonlight."

They all laughed. The tension Josie had carried with her since going into the office that morning started to melt away.

"Nothing so crude," Julia said. "Although I'm not going to criticize anyone's choices of how to dance. You've all seen me on the dance floor, and I'm in no position to judge."

Josie had indeed seen Julia on the dance floor at company parties, a small but elegant presence, drawing the attention of everyone around her. The humble words didn't match that reality, but she still laughed along with the rest before picking at her food some more.

"No, I have something far more serious to discuss today," Julia said. "I want to talk about where the business is heading."

It was as if all the warmth and joy evaporated from the room. Everybody's backs became straight, their postures stiff, smiles sinking into frowns. A few gulped back what remained of their drinks while others set their glasses down. Josie's tension returned.

"We can all agree that Howard's leadership style tends toward the..." Julia hesitated. "The erratic."

"He's pushing too hard in the wrong way," one of the witches said. "This insistence on constant competition is exhausting."

"He's turning teams against each other," another said. "How are we supposed to cooperate in that kind of atmosphere?"

"And his choices of who to hire and fire, some of them are insane."

A lot of eyes turned to look at Sylvia.

"You think I'd disagree with that?" she asked. "He's an asshole."

Somehow, that eased the atmosphere. It was as if Sylvia's words had given everyone else permission to loosen up, to abandon the pretense of civility and offer their real opinions, unfiltered, unreserved. Complaints about funding, restructuring, lack of support, and unwanted interventions. About the chaos breaking out in parts of the business.

Josie drew a deep breath. She still felt like a junior partner here, as though she should be listening and not talking. Maybe that wasn't true anymore. Maybe what she'd seen was part of the discussion.

"I agree," she said when a gap came up in the conversation. "Look at my position. I've not even managed people for a year, and I'm running two whole departments. It's not that I'm not glad of the opportunity, and I'm doing my absolute best, but I never should've been put in this position."

The others looked at each other awkwardly, not sure how to respond.

"Josie's right." Julia laid a hand on her shoulder. "She's doing a marvelous job, but she's doing it despite her situation, not because of it. We were insanely lucky that she turned out to be as talented as she is, but it was still a strange decision to promote her so fast, especially to force a second team on her. If Howard wanted to destroy his own business, he couldn't do a better job of it."

"What do the shareholders think of all this?" someone asked.

"They don't know yet, but things can't stay that way much longer. Once they work it out..." Julia shook her head and pushed her plate away from her. "Then we're all in trouble. They'll insist on sending in a new management team from one of the consultancies, which means all our jobs are at risk. While Howard might be erratic, at least he knows how this business works, and he has an interest in its long-term success. A bunch of consultants whose only job is to shore things up while the shareholders find their exit strategy? That could be the ruin of Philgard."

Josie looked around the table. Almost everyone's eyes were downcast. She drank what remained in her glass and looked around for more.

"We've worked so damn hard to build up this company," a witch said. "It's not only about my career. I don't want to let something I took pride in die."

There were murmurs of agreement. Josie joined in. She might not have been there long, but getting recruited to Philgard had been one of the proudest days of her life.

Seeing the business she'd dreamed of since college collapse would be heartbreaking.

"It won't come to that." Sylvia was the only one still smiling. "That's why we're here, right? Because you have a plan?"

She was looking at Julia, who twisted the stem of her glass between her fingers. The others looked at her too, and their expressions were hungry, expectant, even touched with desperation.

"I do," Julia said. "Or at least the beginning of one."

She looked around as if checking for anyone who might overhear them. However, this was a private room, and the staff had left as soon as they delivered the food. She raised her wand and muttered a spell.

"Tace muros."

The room's walls shimmered with a faint layer of magic, one that would prevent anyone outside from hearing them, whether they pressed an ear to the door or used the most sophisticated bug technology could provide.

"Someone needs to take control of the company," she said. "Proper control, not this chaos we have at the moment."

"You mean a new CEO?" Josie asked.

"Perhaps. Perhaps not. There are different ways to manage it. What matters is that we bring an end to the mess, that we implement sensible, collaborative policies, that we put the right staff in the right positions with the right support. No more teams fighting against each other for attention. A proper business, properly run like we used to be."

"If you want me back, I'll want a raise." Sylvia had a mischievous twinkle in her eye.

Some of the witches laughed. Others had serious, thoughtful expressions as they weighed up what they were hearing.

"Yes, I think we need you back," Julia said. "We're a long way from that yet, and it won't be my place to negotiate the contract."

"If only we still had the head of recruitment here," someone else said, looking at Sylvia, the job's last holder. There was more laughter, but it didn't last long, and when it passed, they were all watching Julia expectantly.

Josie liked the sound of what she was hearing, but she couldn't muster the unfettered enthusiasm she wanted to share. Looking at Julia, she couldn't help feeling that her friend was holding back. She wouldn't have come to them without a plan and a detailed one at that. She was doubtless about to reveal some of the details, but she'd set expectations to hold some back. That made Josie nervous. What was she getting into here?

"For this to work, I need all of you on board." Julia looked each witch in turn in the eyes. "I need your skills, your energy, your commitment. I need my coven at my side. If not, it's not worth the risk. We might as well all go look for new jobs."

Now, in the crucial moment, they hesitated. There were no treason clauses in corporate law, but they all understood what they were considering. This was about launching a coup against Howard Phillips, the man who'd founded the company, the man they all worked for, who many had idolized before they ever joined his firm. They would be taking on a giant of Mana Valley, betraying him to save his company.

It was one thing to vent their grievances and make jokes about what should be. It was quite another to commit themselves, in front of witnesses, to what Julia was asking. To do that, each of them had to trust everyone else in the room, had to be sure that no one would switch sides, and tell Phillips in return for a raise.

Could any of them take that risk?

Josie drew a deep breath. She felt like she stood on a precipice, considering whether to jump. There were only two people in the world she trusted. Julia was one of them. She trusted her judgment, not only about this scheme but about who to bring into it. Right now, Julia needed her. She needed someone to be the first to speak, to take that risk, to show the others that they could.

Should Josie commit to a plan when she didn't know what it was? That was surely holding all of them back. Around the room, witches looked uncertainly at each other, their futures in the balance.

"I'm in," Josie said. "No one understands the business better than Julia. Nobody's supported us better. If this is her move, I'm backing it."

"Fine." Sylvia snorted. "What have I got to lose? I'm in too."

"And me," another witch said.

"And me."

"Me too."

One by one, voices rose until everyone had spoken up. In the silent aftermath, they looked at each other with nervous smiles. Co-conspirators, saviors of the business, maybe both? Julia smiled. They'd said that they were in, but they were still nervous, the whole thing hanging on a thread.

Josie grabbed a bottle of wine, refilled her glass, and got to her feet. "This needs to happen. Only Julia had the courage to make it happen. So here's to Julia, whatever her plan is."

"To Julia." Sylvia stood and raised her glass.

"To the plan." Someone else stood, and the rest followed.

"To Julia and the plan," they said as one and drank.

Julia sat like a queen on her throne, smiling up at them.

CHAPTER THREE

Fran looked around the room. It was dark, cold, and clammy, with trickles of condensation running down walls of black stone blocks.

"Huh." She scratched her head. "How did I get here?" Another thought crossed her mind. "Where is here?"

She put her hand on the simple bed she was sitting on. The mattress was straw. As her hand pressed against it, it rustled. She peered at it more closely and realized that it wasn't simply straw like you might feed to a horse. There were drinking straws too—plastic ones, paper ones, metal ones, some straight and some bendy, some plain and some with decorations on them. One had pushed through a big slice of pineapple. Another had a paper umbrella sticking out of the top.

"That's kind of cool." She spun the umbrella, then sank back on the mattress. Her mattress, because this was her room, she was sure of that, even if it seemed different from her usual space.

She closed her eyes and tried to go back to sleep, but that was hard to do with the sounds of dripping water and the rattling and clinking that came through the barred door at one side of the room. Plus the mattress was moving, wriggling around beneath her feet.

She sat up, pulled back the threadbare blanket, and looked at the straw where her feet had rested. A rat peered back at her.

"Hi there," the rat said in a female voice.

"Um, hi."

"Can you hear someone shouting?" the rat asked.

"No, I don't think so." Fran tilted her head to one side and listened carefully. She felt as though she ought to be able to hear something, but it wasn't there, like watching a TV channel with the sound turned off. "What are they shouting?"

"Mostly the word 'help,'" the rat replied. "Although there's some other stuff too. Human things. I get confused about those."

"Fair enough. I get confused by human things sometimes, and I am human." Fran hesitated as she considered how far that was true. "Well, I'm a sort of human. I'm half Evermore, and half something else descended from a long line of magical warriors."

She probably shouldn't have told the rat that. After all, it was supposed to be a secret, at least, the Evermore part was. Why hadn't she remembered to keep it secret? Winslow would be so mad. He was always going on about protecting the Evermores and the power they guarded.

Wait, hadn't she decided not to listen to Winslow

anymore? That seemed right. In that case, she could tell the rat everything. Except that now she had questions about the rat.

"Why are you here?" she asked.

"Because we work together," the rat replied. "I'm Singar, remember?"

"Are you sure? I thought Singar was bigger and had hands. Shouldn't you be wearing a flannel shirt?"

"I am." The rat flapped the hem of a shirt that Fran didn't remember seeing before. It looked like she'd made it from a washcloth.

"Cool. Why are we here?"

"I'm inventing." Singar the rat twisted two straws together, and a light shone out of the end. "Just like always."

"What am I doing here?"

"You're a captive, remember?"

"Not really…"

Fran looked round. Singar's answer did make sense of a lot of things, like the cold hard walls of the cell, the way that one wall was all bars, and the guards outside, staring in at them. She waved at the guards, and they waved back, then started dancing in unison, a solemn, slow dance, mournful and menacing.

"I got arrested once before," Fran said. "It wasn't much like this. This is more like a cartoon prison or one from a book on Victorian history."

"Like all your pictures of prisons have been jammed together in your brain?"

"Exactly!"

"Well, you know what that means, right?"

Fran felt sure that she should know, that there was a word for a situation like this, something starting with a "D," but she couldn't quite wrap her mind around it. In the distance, she could hear a voice now, someone shouting for her, although she couldn't make out what they were saying.

"Does it mean that Gruffbar's going to come and get me out?" she asked. "He did that before."

"Of course, I'm going to." Another voice emerged from a hole in the bottom of the wall, low and growling.

Fran got up off the bed and crouched by the wall to peer into the hole. All she saw in the darkness was a pair of eyes and the gleaming edge of an ax blade. "What are you doing in there, Gruffbar?"

"Mining. That's what we dwarves do."

"It's not what you do. You're a lawyer."

"Ah, but why do you think I went into business with you? It's a chance to get back to my roots. To make something. To build something. For that, you need to mine metals first."

"That does make sense. At least, I think it does. It's hard to tell with all this noise going on."

The stamping feet of the dancing guards were getting louder and louder, but they couldn't drown out the distant, anguished shouts calling to her for help. If only she could tell what the voice was and where it was coming from.

"Maybe you should go and do something about that?" Gruffbar asked.

"I can't. I'm trapped here."

"You should be able to get out. After all, you built this place."

"I did?"

"Of course. Check your pockets."

Fran reached into the pocket of her prison hoodie. Arrows marked the cloth, like prison overalls in old cartoons, except they were sequins. In her pocket, she found a folded piece of blue paper. She took it out and unfolded it, but the creases never seemed to end. It kept going until it filled the whole cell, covering the floor and climbing the walls. It was a map of the prison.

"That's useful." Fran ran her finger along the outline of a corridor, and as she did, a clear image of the passage appeared in her mind. Then she was there, walking between concrete walls with a smaller blueprint in her hands.

"Just like magic." She giggled. The corridor ahead of her was miles long. "Wait, I've got a trick for this."

She stretched out her leg and passed through the gap between places as her father had taught her. When she put her foot down, she was at the far end of the corridor.

"Woodrow was right. I can do it." She smiled, despite the nightmarish sounds echoing all around. "I'll have to tell him when I get home."

Footsteps echoed down the corridor. She looked back the way she had come and saw a crowd of guards running after her. Singar was sitting on the head of one of them, clutching his long eyebrows like the reins of a horse.

"Run!" Singar screeched. "Run like the wind!"

Fran ran, dashing frantically down the corridor, away from the sound of feet and toward the sound of screams. It wasn't only about escaping. That would never have been enough motive for her. It was about helping whoever was making that terrible sound, about answering the cries that hooked at her heart. It was about doing the right thing.

"I'm coming," she called. "Whoever you are."

As she ran, she held up the map. It was shrinking in her hands, becoming easier to carry but harder to follow. She pressed her finger on a spot in the center, a space labeled "Mirror Room." Once again, a vision of the place came to her, a ballroom with mirrored walls and a mirror ball hanging from the ceiling, its spots of light dancing around the room. The vision became clearer, and she fell through the map, stumbled into the room, found her footing, and looked around.

"Wow," she gasped, looking around her. "This place is so cool."

"No," someone replied, and their voice was like the singing of a heavenly choir. "It is not cool. It is cold, hard, and isolated. It is a cell."

A man was hanging in the air underneath the mirror ball. As least, she thought it was a man. It was hard to tell because he was glowing so brightly that the air around him became a blur, and she couldn't make out the features of his face or the details of his body. He was man-shaped, and there was a richness to that choral voice that seemed distinctly masculine to her.

"I'm sorry to intrude," she said. "I'm looking for the person who was calling for help."

"That was me," the man sang. "Please, you have to let me out of this place."

"I would, but I don't know how."

"You built it. You must know the way out."

He glowed more brightly, and the light reflected from the mirror walls. Fran had to half-close her eyes to keep the light from hurting.

"I didn't mean to build it," she said. "It just sort of happened."

"Just happened? You built my prison, and you put me here."

"I didn't mean to."

"Didn't mean to?" The music of his voice became discordant with rage. "You imprisoned me by accident?"

Fran clapped her hands over her ears and shut her eyes tight. In the distance, she could still hear the tramp of the guards, the sound of their footsteps approaching down corridors on every side. Through her eyelids, the glowing body of the man showed so bright that she couldn't shut him out.

"I didn't mean to," she chanted like it was a spell that could protect her. "I didn't mean to. I didn't mean to."

"You think that helps me?" The glowing man's voice was so clear that it might as well have arrived directly into her head. "You think that intention counts for anything? Action is all that matters, and your actions have trapped me."

"I'm sorry."

In the background, the tramping of feet grew louder. Fran opened her eyes and saw guards streaming into the room. Dozens of them. Hundreds of them. Thousands of them. Each one replicated endlessly in the mirrors that enclosed them. Their jailers surrounded her and the glowing man, and more kept coming, crowding the mirror room.

"Don't be sorry," the glowing man said. "Do something."

"I'm trying," Fran screeched.

The jailers were advancing on her. Some of them grabbed her arms. She wriggled free, but more seized hold of her, and when she shook them off, even more. She was covered, surrounded, closed in from every direction, pulled this way and that. She cried out in hurt and alarm as they dragged her this way and that, pushed her down, and pressed her face against the floor. She couldn't muster her magic, couldn't even raise her voice to scream.

"This is how it feels," the glowing man sang. "What are you going to do about it?"

Fran tried to reply, but she couldn't. She tried to break free, but she couldn't. She tried to shout for help, but she couldn't. She tried to scream so hard that her whole body pulsed with it.

Like that, the world fell away. The nightmare shattered and she sat bolt upright in her bed, in her apartment, sweating in her thick winter sheets.

She called on her magic and summoned light, banishing shadows from the room, and with them the lingering terror. A glance at her phone told her that it was past six in the morning. If it weren't the middle of winter, daylight would've been peeking through the blinds.

Her heart was still hammering at the panic the dream had induced, at the fear and confusion of it all. What she remembered most clearly wasn't the guards grabbing her. It was the glowing man and the anguish in his voice. Imaginary as the rest had been, that part had felt real. Someone had been calling out to her, so desperate that he could reach her even in the realm of sleep. Someone she had a special connection with. Someone she'd trapped.

She unlocked her phone and typed a message to her mom, thumbs darting across the keys.

Hey Mom. Can you help me find the other Evermores? I think the Source needs me.

CHAPTER FOUR

Howard Phillips stood in the wings of a bustling auditorium, looking out at the crowd of journalists, bloggers, and tech enthusiasts waiting to hear him speak. Perhaps one in ten of them had any reach, any impact through what they said. The other ninety percent were there to provide buzz, to add applause, to create a wave of enthusiasm that made it more likely those one in ten went away hyped up, ready to say positive things about him and his company.

It was a thrill to see how these little people, these magicals and humans, danced for him. It would be an even greater thrill when he revealed his full plan, when the darkness came to cover them all.

"We're all set." Julia Lacy appeared at his side with a tablet in her hand. Efficient as always. What would he do without her? Find a replacement was probably the answer. How rare could a good PA be?

"Is Josie here?" he asked.

"She's getting ready. She got held up in another product meeting, then in traffic. We're lucky she made it at all."

He stifled a laugh. He had the business so perfectly tuned. Every moment of the day, his employees were stepping through stress. How many went home with their brains blazing and battered, their nights haunted by nightmares fueled by that stress? It was delicious, this thing he had created, and soon it would be complete.

"It's good that she's here," Phillips said. "Someone else to add a human face to the launch. To talk them through the details, to show that we've thought about how this will affect our customers."

Someone else to take the stress of this occasion. Someone who would feel the pain of it. Someone whose skills he could use while he burned out her spirit.

In the darkness at the side of the stage stood a figure who could have stepped out of a nightmare himself, Phillips' head of security and personal bodyguard, Handar Ennis. The Kilomea cracked his fingers and the muscles in his arms flexed, but the seams of his suit somehow withstood the strain. His tusks glinted in the gloom.

"You've been very quiet," Phillips said.

Handar shrugged. "Got nothing to say."

That wasn't true. Handar had been brooding on something for a while, but Phillips didn't worry about it. Handar was too simple a soul for it to be anything sophisticated or troubling. When he felt that it mattered, Handar would tell his boss. Until then, it could wait. Perhaps, if it was a problem, it might eat away at him a little. Phillips hoped so.

Phillips straightened his tie, although it was already perfect, and checked the edges of the shirt sleeves protruding from his suit. On one of his wrists, the skin wriggled a little beneath the shirt, then went still. Perhaps it was time to get a new skin suit. He couldn't let that part of his disguise fail. Then again, soon it wouldn't matter. Today brought him a significant step closer to the climax of his plans.

"I think we've let them wait long enough," he said. "Let's do this."

He clipped a microphone onto his collar, then strode out onto the stage. The room erupted with applause, a tide of it washing over him. He waved at the crowd and nodded individually to a few serious journalists in the front row as he made his way to the center of the stage. Then he held up his hands.

"Good morning everyone," he called, and the auditorium's sound system amplified his voice. "I know you're all eager to offer your opinions on my company's work. If you quiet down for a minute, I can tell you what we're doing so you know what to complain about."

They laughed, some of them a little too smugly, and silence finally settled across the room. There was a soft buzz as, behind Phillips, a screen descended from the ceiling. It lit up, revealing the Philgard Technologies logo, and in front of it, a picture of their leading product, the Manaphone X.

"Most of you here today covered the launch of the Manaphone X," Phillips said. "I loved reading all your positive reviews and seeing how they helped propel our record-breaking sales. I also enjoyed reading the negative reviews and learning from them. Because there's always more to learn. We're never going to make the perfect product. We can always push to make something better. That's what I'm here about today."

The slides changed, and an image of a Manaphone screen appeared, with the letters "Xy" next to it.

"From most companies, you'd expect to wait six months, perhaps a year, perhaps even longer, before getting the first upgrade to a new phone. At Philgard, we feel that's not good enough. We can do better. We can learn faster. We can improve your experience sooner."

We can drive our employees into the ground rushing to meet a near-impossible self-imposed deadline, he thought but didn't say. His smile widened.

"That's why, today, we're already launching the first upgrade to the software on the Manaphone X. It's an upgrade we're calling Xy. It builds upon everything we've learned from hundreds of thousands of people using our phones and from all the feedback you here in this room gave us, both positive and negative.

"It's a big step up for us as a company, both in the software's sophistication and the challenge we set ourselves upgrading so quickly. It's a challenge whose results make me immensely proud. Late last year, we released the best magically enhanced phone in two worlds. Today, we're making it even better."

He paused and applause burst out. While the serious journalists peered at the screen behind him and frantically made notes, the fans pandered to Phillips' ego and their pathetic enthusiasm. That enthusiasm would ensure that everybody accepted the upgrade, which looked so innocent but carried in it a vital component of his plans. It was one of the last pieces for a work of magic so large that it was beyond the comprehension of the so-called journalists and magic users in this room. A work of magic that would transform the world.

Soon. So soon.

Phillips beamed with pride. Those watching him would assume that smile was all about the phone.

He raised his hands and voice again.

"Please, we're not done here," he said as the applause subsided. "As you must have learned by now, the person at the top is never the right one to fill you in on the details. We're too busy with business lunches to sweat the small stuff like what we've made." Laughter again. Good. Very good. It would make what came later all the more beautifully bitter.

"Rather than bluff my way through your questions, I'm going to hand this over to someone far better-looking and better informed than I am. Please give a big round of applause for one of the executives who made this possible: Josie Bullworth."

Josie stepped out from behind the curtain, clutching a tablet loaded with her notes and the specs for the Xy. As the hall filled with applause, Phillips leaned close to her.

"You've got this, right?"

"Absolutely." She swallowed and tapped the tablet. "It's all here."

"Fantastic." Phillips placed a finger against the back of the tablet, and unseen by her, released a spark of black magic. Why resist the chance to make things a little more nightmarish? "Knock 'em dead."

As he stepped behind the curtain, he turned back to see Josie staring in panic at her tablet's scrambled screen.

"One moment," she called to the crowd, tension hitching her voice. "I'm having a little technical difficulty."

His work done, Phillips stepped out into the corridor. Handar followed, heading swiveling from side to side, looking for any sign of danger.

"Where to, boss?" he asked.

"Back to the office," Phillips replied. "I need to get out of my suit for a bit."

"Got it."

Handar led the way out of the building. A black, armored SUV was parked close to the front entrance between a steam wagon and a vehicle pulled by a lizard. The latter was currently sleeping on the parking lot's tarmac. Handar opened the SUV's rear door, closed it after his boss got in, and took the driver's seat.

"What do you think?" Phillips asked. "Did they like it?"

"'Course they did, boss."

It was always reassuring to hear Handar's obedient tone, to know that he would do his best to please Phillips. That was why he was one of the few people who knew the truth, one of those Phillips could count on to make this happen.

They drove through the streets of Mana Valley with its eclectic traffic. More and more people were importing vehicles from Earth, like their SUV, as status symbols rather than out of practicality. They were still a minority, outnumbered by those vehicles powered by magic or steam, by those dragged by monstrous beasts or carried by vast flying creatures.

Mana Valley was one of the richest cities in two worlds, and it kept on growing. More magicals, more artifacts, more enchantments, more power. That was why it was the perfect place to cast his spell, to rip open the walls of reality. Even if his ultimate target was Earth rather than Oriceran, Mana Valley was the weapon to be turned upon it.

They reached the headquarters of Philgard Technologies, and Handar pulled into the executive parking lot underneath. Phillips considered taking a trip up through the public elevators, stopping off on a few floors for surprise visits to the teams working under him, to give them that extra jolt of alarm that came when the boss turned up.

Still, his real body was wriggling again under the skin suit. He needed to get somewhere he could relax and recharge, somewhere he could be his real self. Instead, he took the private elevator up to his office with Handar at his shoulder, always watchful, always waiting to serve.

In the antechamber to his office, next to Julia's desk, Phillips stopped and turned to Handar. "I won't need you for the next few hours. You can go and get on with the other parts of your job or whatever else it is you do when I'm not around."

"Right you are, boss. If you need me, just call."

"Of course."

Phillips walked into his office, closed the door behind him, locked it, and set the magical seal. He glanced to one side, where a glass wall looked out across the whole of Mana Valley, a dizzying reminder of his corporate power. The wriggling in his wrist was a reminder of his real power, and that was what he had to tend to.

He opened a panel in the wall at the back of the room,

revealing a hidden wardrobe. Piece by piece, he stripped off his clothes and hung them up. His leather-soled shoes took their place next to other pairs, all polished brightly, in a rack to one side. When he was naked, he brought both hands to the back of his neck, pinched the skin there, and pulled it apart. Slowly, then faster, the human disguise slid off and fell to the floor, revealing the Darkness Between Dreams in its true glory, a thing of sickly rippling flesh, tentacles and teeth, of eyes on stalks. A thing from the darkest of dreams.

The Darkness Between Dreams waved three of its tentacles and a portal appeared, a circle of magic that opened a way to another world. It slipped through into a realm more fit for it, one of stark darkness and blood-red light. Acid rain was falling, hissing as it hit the ground. Screams filled the air.

Out of the gloom, creatures ran up to the Darkness, hounds with dripping maws and needle-sharp teeth, their claws gouging the ground. They circled it, a ring of menace, as the portal closed.

"My beauties," the Darkness Between Dreams hissed. "It has been too long."

The nightmare hounds growled, howled, then settled down around it.

The Darkness Between Dreams reached out tentacles to stroke the rough fur of its pets. It closed its eyes and felt the rain burn down its face.

"Oh yes," it said, feeling the full grandeur of its nightmare realm. "Soon a whole world will be like this. I promise you, my beauties, it will be yours."

CHAPTER FIVE

The meeting room wasn't technically separate because the basement of Worn Threads didn't have those. Instead, they'd erected portable partitions to provide some privacy, as well as wall space for monitors, whiteboards, and papers to be put up. An enchantment kept out noise from the surrounding office and meant that no one else could hear what they discussed in that area. Still, it didn't have the solidity of four walls and a ceiling.

"Surely we can do better than this by now." Elethin sat at one side of the table, dressed in a pencil skirt and a silk blouse, legs elegantly crossed. "Hire working space in another building or set up offices at the back of one of the factories. I could tolerate some noise and rough workmen in return for a touch more professionalism."

"We're working on it." Gruffbar exchanged a look with Bart. "For now, we work with what we've got."

"I like this." Fran leaned back in her chair to tap one of the improvised walls.

"You would." Elethin rolled her eyes.

"It's distinctive, improvised, characterful. It's very us."

"Sadly, that much is true." Elethin sighed. "Perhaps we could put some effort into the next steps in professionalizing this firm."

"That's why we're meeting." Bart clicked a button, and a slide show started on one of the wall-mounted monitors. It showed a cartoon bag of money next to an upwardly trending graph, decorated in all the colors of the rainbow.

"Exciting!" Fran clapped her hands together. "What's this all about?"

"Our initial public offering." Bart clicked the button again, and the images gave way to a picture of men in suits. Next to them were the definitions of a bunch of financial terms. "It's time to talk about share prices and targeting investors."

"That sounds a lot less exciting." Fran toyed with her ponytail. "Do I need to be here for this? Accounts aren't really my thing."

"This is very important, Fran." Bart looked at her sternly. "The decisions that we make today could make a huge difference to the reputational and financial wellbeing of Mana Wave Industries for years to come. They will become the foundation for expansion, consolidation, and security."

"Okay, but hear me out, couldn't I be working on new devices while you do this? We've started talking about how to make version two of the FDS, and I have some great things I want to try with Singar."

"This is how we'll fund all your experiments," Elethin

said. "All those lovely machines you want to make, all the grand events we'll use to publicize them. We need this first so you can make your machines."

"Sure, I get that, but can't you guys sort it out?"

"By my beard." Gruffbar shook his head. "How did I end up in the only company where the CEO isn't interested in money?"

"Luck?" Fran grinned.

"Some sort of luck..." Gruffbar leaned forward, looking at her intently. "Listen, Fran. As the CEO, you're legally responsible for what goes on in this company. That means you have to give your approval to big decisions.

"In the past, I would happily have let someone like you sign off on those things without understanding them, to give the rest of us a fall guy if it went wrong, but I'm not that dwarf anymore. As your lawyer and your friend, I'm telling you that you need to understand this, or at least try." He drew a breath. "Please."

"All right." Fran grabbed a Mana Wave branded notepad and pen from the middle of the table. "Can I take notes?"

"Of course!" Bart beamed. "I like it when I have an attentive audience."

Fran decided against telling him that the notes wouldn't all be about what he said, might not even mostly be about that. The odds were good that they would be about whatever technical ideas popped into her brain while she sat there to prevent those ideas from being lost. Of course, some would be doodles because how could anybody get through a meeting without doodling? She would make sure to note down some of what he said, to show that she was paying attention, to help her understand this whole thing, to…

She realized that Bart had already started talking and that she'd missed the contents of at least three slides.

"Could you maybe summarize that?" she asked sheepishly.

"Which part?" Bart asked. "We've already covered—"

"Allow me." Gruffbar had been watching Fran from the corner of his eye, and now he turned to her. "An IPO is when we let people buy shares in the company, apart from the shares we've already promised to ourselves and early investors. It's how we're going to get more money to expand."

"I know all that," Fran said. She'd read about IPOs in the news and biographies of her tech idols, like Howard Phillips. She knew what this was for.

"So you have been paying attention," Gruffbar said pointedly.

"Yes, totally." Fran turned a beaming smile on Bart. "Thanks for that, Bart. Please carry on."

Bart looked with concern at the others. "Shouldn't she—"

"She understands enough," Gruffbar said. "This is an executive briefing, not a course in the fundamentals of economics."

"But my slides…"

"We all appreciate your effort and passion, Bart, but I'm a lawyer, not a student, and my time costs. Maybe you could give us the shortened version."

"Please," Elethin hissed.

"I suppose so." Bart skipped forward a few slides, then a

few more. He frowned as he tried to decide which parts were essential and which ones got him excited as an accountant. "I might have gotten a little carried away, but here..." He settled on a slide. "These are the big decisions we need to make: how many shares, what type, what price, and when we launch them. All of which depend upon our upcoming expenses. So Fran, what do you want the company to do?"

Now they were onto topics she could get excited about.

"We need a way to make more of the FDS more quickly," she said. "Loads of people want it. It would be awesome to develop a load more software, games, and other entertainment, maybe even some useful apps for around the house. I know that's off-brand, but Josie and my mom said it might make people use the system more.

"We're already working on developing version two. We can take longer over that than the first one, but it will be more complicated. We need to research what our strange circuitry from the kemana does, refine the spells we're running through it, explore alternative power forms for the battery, and Smokey has some great ideas about making the core software more adaptable."

She paused for breath, and Gruffbar held up a hand.

"To summarize," he said, "expansion and refinement of the FDS line."

"Sure, you could put it that way."

"What about our security work?"

Fran hesitated. She knew what she wanted to do, which was to move on past it. She also knew that the containment units were providing them with good money and providing jobs for many of their employees at the factory sites. She couldn't let that go.

Plus, Singar had been working on her new version, and that was kind of cool. Fran wanted to see how it worked.

"We should keep going and develop a new version of the unit."

"Given the orders we have coming in, we could easily set up another production site just for this," Bart said.

"Sure." Fran shrugged. "Why not? It's good money, and we're helping keep people safe, right?"

"We are." Gruffbar looked at Bart. "I assume you have some expense projections that cover all this?"

"Oh yes." Bart clicked forward through a series of slides with different predictions of Mana Wave's financial future. "I prepared for a range of possible options, and I'm pleased to hear Fran wants to be ambitious. As the young people say, we should go big or go home."

"People who say that haven't been young for decades," Elethin interjected. "But please continue."

"Right, well, this is my projection for what we'll need to support the expansion of both product lines, as well as research into the underlying magic and technology. I've budgeted for a small discretionary fund too, assuming that we'll think of something else we want to start developing."

There was a *click* and another slide. Like the one before it, it contained financial figures that seemed mind-boggling to Fran. "This is the earnings we can reasonably expect off these product lines and their timings. As you can see, we'll end up with a substantial profit, but to get there, we need a significant boost at the start."

A third slide showed the gap between the two figures.

Fran's mouth hung open. "We need people to give us that much money? That's... They can't possibly... Surely no one will..."

"Oh, Fran." Elethin reached across the table and patted the back of Fran's hand. "We're the hottest new thing Mana Valley has seen in years. People will be lining up to give us this money."

"Really?"

"If we get the IPO right, yes." Bart clicked to another slide. "Which brings us to the big decisions, as mentioned before: number and type of shares, price, and launch date."

He waved, and a little magic sparkled in the air. At the side of the room, a huge sheet of paper unfurled, hanging down one of the temporary walls. Charts and figures covered it. Smiling like a kid at Christmas, Bart walked over to it.

"This is our target figure," he explained, using a laser pointer to indicate a top corner. "This is how that breaks down in different scenarios. Bear with me because the cash flow calculations are a little complicated at the start, but as you'll see, they get more exciting as we go along..."

Fran normally trusted Bart's judgment, but when it came to what numbers could be exciting, he had a very different worldview from her. Within minutes, her eyes glazed over while he and Gruffbar talked back and forth about different numbers, and Elethin occasionally interjected with a question.

To keep herself focused, Fran started doodling, sketching out new circuitry for the FDS while she listened to what Bart was saying. Then she had a different idea for the circuit, which could make brighter, clearer images. She tore off one sheet of paper, started scribbling frantically on another one, then looked up guiltily as she realized that Bart was still talking and she hadn't listened for at least five minutes.

"That's great." She pointed at the cluster of figures he was standing by, hoping no one would notice her bluff. "You've really thought this through."

"I have," Bart agreed. "I'm glad that you like this model, because I think it's the best financially."

"Great. It's decided." Fran stood, clutching her diagram. She wanted to get back to the workshop and see if this idea worked in practice.

"That part's settled." Gruffbar stood. "Now we need to talk about our legal and regulatory obligations."

"About what?"

"About how we make sure to do this legally."

"Shares can be illegal?"

"There are a lot of regulations around financial transactions, especially when a lot of money's at stake."

"This is a lot of money." Fran looked at the top figure again, wide-eyed. She could barely believe that she'd made a business worth that much. "So we need to meet again to talk through the legal part?"

"No." Gruffbar shook his head. "We need decisions on this now."

Fran sighed and sat back down. "I was afraid you'd say that." She flipped over a notepad page and did her best to pay attention to the cramped text Gruffbar had brought up on a screen.

Exciting new devices would have to wait for later. Now it was time for her to behave like a responsible magitech executive. If she got bored, all she had to do was remember that this would buy them the coolest new tools, the biggest new factories, all the pieces they needed to build her new circuits.

"Go ahead," she said. "I really am paying attention now."

CHAPTER SIX

Handar woke and immediately opened his eyes. If there had been a time when he slowly emerged from sleep, it was far behind him. The military life had broken off any soft edges he had, and there weren't many of those in the first place. Waking up quickly, being ready for immediate action could make the difference between life and death in the field.

He took a moment to absorb his surroundings, to remember where he was and why—his bedroom in his apartment. Weak winter sunlight seeped through the blinds and cast pale lines across the wall. Sheets lay across him, a simple design like most things in his apartment. Next to him was a warm body, her breath easing gently in and out.

He smiled as he turned his attention to her. Who would've thought he'd meet his perfect woman in a tunnel bar? It made sense, in a way. After all, he'd lived a lot of his life underground and in rough bars making shady deals, whether for black market provisions in a war zone or information his boss wanted around the city.

He'd never thought of those places as holding anything more for him. They were for work, like everything else. For a mission, whatever it was at the time. Not for comfort or compassion.

Not until now.

He tugged the sheets back a little, admired the muscles of Berra's arm, the angle of her jaw, the dark hair draped across her tough skin with its intricate tattoos. She was his sort of Kilomea.

Berra's eyes opened a crack, and she looked up at him.

"Cold," she mumbled around her tusks.

"Sorry." Handar lowered the sheet and tucked it back in around her. "You keep sleeping."

She muttered something affirmative and rolled over, wrapping herself up snug and warm. That drew the sheets off of Handar, but he didn't mind. He wanted her to be comfortable, and he was too awake to keep sleeping now.

He got out of bed, and pulled on loose trousers and a sweatshirt. Normally, he started the day with a workout, but that could wait until later when he wouldn't disturb Berra. Instead, he unlocked the metal cabinet in the corner of the bedroom, took out a box full of papers, and took them through to the table in the apartment's main room.

Returning to the bedroom, he hesitated in front of the cabinet. Was it even worth keeping this thing, given that intruders had already breached it once? Maybe he should give up on it in favor of off-site storage so it was harder for his competitors to find out where he was storing the prophecies. Maybe he should get better locks.

Or maybe he should crush the little worms who'd dared to intrude on his space. His hand tightened around the edge of the metal door, knuckles pale, and if not for Berra, he would've slammed it. Instead, he eased it shut and locked it. For now, it would have to do.

In the kitchen, he made himself strong, black coffee in a small stove-top pot that he'd been carrying from one barracks to another, one field camp to the next, for over twenty years. There were a few scratches on the surface, inevitable after this long, but it was still in good condition, like all the tools that mattered to Handar. Like the viciously sharp knives on a magnetic strip above the kitchen counter. Like the backup handgun in a drawer underneath.

He carried his coffee into the living room, sat at the table, and carefully took the documents out of the box. They were only a part of all that he'd accumulated over the past six months, a whole safe full of books, notes, and scrolls, more reading material than he'd ever owned in his life. Legally, he didn't own some of these, but none of their owners would be coming for them. If they were still breathing, they would know better than to seek him out.

He set aside a single red folder and spread the rest of the documents in front of him, trying to work out where to start. Drinking his coffee gave him a moment to think, but otherwise didn't help. If this stuff made you smarter as the memes said, he must be pretty damn dumb in the first place, at least compared to the other people who dealt with this stuff. The words overwhelmed him, a mass of signs and symbols that blocked his path to meaning, not opened it. He had to start somewhere, so he picked up one of them.

It was one of the prophecies themselves. He didn't know who'd written it or when despite all the books he had that were supposed to explain this stuff. Those books were as bad as the prophecies, worse even. How could smart people make language so incomprehensible?

Reading their work was supposed to fill him with knowledge, to increase his smarts. Instead, he felt stupider with each passing page. He persisted because this mattered. Because it was a way he could help the boss, even if the boss didn't know about it yet. Also because he wasn't going to be beaten by some punk kid and his idiot girlfriend.

Handar glanced at the red folder and sneered. Oh, no. He wasn't going to let them beat him.

He turned his attention back to the prophecy. Like several of the others, it was obsessed with doors and gates. Handar could understand that if it was giving instructions for how to fortify and defend a building or how to assault it, but this was supposed to be about big events coming in the future, maybe even here in Mana Valley. Could doors really be so important?

Maybe there was a fight coming, and this was supposed to help plan for it. He got out a sheet of paper and started copying out all the passages about doors and gates or any other building feature. Maybe he could use them to work out where the big event would happen. He could put a map together, work out what they would have to fight for, even come up with a plan to assault or defend it. That was the sort of work he could deal with.

"I smell coffee."

Berra stood in the bedroom doorway, a sheet wrapped around her. It accentuated the muscular curves of her body, the little scars the tattoos didn't quite hide near the top of her chest. Handar grinned at the sight. He could see himself heading back to the bedroom real soon.

"You got a cup for me?" Berra said. "Or are you one of those boyfriends who does nothing for his girl?"

"So I'm your boyfriend now?" Handar went through to the kitchen and set his little pot to start brewing. It wasn't big enough to make coffee for two at once. Should he buy a bigger pot?

"You'd better be." Berra punched him on the arm, then pressed her body against his, pushed her face against his shoulder, and caught the side of his neck playfully between her teeth. "Else things are gonna get rough in here."

"Sounds like I win either way."

Handar turned and kissed her, losing himself in her presence. Only when the coffee pot hissed did he drag his hands off.

"Here." He poured the coffee into a mug and handed it to her.

"You got milk, sugar, anything like that?"

He shook his head. "Never bothered."

"Damn, Handar, you still act like you're passing through this town." She laughed and carried her coffee into the other room, then looked back at him. "That ain't true, is it?"

"No." He followed her through and sat back down at the table, his attention drawn to the prophecies. "I'm here for the long haul."

"Good." She rested a hand on his shoulder. "What's all this?"

Handar frowned at the pages. There were things he

couldn't tell anyone, not even her, not even once time passed and they'd known each other for years instead of a few precious months. There were other things he'd only chosen to keep secret, things that were his decision. Surely it was okay to tell her about those?

"It's a project I'm working on," he said. "Something secret for my boss."

"He's got you doing secret projects?"

"No. I mean yes, he does, but that ain't this. He don't know I'm doing this. I'm gonna work it all out, then show him."

"Like a surprise present?"

"Yeah."

"'Cause you know he'll want it?"

"'Cause I know he needs it, no matter what he thinks."

"Loyalty and hard work. You're one of the good ones, Handar Ennis."

Any way he cut it he was pretty sure that wasn't true. He'd left too much carnage in his wake to ever count as righteous. He had his principles and did what was necessary for the people who mattered to him. For someone who'd lived his life, that was as close to good as you could get.

"Problem is, I'm getting nowhere." He held up a parchment for her to see. "All this stuff's prophecies. It's supposed to tell me the future, but all I see coming is that I'll get mad and tear this stuff to shreds."

"Huh." Berra opened a book sitting at one side of the table and flicked through its contents pages. "'The Power of Metaphor,'" she read aloud, slowly and carefully, sounding out each syllable. "That's what this part's all about. Things standing in for other things, right?"

"Uh-huh."

"And here, you keep writing down bits about doors."

"I do."

"Well, what if they ain't real doors? What do doors mean to you?"

"They mean I can get into buildings. What else are they gonna mean?" He clenched his fist. This sort of thinking was why he found this so frustrating.

"Calm," Berra said. "Don't force it."

She went to stand behind him, her belly pressed against his back, and took long slow breaths. He found that his breath started following hers, and a sense of peace came over him. His fist unclenched.

"I guess they're other things too," he said slowly, as the idea unfurled with his fingers. "Like weaknesses, places you can break through."

"Weaknesses. That's good. Could be that's what they stand for here."

Handar grinned. Maybe he could do this after all. He could unravel the secrets of these papers. He could find the meaning in them. All it had taken was the right help.

He got out of his seat and took hold of Berra.

"You're so smart," he said.

She shook her head. "I just got lucky."

"I'm the one who got lucky, finding you."

"Quit talking like an elf." She punched his arm, but she was smiling.

"You can help me with this. Work out what it all means."

She shook her head again. "That ain't me, Handar. I can keep your secrets, but I can't untangle someone else's. Not this sort of secret."

"I can't do it on my own."

"Then find someone else who can help. Someone who's proper smart. You and me, we're good with our bodies, but you must know someone good with their brain. Someone you can trust."

Handar ran a hand down her side, but his mind was only half in the room. He did know someone else, someone who would be motivated to help the boss. He'd never thought about whether he could trust her. It never occurred to him to trust people he hadn't fought alongside. He trusted Berra enough to tell her about this. Maybe he could trust someone else too.

"What's this?" Berra flipped open the red folder to reveal the first sheet of its contents, pictures of Fran Berryman and Cameron Kowal. "Who are these two?"

"The enemy," he growled. "The people trying to work this out before me."

"They don't look like much of anything." She flipped the folder shut and pressed her hand against his chest. "Barely a muscle between 'em. I bet they ain't worked out the metaphor here. Not like you." She tapped him on the forehead. "They're gonna regret ever crossing my Handar."

"Your Handar." He grinned and pressed her close. "I like that."

"You'd better." She pushed her fingers through his hair and pulled him closer, so he felt her breath against his cheek. "I don't plan on letting you go."

He wrapped his arms around Berra and lifted her off her feet. She laughed.

"What you doing?"

"Going to the bedroom. All this thinking, we've earned ourselves a lie-in."

"What about your prophecies?"

"Future can wait. Right now, I'm gonna live for today."

CHAPTER SEVEN

Fran stood in the street outside the Blazing Bean coffee shop, wrapped in a padded coat, mittens, and a thick woolen scarf. It was the coldest winter day so far, and she wasn't taking any chances. On her shoulder, a crow was also taking shelter from the cold. It had caught an edge of her scarf in its beak and was trying to pull that edge over its body.

"You don't have to be here, you know," Fran said. "You could go find somewhere warm to perch."

The crow croaked in disagreement and kept tugging at the scarf.

"I know you're proud of what you found, but that doesn't mean you have to come along," she continued. "I can tell you later whether it was any good."

The crow let out another disgruntled noise and pressed itself closer to her. Now it was trying to take shelter under her hair.

"In fact, you probably shouldn't be here. It's kind of creepy, having my dad following me out on a date."

The crow croaked indignantly.

"All right, fine, you're not my dad. You're his messenger, his observer, his information-gatherer. Heck, you might be the closest thing he has to a friend. All of that makes it bad enough that you guys have been following me for years without you coming along now."

The crow shrugged, but only slightly. It had layers of scarf and hair around itself and wasn't going to risk shaking them off.

The door of the Blazing Bean opened, and Cam stepped out into the street.

"Hi there." He leaned in to kiss her hello. "You know you could've waited inside, right?"

"I felt guilty about coming in and distracting you when you're at work."

"Since when?"

"Since I started having employees as well as colleagues."

Cam laughed. "I see. So now that you're a boss, you're going to object to people slacking off? What next, a bit of union-busting?"

"No! I just..." Fran shrugged. "I didn't want to be competing with little old ladies for your attention."

"All right, I'll take that one." Cam followed her lead as she wrapped an arm around him and ambled down the street. "So, where are we going tonight?"

"That would be telling."

"That's the idea."

"Well, I have other ideas."

A flying taxi was waiting at the corner, a basket big enough for both of them with a pair of giant eagles sitting ready to carry it aloft.

"No expense spared tonight, huh?" Cam climbed in alongside Fran.

"We couldn't get where we're going without it." She smiled at him. "I think you'll like this one."

The taxi took off, the basket creaking as its slats settled under their weight. The eagles beat their powerful wings, and within moments they were soaring over the heart of Mana Valley. The crow peeked out from under Fran's hair and looked up enviously at the eagles.

"You can come with us as far as the entrance," Fran said to the bird. "After that, you go find your own entertainment, understand?"

The taxi swept out across the sea of lights that was Mana Valley. There were lights from homes, offices, vehicles, street lamps, flashlights, and festive decorations that were still up—almost as many points of light on the ground below as in the clear sky above.

"I could fly around like this all evening." Cam pushed his glasses up his nose. "It's amazing."

"I couldn't." Fran pressed against him and huddled close, trying to shelter from the wind. "Too cold."

The taxi reached the top of a towering office block and settled down on a landing pad. At a gesture from Fran, the crow reluctantly flew away while she and Cam got out of the basket and into a bubble of warm air.

"Wow." He looked around. "This is quite a place."

The owner had transformed the rooftop into a restaurant, with tables and chairs scattered across its tiled surface. There was a bar to one side, and at the back, chefs labored at a set of exposed cookers, their work open for anyone to see.

"You must be Ms. Berryman," said a sharply dressed elf waiter. "Can I show you to your seat?"

They followed him to a table with a view across the city's lights to the distant mountains.

"Still wish you were flying around in that basket?" Fran asked as she took off her coat.

"This will do just as well." Cam also stripped off his winter layers. "Better, even. How do they keep it warm?"

"There's a magical field. Keeps the rain off, too, although we won't need that."

"It's great, but it must be difficult to get a table at a fancy place like this."

"Not when you're the hot new thing in Mana Valley."

Now seated, Fran glanced around. Sure enough, she caught a few people covertly looking her way. Some were probably trying to work out why they recognized her, but others had a knowing look that came from trying not to gape at a celebrity openly.

"This might take some getting used to," Cam said. "Especially for a poor barista who normally only gets attention from people who want drinks."

"It is a bit weird." Fran leaned forward to whisper to him. "It's cool too. Elethin says I could get a reservation anywhere I want, so when the crows spotted this place, I thought we should give it a go."

The waiter reappeared with a notepad in one hand and a bowl of dice in the other. "Are you ready to order?"

"Could we see a menu first?" Cam replied.

"That's not how things work here, sir. You roll the dice, and they pick dinner for you."

"What if I roll something I don't like or I'm allergic to?"

"That's never happened yet. Please, pick a die, give it a go."

Cam shrugged and picked out a ten-sided die. The air around it glittered as he rolled it into the table's center. "A seven. What is that?"

"Let's wait and see." Fran picked out a different die. "I don't want to spoil the surprise."

They rolled dice for their drinks and three courses, then the waiter swept the polyhedral shapes into his bowl and headed for the kitchen.

"Are you sure about this?" Cam asked. "This place looks pricey, and for all we know, we might have picked the most expensive dishes on the menu."

"Don't worry. I'm paying for this one."

"That's not how it works." Cam frowned. "We always split the bill."

"That's great normally, but we couldn't afford to try a place like this that way."

"Fran, how can we afford this at all?"

"Well, you know…" She trailed off, one hand pressed against the back of her neck, suddenly feeling unaccountably uncomfortable. "My business."

"Really?" Cam raised an eyebrow. "I knew things were going well, but this…" He gestured around them at the finely furnished restaurant and the other diners in their designer clothes. "You're earning this kind of money?"

"This and more." Fran blushed. "I wasn't sure how to tell you or if you already knew from all the things in the news."

Now it was Cam's turn to look embarrassed.

"I haven't had a lot of time for the news," he admitted. "I

mean, I'm still keeping an eye out for anything relating to the prophecies, and I try to keep on top of the headlines. It's great when I see something about you guys, but I haven't exactly had time to read it all."

"Well, we're earning big money, and it's about to get even better. So I thought I'd treat you to this." Fran grinned. "Isn't it great?"

"It is, but..."

Cam hesitated uncertainly. The arrival of a pair of waiters carrying their drinks and starters saved him from deciding.

"That was quick." Fran took a sip of the tastiest fruit spritzer she'd ever had.

"It's not only the dice that are lucky," one of the waiters said. "Anyone cooking in our kitchen finds that if they get started on a dish, it will turn out to be what's wanted." He gave them a small bow and backed off. "Bon appetit."

Cam used his fork to break off the corner of a pastry parcel full of vegetables and cheese, then took a bite.

"Oh, wow," he said. "Those dice really are lucky."

To Fran's surprise, he followed that comment by setting down his fork and pushing the plate away.

"What's the matter? Isn't it good?"

"It's delicious. That's not what's putting me off."

"What is?"

Cam ran his fingertips over his forehead as if he was trying to press away the wrinkles of stress. It didn't work.

"It's all of this, Fran. When we met, we were equals. You were starting a business from nothing, and I was working a low-wage job in a coffee shop. Even when we got together, we were on the same level. We went where we could afford to go, and if we sometimes spent a little more than we ought to, we knew that we'd both feel the pain the same way. Now you've got all this money, and you're paying for expensive dinners, and it's..."

"It's great, right?" she asked hopefully. "Because we get nice things."

"No. It's uncomfortable because you can afford the nice things and I can't. It's emphasizing the difference between us. There's a power imbalance there."

"Does that matter?"

"Of course, it matters!" Cam snapped. "How can you not see that? It means we're not equals in this relationship."

Fran reached across the table and took his hand. She squeezed it gently until he looked her in the eye.

"Cam, I don't know much about relationships, but there's something I can see, which is that there were always going to be imbalances between us."

"You're not making things better."

"Hear me out. I was always going to be better with technology than you. You were always going to be better at understanding people and society than me. You're smarter. That's why you almost have a Ph.D., and how you worked out that something was going wrong in the Valley with all those prophecies. I'm better at applying what I learn. I'm also way better at skating, but I can't make coffee as well as you."

He smiled a little. "You certainly can't."

"Hey, no need to rub it in!" She smiled too. "I get that right now the professional difference is huge. I've got all this money and prestige, and that's thrown part of our life out of balance.

"I still need you as much as ever, more even. I need someone to keep me grounded, to calm me down when I get stressed, to value me for something other than my work. I love you, and that's not changing. I just get to express it differently, like taking you nice places."

"I love you too." Cam shook his head. "I guess I need time to get used to this. We might need to set some rules, so I get to pay once in a while."

"I can accept that." Fran tried a spoonful of her soup. "Oh wow, that is so spicy! And in, like, a totally awesome way."

"I've got to admit; this place is pretty cool." Cam ate more of his starter. "I feel bad now. I didn't mean to complain."

"You've been busy. That makes it harder to deal with things." Fran pursed her lips. "Wait, I never asked. Why are you so busy?"

"Ah, that..." Cam tapped his fork against his plate. "It's the doctorate. I'm running out of time to finish it."

"So you've been rushing to get it done?"

"Sort of. I've mostly been talking to my supervisor and stressing myself out, trying to decide what to do."

"What do you mean?"

"I should've finished this thing ages ago, and the fact that I haven't shows that maybe academia isn't for me. I could stress myself out and work myself to the bone and maybe get it finished, or I could accept that it won't happen. I could let go, relax, move on. I have to admit, that sounds pretty appealing right now."

"What would you do instead?"

"For now? Make coffee."

Fran carefully ate the rest of her soup while she thought that one over. With the last mouthful done, she set her spoon down.

"No," she said.

"Excuse me?" Cam looked at her uncertainly.

"I said no. Cameron Kowal, you're one of the smartest people I've ever met. You're insightful and hard-working. You love history, and you're passionate about...about that thing you're researching."

"The unseen influence of magical factions on the politics of seventeenth-century Europe?"

"Exactly, that. You could still have a career in academia, become a professor with an office full of books, make as much difference in the world as my business does. Even if you decide not to do that, you'll feel so much better for finishing what you started."

"I guess you're right..."

"Plus you'll get to call yourself Dr. Kowal, and that's awesome."

He laughed. "You think I should work myself ragged to call myself a doctor?"

"If that's what it takes to motivate you, yes."

He laughed, then leaned around the table to kiss her.

"Fran, your encouragement is far more valuable to me than all the fancy dinners you can pay for. Thank you."

"So you'll do it?"

"I'll do it. I should warn you. This might mean I don't have much time for a little while for us or the things we do together."

"I don't like the sound of that." Fran pouted, but only for a moment. It was hard not to smile with Cam around.

"It'll be totally worth it." She raised her glass. "Here's to you, future Dr. Kowal."

"Here's to us." Cam raised his glass too.

Flying high overhead, the crow looked down on them. It croaked in approval.

CHAPTER EIGHT

"I hear that you ate at the Sky Dice last night," Elethin said as they sat in the back of a limo, making their way through the early evening traffic.

"Did Bart tell you?" Fran asked. "He helped me find their booking line."

"No, it was on one of the gossip sites. You're a celebrity worth reporting on now."

Facing them from the seat behind the driver, Gruffbar snorted.

"Worth is a low bar where gossip sites are concerned," he muttered.

"Don't be a party pooper, Steelstrike," Elethin said sharply. "When our Fran gets attention, that's good for all of us."

"When she gets attention for her work, sure. When it's for eating dinner? That hardly helps."

"You're only sulking because you couldn't wear that grease-stained jacket of yours."

"I'm in a bad mood because this thing is strangling me." Gruffbar reached under his neatly trimmed beard, stuck a thick finger through his collar, and tugged at his bow tie.

"Don't you dare undo that. Not until it's late enough to be stylish."

Gruffbar crossed his arms and glared at them. "It's all right for you. Feminine black tie doesn't mean throttling yourself."

Fran looked down at her outfit. The dress was the most expensive one she'd ever worn and more revealing than she was used to, but at least Elethin had let her choose one covered in sequins. Even her shoes were sparkly enough to make up for the difficulty of balancing on them.

Elethin, meanwhile, looked like she'd been born for moments like this. She wore a clinging gray dress slit most of the way up her thigh, showing off legs that would make a model jealous. She walked as easily in her heels as if she was barefoot on a carpet.

"Here we are," Elethin said as the limo pulled up in front of a grand hotel. "Remember, tonight is about raising Fran's public profile. Personality trumps trade talk. Only bring up business issues if someone else mentions them first."

"Then what do I talk about?" Gruffbar growled.

"The usual. Gossip. Outfits. That new exhibition at the city gallery. How good the DJ is. You know, small talk."

"Sounds awful."

"Don't give me that. I know you went to the art exhibition."

Gruffbar let out a discontented *humph,* then opened the

door and stepped onto the red carpet leading off the street. Immediately, cameras started to flash.

"You go last." Elethin stepped out, then gestured at Fran to join her.

As Fran stepped out, the flashes grew more frequent, as did the cheering from the crowd held back behind security barriers.

"This is so weird," Fran whispered, trying to maintain a smile.

"Get used to it," Elethin replied. "You're a celebrity now. Don't forget to wave."

The three of them walked up the red carpet, Fran waving as she went. It was kind of fun.

"All this is because people want to fund a new hospital?" she asked.

"No, this is because people love *Orchard of Stars*. Celebrities are a useful way to get a charity funded."

"Orchard of what now?" Gruffbar asked.

"You know full well, Steelstrike, that the cast of *Orchard of Stars*, one of the most ground-breaking soap operas in modern entertainment, put this together."

"It's Elethin's favorite." Fran waved at a TV camera.

"I will admit, I quite enjoy the show."

"So we definitely shouldn't do anything to embarrass you?" Gruffbar grinned.

"Whatever you're plotting, don't you dare." Elethin's tone was acid but her smile sweet. "Fran's profile, remember?"

"Fine, I'll behave myself. Only for Fran."

They reached the hotel's entrance, where the doors

were held open by a pair of dwarves in dinner jackets, and walked from there into the lobby.

"Hi, there!" An Arpak in a ballgown swept up to them, her wings spread wide behind her. She had the most beautiful golden feathers that Fran had ever seen and a face that had beamed out at her from a dozen gossip magazines in corner shops and supermarket checkouts. "I'm Heidi. I play Encanterel in the show. You're Fran, right?"

"Um, yes, hi." Fran tried to reciprocate as Heidi air-kissed her dramatically on both cheeks. "These are my friends, Gruffbar Steelstrike and Elethin Tannerin. They're on the board of my company."

Was she supposed to say that? Elethin had said no business talk, but Fran wanted to let Heidi know that the others were as important as her.

"It's an absolute delight." Heidi bent to greet Gruffbar, then turned to Elethin. "Oh my skies, your dress is exquisite."

"You're too kind." Elethin smiled and pushed back a few stray strands of hair. "I have to admit that I'm a fan of your work."

"No!" Heidi laughed. "That is so sweet of you. Now, why don't you all come this way? The party's just getting started..."

She led them through to the ballroom while another actor took her place, ready to welcome the next arrivals.

The ballroom was full of people, all of them dressed as elegantly as Fran and her friends and looking as comfortable about it as Elethin did. Waiters of all shapes and sizes walked between them, carrying trays of drinks and tiny morsels of carefully sculpted food. The bodies of many of the guests were also carefully managed, with the faces and physiques of actors, models, and music stars.

Within a few seconds, Fran had recognized the leads from two of her favorite films and a folk singer her mom loved. Mingling with the gorgeous and the glamorous were Mana Valley's other elite, the money and the power. Business leaders, investment bankers, and hedge fund managers, all dressed as expensively as the stars.

"Is that Talthin Crane?" Fran asked as a dark-haired elf strode by.

"Uh-huh." Gruffbar watched the elf with narrowed eyes. "Looks like he's gotten over Smokey beating him at the ballot box."

"Hard to stay sad when you've got his money. Ooh, and look, Howard Phillips!"

"It would hardly be a Mana Valley fundraiser without him," Elethin said. "Those aren't the people to focus on." She gestured at the balconies around the edge of the room, where photographers were lining up their shots. "Tonight is about the stars. If you want to be in tomorrow's news, you want to talk to them."

"That's what we want, right?"

"If anybody else asks, you want to raise money for the hospital. As far as I'm concerned, you get yourself in front of the cameras and have fun doing it. These are the beautiful people. Enjoy the moment." Elethin looked out across the sea of money, power, and glamor. "Gods, I've missed this."

She stepped into the crowd and within ten seconds was

deep in conversation with a sports star. Fran stood uncertainly for a moment, then shrugged.

"Guess we go for it." She turned to the nearest guests and held out her hand. "Hi, I'm Fran, and I'm totally out of my depth here. How are you doing?"

A wizard with a red bow tie laughed and shook her hand. "Hi, Fran, I'm Dirk, and it's a pleasure to meet someone so upfront. Would you like to meet some other people from the show?"

As they headed into the crowd, Gruffbar reached up to stop a passing waiter.

"You got whiskey?" he asked.

"Yes, sir." The waiter handed him down a glass. "Can I get you anything else?"

"Another whiskey?"

The waiter looked at his tray, which mostly held champagne. "I could fetch another?"

"Great. I'll be at that table in the corner. Bring me three whiskeys and whatever food here is closest to a steak sandwich."

"I'll see what I can find." The waiter looked at Gruffbar uncertainly. "I hope you don't mind my asking this, sir, but are you sure you belong here?"

"Absolutely not. My colleague invited me to make me miserable. By my beard, I'm not going to let her win. So you bring me my whiskeys and my sandwich, and I'll have my kind of party. Clear?"

"Crystal clear, sir."

The waiter rushed away, and Gruffbar went to find his seat.

Across the room, Elethin was in her element, talking

casually with powerful and beautiful people, laughing at their jokes, looking enraptured by their anecdotes, saving her stories for the perfect moment to keep everyone engaged.

This had been her life once, although those parties had held a few dark dealings. Whispered conversations that hinted at blackmail without ever stating it out loud. Letting toxic rumors out to poison rivals' reputations. Making sure the right people met or were kept apart to ensure that the right deals happened. Or perhaps the very wrong deals.

She almost missed the Machiavellian scheming for the challenge it had given her, but she hadn't missed it half as much as the glitz, the dizzying feeling of being part of a true elite.

"No, you didn't!" she exclaimed, laughing lightly at an athlete's anecdote.

"Swear I did." He winked. "Don't ever tell my coach though."

"Don't worry, your secret's safe with me." She let her hand linger a moment on his forearm. "I won't tell a soul."

He held up his glass, then glanced at hers.

"Can I get you another? They do some great cocktails here."

"That would be divine. Get me something spicy."

"Feeling adventurous?"

"Always." She raised her eyebrow a fraction and enjoyed the way his smile responded.

"I'll be right back."

She watched as he hurried away to the bar. He had a good body for a human, but there were lots of fine bodies here, and the night was young. Much as she was enjoying his attention, she really should keep mingling.

"Champagne, ma'am?" a waitress asked, holding out her try.

"No, thank you." Elethin surveyed the room around her. "I have a drink coming."

"Are you sure?" the waitress asked. "I can't get you anything, El?"

That name brought Elethin's attention down with pointed force onto the waitress. There was only one place where people called her El, and she thought she'd left that behind.

Now that she looked, the waitress was familiar. A short Arpak with dark wings and pale skin, her hair had grown out almost to shoulder length, but there was no mistaking the bright gleam of her eyes.

"Kotia." Elethin's voice turned cold although she kept her smile bright for the rest of the room. "I didn't expect to see you here."

"Thought I was still in Trevilsom?"

"Honestly, I didn't think much about you at all."

"Figures. You always were a selfish bitch."

"You weren't exactly a vision of virtue yourself. That's how you ended up in jail."

"Yeah, well, I'm out now, and I need help with something."

"A better job or a better haircut? Either way, I'm the wrong woman to talk to. I'm as bad with a resume as with a pair of scissors."

"Funny, I remember you being pretty handy with one scissor blade." Kotia's eyes narrowed. "But then, I remember a lot of things that you wouldn't want people out here to know."

"You don't know anything about me." Elethin felt her spine stiffening, her jaw setting. She couldn't help herself. Tension was rising through her, a fight or flight response like she hadn't felt since she'd stepped out of that cold, hard place and back into the fresh air of freedom. "You don't know what I am out here."

"I know you're the sort of person who goes to parties like this. I know that they're what you dreamed of on the inside, what saw you through. And I know that, with a rumor in the wrong place, you could lose them again."

"You wouldn't."

"I won't need to because you're going to help me, right?"

With gritted teeth, Elethin slid a hand briefly into her purse. When she reached out to take a glass of champagne from Kotia's tray, she left behind a business card in its place. "Call me tomorrow. We can meet for coffee."

"Sounds real civilized." Kotia whipped the card away into her pocket. "See you then."

The waitress headed off into the crowd, just in time for the athlete to return, holding out a glass of something red. "Here, try this. It goes down really smooth."

"You're so sweet." Elethin took the glass. "I'll be back shortly. I need to check in with my colleague."

"Sure, sure," the athlete replied, confused by the sudden change in her mood. "You want me to come with you?"

"No, no, you keep mingling. Don't you worry." She touched his upper arm, a fleeting brush of her fingers that hinted at far more. "I'll find you soon."

She left him grinning as she headed through the crowd, fighting back a scowl. How dare Kotia do this, ruining her perfect evening with memories of prison? And how dare she make demands?

Elethin gulped her drink. It was warm, smooth, and delicious, but it still felt bitter going down.

As she'd expected, Gruffbar had found the single dark corner in the room, the one place where a person could go unnoticed while the bold and the beautiful whirled around them. She flung herself down in a seat next to him and finally let her mask of happiness slip.

"Thought you loved these parties?" He grinned.

"I do."

"Then why do you look like someone pissed in your cocktail?"

"Because they might as well have done." She downed the remains of the drink and set the glass aside.

"Somehow, my evening just became perfect." Gruffbar picked up a whiskey glass and held it out to her. "Peace offering? You look more miserable in this place than I could ever be, which means I win."

"There are no winners here." She snatched the glass and took a sip. The burn of liquor down her throat was more satisfying than the sweet cocktail. "Only losers making my life worse."

"Anything I can help with?"

She snorted. "Of course not."

"Guess I'm keeping these to myself then." He picked up two other glasses. "How's our girl doing out there?"

They peered from their shadowy corner into the crowd. Fran stood at a table, improvising a steam turbine from candles, napkins, and a bottle of mineral water, to the delight of a laughing crowd of actors and singers. She wore the excited smile that suited her so well. From the balconies above, the flash of cameras rained down on her.

"Fabulously, of course," Elethin said. "At least we got that much right."

CHAPTER NINE

Fran yawned and stretched. At least there was plenty of space to do that out here in the hills. If she tried to stretch in the office, she was likely to hit one of her new co-workers as they hurried past on some administrative errand.

"Bored already, Francesca?" Irene Berryman raised an eyebrow at her daughter. "I thought you wanted to do this."

"I do. I'm sorry." Fran stifled another yawn. "We've been really busy at work, and Elethin keeps dragging me out to parties and galas on the weekends. They're fun and all, and I've met some awesome people, but I'm not sure when I'm supposed to catch up on sleep."

"You poor dear, caught up in the horrors of celebrity parties while I'm free to sit at home dying my hair and watching the news."

"I know, I know. I should be grateful for what I've got. And I am. I just wish that what I had included a few more hours in bed."

A crow swept past them, croaking as it went. Fran waved a gloved hand at it.

"For what it's worth, I'm glad you gave up some of those hours for us to come out here," Irene said. "It feels like forever since we've gone for a walk, only the two of us."

"It does. I'm sorry it couldn't simply be a relaxing hike."

"I'm not. It's nice to feel that I can still be useful to you, even when you've become this strong, assertive, independent young woman."

"Aw, Mom." Fran squeezed Irene's shoulder. "You'll always be the one I come to when there are monsters under my bed."

"Or Evermores in the hills?"

The crow landed on Fran's shoulder and peered suspiciously around.

"Especially Evermores in the hills." Fran looked across the wooded slopes. "Speaking of which, are you sure you can find them out here?"

Irene nodded, and a mischievous smile slid up her face.

"Oh, yes. After one of my previous problems with Winslow, I had a friend put a tracking spell on him. It's gotten weaker over the years, but when I need to, I can find that old goat."

As if to reinforce her point, a real mountain goat stepped out onto the path and stood glaring at them. Thanks to the background magic of the foothills and the mountains beyond, it had transformed into something more than a mundane beast. Instead of a single pair of horns, ten of them thrust out across the top of its head, forming a halo, and the creature's eyes flashed from red to green and back like a broken light on a Christmas tree.

"Wow." Fran's breath frosted as she stood staring at the goat. "Look, it has a family."

Four smaller goats with the same pattern of horns and eyes flashing in different colors followed their mother onto the path, then into the trees and away. The crow tilted its head, stretched its wings, and flew after the goats, following them down the hill.

"They were cute," Irene admitted. "But slightly beside the point. We're nearly there, wherever there is."

They trudged up the rough trail, small stones and dirt crunching beneath their walking boots. They were both wrapped up in thick coats, gloves, scarfs, and hats until very little of their skin was exposed, but the mountain air still stung the bare spots on Fran's cheeks.

"Are you sure you want to do this, dear?" Irene said as they approached a ridge. "I think you'd be better off without Winslow and his people in your life."

"I get why you say that. Heck, I tried to shut them out. The Source has come to me in dreams three times now. It needs help, and I don't know who else could give it."

Irene smiled sadly. "I'm so proud of you. Now let's see what sort of hole Winslow has found for himself this time."

They strode to the top of the ridge and looked down into the valley below. The slope beneath their feet was steep and broken as if someone had viciously hacked away the earth itself. Farther down, it turned into a gentler but no more pleasant-looking slope of loose rocks. The far side of the valley was the same, torn and filthy with debris, and the low ground between them was why.

An aging mining complex took up the valley floor. There were brick and wood buildings in a style not used in at least fifty years, and they'd been falling apart since then. Rusted iron roofs sagged over crumbling walls. Hulking equipment stood at tunnel entrances, weeds growing across pulleys and gearwheels rusting into brown scab lumps.

"Dwarves?" Fran asked.

"No, dear. Dwarves keep their mines far better than this."

"Maybe they abandoned it?"

"Dwarf miners are tidier about leaving too. This was some other sort of magicals, probably one of the businesses down in the valley, back when they got their hands dirty with things like mineral extraction."

"I thought you didn't know much about Mana Valley."

"I've been learning."

Their conversation was interrupted by a ripple of magic, and a sound like the earth itself was screaming. The ground gave way beneath their feet, and they slid down the slope, faster and faster toward the valley floor. The rough ground scraped Fran through her jeans.

Large, jagged stones rose ahead of them, like the teeth of a hungry giant. At their current rate of descent, they would wind up impaled on those rocks.

In the bare seconds available to her, Fran summoned one of the powers her father had taught her. She raised her leg and took a far step, appearing on the far side of the stones. There, she spun and unleashed a blast of Evermore sound magic that knocked a stretch of the sharp stones flat. Irene slid through it and halted by Fran's feet.

"Ouch!" Irene exclaimed. A bolt of light sizzled past her head and melted a hole through one of the rocks. "Double ouch!"

Fran spun and raised her hands, flinging up a protective field of powerful sound waves. It rippled the air in front of her in time to disrupt two more bolts of burning light so both hit the ground instead of her and her mom.

She flicked her wrists, and the wall of magical sound rushed away from her. It hit a half-collapsed shed at the edge of the mine workings. The shed collapsed and flung the magical inside from her feet.

Fran took another far step and appeared at the magical's side. As she arrived, Fran extended a hand, calling for whatever weapon was closest. A rusted ax hurtled through the air, and its handle slapped into her hand. She raised it and stared down menacingly at the magical.

"Quit with the magic. Now."

The magical stared up at her. She looked human, which would normally have meant a witch or a shifter, but something about her magic felt familiar to Fran. As the woman pulled her scarf down from across her mouth, Fran realized that she knew the face too.

"You're one of the Evermores, aren't you?" Fran asked. "Taldiss, right?"

"Is that Fran Berryman?" Taldiss blew short dark hair out of her eyes and pushed into a crouch. She looked warily at Fran's ax. "What are you doing here?"

"What are you doing attacking us?" Fran asked as Irene joined them.

"Rock monsters attacked us. Thought you might be them again."

"Do we look like rock monsters?" Irene asked indignantly.

"I saw silhouettes on the ridge, then a blur of movement down to the bottom. After the past few months, I wasn't taking any chances. Not with everything that's at stake."

Fran sighed and lowered her ax. It hadn't been the most reasonable response, but if she got violent every time the Evermores got defensive, things would get ugly fast.

"Is Enfield around?" she asked.

"He is, but..."

"I should see Winslow first?"

Taldiss nodded. "He is our leader, and he'll want to know that you're here. Plus, I don't know whether Enfield's in a state for visitors today."

"Why?" Fran was alarmed. "What happened to him?"

"I should let him explain. Come on."

Taldiss led them across the abandoned mining site to one of the tunnel entrances.

"This place looks rough," Fran said as they walked down a tunnel lit by small globes of magical light.

"It's a lot better than when we found it," Taldiss said. "We've cobbled together a heating system and got the ventilation up and running. But yeah, it's no match for the house in the hills. Whole time we were there, I was mad that we weren't home. Now I miss it."

They turned off the main tunnel into a smaller chamber, still lit by magic. If there was one thing the Evermores would never be short of, it was light. It illuminated a room lined with reclaimed wooden boards, carpeted with old rugs and offcuts. There was a rough cot in one corner. In the center of the room, four slices cut from a tree trunk served as seats around a packing crate table.

An Evermore with flecks of gray in his dark hair rose serenely from one of those seats.

"Winslow." Fran tried her best to sound pleased to see him. "How are you?"

"Fran." Winslow nodded at her. "And Irene. I thought you were both done with us."

"You also thought I'd be back, I bet." Fran crossed her arms.

"I did have certain expectations. After twenty-six thousand years, people become predictable."

"If I'm so predictable, what brought me back?"

"Beneath it all, a desire to be with your own. I'm sure you found a way to justify that. Curiosity about the Source, perhaps, or your concern for Enfield."

There was a stiff silence while Fran considered her next words. She didn't like to lie, but she didn't think honesty was the best policy where Winslow was concerned. He'd made clear that he thought they could never release the Source. If she let him know that was her ultimate goal, he would do his best to stop her, and despite his circumstances, he held the power here.

"Where can I find Enfield?" she asked.

Winslow smiled smugly. "Taldiss will show you. Perhaps, Irene, you could stay here and talk to me, let the youngsters have some time to themselves?"

Fran followed Taldiss back into the tunnel and down its cold course, deeper into the mountainside.

"Whatever you want with Enfield, don't push it," Taldiss said. "If I think you're risking his recovery, I'll kick you back out into the rubble. You might think you're tough, but I know a few tricks too."

"I don't think I'm tough."

"Yeah, right."

Taldiss opened a creaking door into another chamber. This turned out to be a communal room where other Evermores had gathered. They watched in silence as Taldiss and Fran crossed the room and went through a door on the far side.

"Enfield?" Taldiss softly asked as they entered a small, dimly lit space. "Are you awake?"

"Just about."

Someone moved in the gloom, and the light level rose. Pushing aside his blankets, Enfield sat up on the edge of a bed, wincing as he did so.

Fran almost winced too at the sight of him. Beneath loose clothes, she could make out the shapes of bulky dressings covering large parts of his body. One hand was bandaged, the bandages disappearing up his sleeve. His blond hair was growing back from stubble, but only patchily on the left-hand side, where raw scars ran almost from the top of his head down across his face.

"Oh, Enfield." Fran ran over and hugged him. He yelped in pain, and she immediately let go. "I'm so sorry. I didn't mean to... What happened?"

Enfield stretched out his legs, using his hands to move one of them, and leaned back against the wall. "The Source. It escaped. We went after it, and things got messy."

Fran stared in horror from his face down to his leg, which lay at an odd angle.

"The Source did this?" she whispered.

"Good thing we caught the damn thing again, huh?" Taldiss said. "It's a menace."

"It's more complicated than that," Enfield said.

"I can't believe that you of all people are saying that. It almost killed you."

Enfield closed his eyes. "I'm sorry, Taldiss, I don't have the energy to fight this one out again."

"I…" Taldiss clenched her fist and pressed it against her stomach. "Fine, whatever. I'll leave you two to catch up. Shout if you need me."

She strode back into the other room, leaving Fran and Enfield alone.

"Seriously." Enfield opened his eyes. "It was more complicated. I've seen a side of the Source I never saw before. I think it needs our help."

"I'm so glad you think that," Fran said. "We should talk about it later. First, tell me what happened to you."

"That's not only a complicated story. It's a long one…"

CHAPTER TEN

Fran's trip into the mountains was still on her mind two days later as she sat in the Blazing Bean coffee shop with Gruffbar, watching two crows peck at a discarded muffin outside the window.

"Do dwarves clear up when you leave a mine?" she asked.

"Of course." Gruffbar looked up from his laptop. "At least, most do, but as with anything, you get a few bad actors who don't do the right thing."

"Like the sort of people you used to work with?"

"Absolutely not!" The dwarf stared at her indignantly. "I've helped arrange kidnappings, thefts, blackmail, and extortion, but I draw the line at bad mining."

"Sorry. I didn't realize it was such a touchy subject. Can I get you a cake to make up for it?"

She glanced at the counter. Buying cake would get her a few seconds of talking to Cam, who'd drawn a long shift today.

"Maybe later." Gruffbar stood. "Our meeting is here."

Fran stood and held out her hand to the woman approaching them. "Hi, I'm Fran. You must be Dot."

"That's right." Dot shook Fran's hand. "Pleased to meet you."

Dot was around Fran's height, with a wild mass of hair in brown and blond streaks. There was a little fur on the back of her hand, and the tips of her fingers were claws, a limited piece of transformation that a lot of shifters chose to adopt when coming from Earth to Oriceran on business. It was as if showing their magical side justified their presence on the other world and made them feel more confident that they could fit in.

"You've met Gruffbar already?" Fran asked.

"That's right." Dot shook his hand anyway, then took one of the spare seats at the table. "Thanks for meeting with me."

"I'm happy to." Fran smiled. "It's always exciting to see what technology other people are working on."

"Well, I don't like to brag, but this is particularly cool."

Dot took a black cube out of her bag and set it on the table. On one side were three lenses. She pressed a button on the top, the lenses brightened, and a three-dimensional image of a house appeared in the air next to the box.

"I run a startup, like you," Dot said. "Well, not quite like you, or I'd be living in a nicer apartment."

Fran decided against telling her that she lived in the same cramped rooms she and Josie had found when they first came to Mana Valley. It didn't matter right now.

"We've been working for several years on a new magitech projector," Dot continued. "It uses a combination of technology and enchantment to create three-dimensional images in the air. Like you've done with the FDS, but we haven't got consistent movement yet."

"Ooh, I can help you with that!" Fran said. "What we did was—"

"Fran," Gruffbar interrupted, "now's the time to listen, not give away our technical secrets."

"Oh, right, yes!" Fran laughed. "Sorry, I get distracted easily. Tell me more about your projector."

"Well, there's one thing we've done that I don't think you have yet." Dot gestured at the hologram. "Touch it."

Fran reached out and prodded the miniature house. Instead of pushing through the image, her finger pressed against something almost solid. Its texture was as rough as real bricks, but it gave a little beneath the pressure of her touch, like rubber. She grinned and ran her fingertips across the roof, then squeezed the tiny chimney.

"That's so cool," she said. "Is it really solid, or is that part of the illusion?"

"That's a simple question with a complicated answer," Dot said. "One I'd be happy to go through in detail with anyone I was collaborating with."

"Which is why you're here."

"Exactly. I think what we've developed could be a great addition to the FDS, allowing you to create more interactive games and more convincing entertainments."

"Why don't you finish developing this by yourselves? I'm sure you could sell it to other people, not only Mana Wave."

"Our funds are getting tight. We haven't been able to attract the right backers."

"Which is why you contacted us," Gruffbar said.

"That's right." Dot shifted in her seat. For all her show of confidence, she wasn't comfortable with this sort of talk. "We need money. You have money. We have new technology, and I think you might need that, to keep improving your product. So…"

"Ooh ooh ooh!" Fran clapped her hands together. "This sounds like a great—"

"Fran." Gruffbar cut her off again. "This is something we should talk about." He turned to Dot. "Could you go get fresh coffee and some cakes? Tell the guy behind the counter that Fran and I will pay for it later."

"He knows you?"

"You could say that." Fran blushed.

"Okay then." Dot got out of her seat and went to join the queue for service. As she went, she glanced back uncertainly over her shoulder.

"We're going to work with her business, right?" Fran said once Dot was out of earshot. "You're not showing me this cool new toy just to take it away. That would be too cruel, especially for a reformed character like you."

"We're going to go one better," Gruffbar said. "We're going to buy her business."

"We are? Why?"

"Because we have the money to do it, and they have technology we want."

"So why not work with them?"

Gruffbar leaned back in his seat and stroked his beard. "Fran, there are many advantages to doing this through a takeover. It will give us more control over the technology, meaning that we can't lose access to it at some future point. We can integrate it better into our designs and production process to create better products.

"By bringing our businesses together, we create something larger and more powerful to the advantage of all involved, including Dot and her colleagues, who will get well-paid positions at Mana Wave. It shows the world that we're a growing, dynamic company, the sort that can afford to make a power move like this."

"What if I don't want us to be that sort of company, taking over everybody else's toys?"

"Then you'll be setting serious limits on our potential as a business." Gruffbar folded his arms. "Is that what you want?"

Fran ran her fingers across the hologram house. It was very cool, and she could already think of a dozen different things she, Singar, and Smokey could try with this tech. Still, there had to be more than one way to do this.

"All that stuff you said about access and integrating processes, surely we can make contracts that would let us do those things without a takeover? Like, if we make some sort of alliance."

"Theoretically, maybe, but it will be more awkward and complicated, less secure."

"I can live with that. Dot's clearly worked hard to create her company. She shouldn't have to give it up to get the money to finish her work."

"Fran, I'm a lawyer, not a business analyst, but even I understand that this is how the world works. People create startups so that someone else will buy them. It's the quickest way to make good money if you've got a product worth selling."

"That's not what I did. I set up a company because I wanted to run it. I wouldn't give up Mana Wave because someone offered me a big check."

"That's great, but doesn't Dot deserve her chance to get that big check? She's been working on her company years longer than you have, and she still doesn't have the investors she needs. She's not going to the fancy parties like you."

"Then she should have a chance to do all that. I won't take away her dreams by taking over her company."

Gruffbar groaned and pressed his fingers against his temples. "Bart warned me the conversation would go this way, but I didn't believe him. I thought you understood how the Valley works by now."

"I do, but that doesn't mean I have to act like everyone else. If I did, Mana Wave never would've gotten as far as we have, right?" Fran smiled brightly at him. "Don't worry. This can be part of making our brand distinctive like Elethin's always talking about."

There was a long pause while Gruffbar drummed his fingers against the table. He stared across the illusion of the house at Fran, and she could almost see the words gathering behind his eyes as he looked for another line of argument. Even that made her smile, a reminder of what a good lawyer her friend was.

"This comes down to fundamentals," he said. "For a business, growth is good. It's how we reach different markets. It's how we increase profits. It's how we get to entertain more people."

"You put that last one in for me, right?" Fran said. "You wouldn't have said it to a normal CEO."

"I wouldn't have had to."

"I'm not a normal CEO."

"Very, very true."

"Here's the thing. I've heard all this stuff about growth is good, but I've seen the other side as well. Businesses that get so big they lose their heart. Industries where there's almost no competition, so customers get no choice. All those folks on Earth who've had to build new economies so growth wouldn't kill the environment. People grow until they're big enough to run their own lives, but cancers grow until they kill you."

"You're comparing Mana Wave to cancer?" Gruffbar raised his eyebrows. "That I didn't see coming."

"No, silly. I want to make sure we don't turn into a cancer-type business, the sort that grows and grows and kills the things around it. It's good to have diversity in the industry, with different businesses making different things in different ways. That's how you get more innovation, more ideas, and more people with a share of the pie.

"I don't want to take over magitech entertainment. I want to make it more varied and brilliant, with more choice for what people can buy. Yes, that makes it tougher for us, but it'll push us to do better, and that's a good thing."

"Fine." Gruffbar flung his hands in the air. "I give up. What do you want to do instead?"

"You'll see."

"That's not how this—"

"Hi, Dot!" Now it was Fran's turn to cut Gruffbar off as the shifter returned to their table, carrying a tray full of coffee and cake.

"Hi." Dot nudged her projector aside and put the tray down. "I wasn't sure what to order, but that nice guy behind the counter said you'd like these."

She handed Fran a cappuccino with silvery sprinkles and a rainbow-colored slice of cake. Gruffbar got black coffee and a donut. Dot perched on the edge of her seat with a Danish pastry in one hand and a tea in the other.

"So, um…" She looked nervously from Gruffbar to Fran. "What do you think?"

"Gruffbar thinks we should buy out your business."

"Oh." Dot sagged. "I mean, it's not what I hoped for, but it's better than going bankrupt."

"I've got a better idea, though." Fran pointed at the projector. "This thing is cool, and I want to make it happen, but I don't want to take your company from you. So let's make a deal.

"You give us exclusive access to this technology for, like, some years, and in return, we'll support you in making it better. We'll give you advice on funding, publicity, and technical issues. We'll even collaborate on building devices. Meanwhile, this technology will make the FDS even more awesome than it already is."

"Really?" Dot blinked and stared, open-mouthed. "Are you sure?"

"Sadly, she is." Gruffbar set his laptop on his knees and started typing. "I'll turn this woolly nonsense into a real contract. Do you have a legal team?"

"No."

"But you have a lawyer?"

"I'm not sure we can still afford her."

"I'll lend you the money." Fran waved her slice of cake. "We have to make sure this is fair."

Dot smiled so wide it looked like her face might split in two. "You guys are amazing."

"She's amazing." Gruffbar pointed at Fran. "Me, I'm here to bask in her glory."

CHAPTER ELEVEN

"Remind me, what is this one?" Howard Phillips asked as the steam car pulled up to a hall with its outer walls covered in gigantic clockwork mechanisms.

"The Worshipful Company of Watchmakers," Julia said while Handar reached for the door handle.

"Why are watchmakers important?"

"They were one of the first real technical industries in Mana Valley, back before electronics. When mechanical watches went out of fashion, they evolved into a gentlemen's club and benevolent society for the more traditional sorts of technologists."

"Aren't technology and tradition at odds?"

"Some people like tweed suits and chainmail as well as microelectronics and cutting edge spellcraft."

"This is a place where those sorts of people get to feel important while raising pittances for charities?"

"That would be one way to describe it, yes." Julia peered out at the building. "A fairly accurate one."

"Well, then." Phillips straightened his tie, then stepped out onto the sidewalk. "Let's go be charitable to them."

A few journalists were waiting outside Watchmakers' Hall, but not the bustling crowds that had reported on some of the events Phillips had been to in the past few weeks. There was a limit to what even the trade press and gossip magazines could be bothered to cover, and his fifteenth public appearance in sixteen days was almost as far down that list as this outdated club for outdated inventors.

If he did something memorable tonight, more of them would be back for tomorrow's function, just in case, but he didn't plan to make this into anything newsworthy. Contrary to appearances, publicity wasn't his main concern tonight.

"Mr. Phillips." A gnome journalist approached him, the trace of a sound recording spell shimmering in her hand. "What do you say to commentators who've labeled your recent charity drive as nothing more than a shallow attempt to sell Manaphones?"

Phillips let out a small, patronizing laugh that he'd been practicing for occasions like this.

"If I didn't sell my company's products, I wouldn't be doing my job. If I weren't concerned about the plight of the needy, I wouldn't be human."

Of course, he was neither human nor concerned, but the journalist had no reason to know the first part.

"What do you think of Deltaspell's decision to fast-track the new Deltaphone, which shares so many features with your Manaphone?"

"I think competition is good for the market, and I look

forward to one day having real competition. Now if you'll excuse me, I'm off to help a good cause."

He walked up the steps into the clockwork building, with Handar following to his left and Julia to his right. Around them, the walls ticked and whirred, every surface a part of some grand and intricate mechanism. Handar watched it all with a suspicious eye.

"It would be easy to hide a trap in all of this," he said.

"That's why you're here," Phillips said. "I didn't hire you for your looks."

At the end of the lobby, a pair of nervously smiling dwarves stood in front of a huge doorway, its double doors open wide. Beyond them, a couple of hundred magicals in suits and stylish dresses sat around tables laden with crystal cut glassware and silver cutlery, most of them talking a little too loud.

"Mr. Phillips." One of the dwarves shook his hand. "So good of you to join us this evening. Everybody's been looking forward to hearing you speak. They're so excited I can barely keep them in their seats."

Excited or impatient? Phillips had timed his delayed arrival to cause real discomfort for his hosts, as they fretted about whether he would turn up without leaving it so long that they gave up on him. It was good to spread some tension, but his other task here was too important to risk.

"Thank you for having me," he said. "Do we have time for a drink first, or would you like me to get straight to my speech?"

The dwarves exchanged a nervous look. No one wanted to rush one of the most powerful men in Mana Valley, but behind them, a pair of half-drunk wizards had started throwing bread rolls around the room.

"If you don't mind, perhaps the speech first, and we can arrange a drink while you're giving it?"

"Of course. Handar knows what I like."

While his bodyguard dealt with their dwarf hosts, Phillips strode through the doors and across the hall with Julia at his side. There was a ripple of excited chatter as he crossed the room and plenty of eyes turned to follow him. He waved to a few acquaintances along the way and stopped to shake hands with two, giving more time for everyone to notice his arrival. By the time he reached the dais against the far wall and climbed up behind its podium, everyone watched him.

He tapped the microphone attached to the podium, and a thudding filled the hall. Conversation died away, leaving only the ticking of a gigantic clock on the wall behind him.

"Sorry I'm late." Phillips pulled a copy of his speech from his pocket and flattened the papers on the podium. "It seems particularly ironic here."

He pointed at the clock behind him, and there was a mixture of drunken and dutiful laughter from his audience.

"As some of you know," he continued, "the Worshipful Company of Watchmakers has always held a place close to my heart. How could it not, when this venerable institution has played such an important role in shaping the city where we all live and the industries in which we all work? In a very real way, the history of the Worshipful Company is the history of Mana Valley, and the history of Mana Valley is that of the Worshipful Company. It's a proud and bold history, in which progress has sounded out with power and constancy, as reliable as the ticking of a clock."

He faked a smile. What sickly garbage. The Watchmakers were a tick on the skin of Mana Valley, as important to the modern city as a discarded candy wrapper. Still, the Worshipful Company and their guests were lapping his words up, basking in the recognition of one of Mana Valley's greats. He would have to arrange a bonus for whoever had written tonight's speech. They'd done exactly what was needed, no better and no worse.

"If this Worshipful Company is important to me, tonight's cause is even more so." Whatever the cause was—he hadn't paid attention to the charities when he did these things once a year. He certainly wasn't paying attention now. "Loss of life or sanity remains a constant risk for those involved in experimental magic, and it's heartbreaking to see the grief of their families."

That part at least was true. You couldn't mess with powerful forces without risking destruction, and there were few things that magical researchers loved more than pushing a little too far. The horror and loss felt by those they left behind were delicious treats to Phillips. Or perhaps it was more accurate to say that they were delicious treats to the monster behind the Phillips mask.

"That's why I'm here tonight, to support the Esoteric Scientists' Widows and Orphans Fund, not only through my presence but through a gift from my foundation, to care for those left behind."

Julia reached into the enchanted handbag they'd hired for the occasion and pulled out a giant check twenty times larger than the bag. She rested it on a rail on the front of the pedestal, and the crowd gasped as they saw the number on the check, then burst into applause.

Phillips kept smiling. He could afford to give the money away. It was a drop in the ocean compared with what his company was worth, and besides, all the money would soon be meaningless when his plans came to fruition.

He waited for a minute, letting the audience take time to absorb his fake generosity, then waved for quiet.

"That isn't all I've brought." He extended his hand.

Again, Julia opened her handbag. This time she took out a clock. It was a mixture of ancient and modern, some of its components old and worn, some shiny and new. Its face had a crack down one side, but below it was a bright new digital display. The combination shouldn't have worked, but Phillips and the people working for him had found a way to combine the parts so old and new complemented one another.

"When I bought my first office, it was an old building," he said. "In the basement, I found the pieces of a broken clock. I recognized them immediately as belonging to an Angam 38, one of the rarest and finest clocks ever produced in this valley."

There were murmurs of agreement and curiosity from around the room.

"Sadly, I didn't have all the parts to repair it. Many were lost forever, and I didn't have the heart to replace them with imitations, but I couldn't bring myself to let these parts go either. Now, years later, I've found a solution—a mixing of the old and new, progress and tradition, the most fitting reminder of the good work that Philgard Technologies and the Worshipful Company of Watchmakers can do together. I present it to you, Watchmaker President, a tribute to your work and an eternal reminder of our bond."

Philips stepped down from the podium and held out the clock. Amid a roar of applause, a fat dwarf in an old-fashioned suit bustled over to receive it, beaming from ear to ear.

"Thank you so much, Mr. Phillips," the dwarf said. "This means so much to us. Your clock will sit in pride of place here in the great hall."

"Really, it's my pleasure." Phillips shook the dwarf's hand, then turned to smile for photographs. "This clock means as much to me as it does to you."

In fact, it meant far more to him, but he wasn't going to say that. Hidden within the clock's workings were runes and magical circuitry with a very different purpose, along with a crystal holding power from Phillips' nightmare realm.

When the time came, this gift, like all the others he'd spread across Mana Valley during these last few weeks, would unleash their true potential. They would become a network of power, parts in an intricate web of magic that he'd spent years weaving. With their help, he would rip the walls of reality open and let his world through.

"Such a good cause," one of the other guests said, vigorously shaking Phillips' hand. "So kind of you to help."

"It is, isn't it?" Phillips smiled back at her. "Please excuse me. I haven't had anything to eat or drink yet."

"Of course, of course, please, don't let me keep you. Perhaps we could talk later? I have a business proposition that might be of interest."

Phillips doubted it, but he smiled and made polite noises, then followed Handar as the bodyguard made a path for him through the excited mass of people. At last, they reached a table in the corner, empty except for Julia, and Handar pulled out a seat for Phillips.

"Was that true, boss?" Handar asked quietly. "The story about the old clock in the basement?"

"Of course not, but it sounded good, didn't it?"

"I liked it."

"More importantly, so did they."

In the middle of the room, the Watchmaker President had placed a chair on a table and set the clock on top so more people could see. The members of the Worshipful Company crowded around, admiring the craftsmanship, old and new, discussing their theories on how those splendid people at Philgard had made the whole thing work.

As he tucked into his food, Phillips listened to fragments of conversation, people retelling his speech writer's story, embellishing it, helping it to grow. Perhaps they would still be telling the clock's story when it helped to wrench reality open and channel a world of nightmares through this one.

He hoped so. And he hoped that he could see their faces then.

CHAPTER TWELVE

"I'm sure it was this way," Fran said as she hiked up the woodland trail, heading toward the mountains that loomed above them. "At least, like, ninety-five percent sure."

Cam laughed. "That's what you always say right before you turn us around and head back in the opposite direction."

"I always get to the right place in the end, don't I?"

"So far, yes, but couldn't we use a map?"

Fran stopped and looked around. Did those trees up ahead look familiar? She thought they did, but she'd thought the same thing about some other trees a mile back, and those had turned out to be the wrong place entirely.

"I don't think there are good maps for up here," she said. "Not a lot of people come this way. That's why Winslow chose it."

"Then how did you find it before?"

"My mom."

"She couldn't come now?"

"She's got work. Besides, I didn't want to worry her with all this prophecy stuff."

"Fran, she was the one selling prophecies for cash. She got kidnapped over it. I think it's a bit late to protect her."

"Would you stop trying to keep your family safe?"

"I guess not."

"Well then..." Fran looked up. "Hey, someone's come to help us."

A crow was circling in the sky above their heads. It dipped its wings, acknowledging Fran's attention, then turned its course, heading away from the trail they were on and above denser trees.

"This way." Fran followed the crow.

"Are you sure?" Cam asked as they pushed through thick undergrowth and up a rough slope.

"Totally. Would the crows lie?"

"I don't know. Maybe. Depends on what they want."

"They're my friends." Fran's breath came in frosted puffs as she scrambled up the slope, grabbing branches to keep her steady. "Or maybe more like pets. Or messengers. Kind of spies from my dad, but that's not the point right now."

"It sounds like it could be the point."

"It doesn't matter because..." Fran reached the top of the slope and gazed into the valley below. "We're here."

Below them was the set of dilapidated mine buildings and entrances to old tunnels that the Evermores had made their base. The inhabitants had done more work since the last time Fran was there. Walls built out of rocks and old mine props stretched between the ruined buildings, and one of those buildings had a new roof made from pine branches. Still, the valley's overall tone was that of an industrial waste ground, in which even the weeds looked unhealthy.

Taldiss was on guard duty again, standing behind one of the walls. She pointed at Cam as the two of them approached.

"Who's this?"

"My boyfriend, Cam," Fran said proudly. "We're here to talk to Winslow and Enfield."

"You know this is a hideout, right?" Taldiss asked, scowling. "It beats the point of a hideout if you keep showing it to random passersby."

"Not passersby, just Cam. And it's important."

Taldiss shook her head.

"Whatever. I'd walk you in, but we've had more trouble with the rock monsters, and someone has to keep watch."

The crow landed on Fran's shoulder and gave Taldiss an inquisitive look.

"He has to stay out here," Taldiss said. "I don't trust him."

Fran wasn't going to protest. It wasn't as if the crow could contribute much to the conversation ahead. She waved him away, and he settled on top of one of the buildings, glaring down at Taldiss.

"Same tunnel as before." Taldiss pointed to one of the mine openings. "If Winslow's not in the first room, someone there can tell you where he is."

Fran and Cam headed down the tunnel to the room where she'd found Winslow before. Sure enough, he was there, and Enfield was with him, sitting on the log seats around the packing crate table, eating soup.

"Hi guys." Fran took one of the other seats. "You've met Cam, right?"

"Cameron Kowal." Winslow watched the new arrival. "You come from a distinguished line, as such short-lived creatures go."

"Thanks, I think." Cam took a thick lever arch file out of his backpack and thumped it down on the table. "We brought something for you to see."

"What is this?" Winslow asked.

"It's about the Source," Fran said. "You've still got him captive, right, somewhere around here?"

She looked around the room, which didn't contain a caged magical of ancient and immense power. With all these tunnels, it would be fairly easy to hide him away.

"We have it, yes," Winslow said. "As soon as we can find a way to transport it to Earth safely, we will. The kemanas need stabilization before their power unravels forever." He opened the file and flicked through a few pages. "What is all this, copies of prophecies?"

"That's right." Fran turned the pages until she reached the section they were after. "Prophecies, commentaries, and analysis. Cam gets this stuff way better than me, so he can explain."

Winslow and Enfield turned to look expectantly at Cam.

"Something bad is coming to Mana Valley," Cam said. "I've been investigating it for years, gathering and analyzing prophecies, putting the pieces together. It connects to you guys, to the Evermores."

"Many things connect to us," Winslow said. "That's what happens when you've lived for thousands of years."

"Right, well, up until recently, I thought that you were the threat. I mean, I didn't know who you were, but I thought you would cause whatever's coming. Now, I think it's more complicated than that. I think it's about this Source of yours. Here, see this…"

He pointed at a section of the text.

"'When the darkness comes, the origin shall be the key,'" Enfield read aloud. "'But the hammer blow shall fall, as surely as the skies, and there shall be no safety if there is none for the origin of these things.'"

"This isn't the only reference to an origin," Cam said. "It's scattered through different prophecies, all of which I've connected. We're pretty sure that the Source is this origin, and as you can see, it's connected to what's coming. If we want to protect people, we need to keep the Source safe."

"The Source is perfectly safe already," Winslow said. "We're holding it in one of Fran's containment units, which is as secure as it could be. Unless you doubt Fran's work?"

"She told me that the Source got away from you twice already. What's to stop that from happening again?"

"We are."

"We don't need to keep the Source confined," Fran said. "He can be friendly, I'm sure of it. He just doesn't like being held prisoner. If we can find another form of power to use instead of him, if we can get the kemanas working without the Source, we can let him out and make friends with him. Won't that be way better than relying on someone who's mad at us, who only wants to get away?"

Winslow shook his head and pushed the file full of prophecies away from him.

"Leaving aside the number of 'ifs' your plan relies upon, you are ignoring the very nature of the Source. It is a wild force and a dangerous one, something we must contain. When it got out the last time, it nearly killed Enfield. Do you want that to happen again?"

Winslow looked pointedly at Enfield, still heavily bandaged and scarred down one side of his head. Fran felt guilty looking at him, wondering if she could've saved him from this by building a better containment unit or being there for the Evermores when they needed help. But they'd made their choices, she'd made hers, and they couldn't undo the past.

"There has to be a better way," she said.

"Perhaps your prophecies are true." Winslow pointed at the folder. "Although in my experience, many turn out to be false. If this one is true, we need to keep the Source safe, and I can't think of a better way than what we're doing now. Keeping an immense well of power safe for the world, and keeping the world safe from the carnage that can come when the power breaks free."

"Please, Winslow, the Source came to me in my dreams. It's desperate to get out."

"This is about dreams now?" Winslow shook his head. "Most of those come from the inside. It's a sign of how much you've worked yourself up about this. Let it go. Help us find a way to transport the Source instead. Once we get it back to our home on Earth, once it's in the chamber that held it for millennia, it will be secure."

"I still think you're wrong." Fran sighed. "But if you need my help to do the transport safely, then I guess I'm in."

"Such enthusiasm." Winslow smiled slightly. "You remind me of your mother."

An awkward silence fell.

"Let me talk to them." Enfield laid a bandaged hand on Winslow's shoulder. "Everyone here respects your wisdom, but sometimes that respect can create distance and make it harder to find agreement."

"You're learning, Enfield." Winslow rose from his seat. "Very well. I will see you all later."

He headed out of the room, leaving the three of them.

Fran wanted to be mad at Enfield for taking Winslow's side, but it was hard to be angry at him when he was still in such a sorry state. His wounds had healed a little since the last time she was there, but it looked like some of them would never entirely go away. The Source had done this, and it was understandable if that affected his perspective.

"You agree with Winslow now?" she asked sadly.

"Not at all." Enfield pulled the file closer so he could look at the prophecies again. "It's easier to talk properly now that he's gone."

Fran grinned. "I should've known."

Enfield shrugged, then winced as the movement shifted one of his bandages.

"The Source saved me at least once while I was hunting him," he said. "We made a connection. I still don't understand what's going on here, but I do understand that we've been holding a thinking, feeling, caring creature prisoner because it was the easiest way to get what we wanted. That has to end."

"Have you talked with the other Evermores about this?"

"They don't see Winslow or the Source the way I do.

Maybe if they spent as much time with you as I have, they'd view the world differently." Enfield flashed her a smile. "You've changed me for the better, Fran, and so has the Source, despite all of this." He gently tapped the scarred side of his face. "Now it's time to take that better out into the world."

He flipped pages in the file, skimming through the prophecies they'd copied and the notes they'd made. Most of it was Cam's work, built up over years of careful study, but Fran had made some contributions since they started collaborating.

"What do we do now?" Cam asked. "Can you lead us to this Source so we can set it free?"

"It's not that easy," Enfield said. "Winslow's right in one regard. If we let the Source go without finding an alternative to fix the kemanas, all magical power on Earth could fail. Too many people's lives depend upon that power for us to willfully destroy it.

"We have to find an alternative way to generate magic. Then we fix the kemanas and persuade my fellow Evermores to let the Source go." He looked at Fran. "Can you make that alternative using your magitech?"

"Not yet," she admitted. "I have some ideas. Turning Chasmodar's power into a substitute for mine in the Mana Wave batteries taught me a lot about energy conversion. I think I can apply similar principles here, but to do that, I'll need to spend time studying the Source."

"I can arrange that. We'll go back to the old pretense, claim that we're looking for a way to transport him safely home. I know it's more awkward for you to come out here than it was to work at the house in the hills, and it sounds like your business is taking off. Can you spare the time for this?"

"I've got more time free while Cam finishes writing his thesis. Plus Mana Wave Industries has staff now, so I can hand off some tasks to them. I'll make it work."

"Great. Do you want to go see the Source now?"

"That would be brilliant, right Cam?"

"Absolutely. I'm curious to see what this is all about." Cam patted the thick file of prophecies and analysis.

"One other thing first, though." Fran pointed at Enfield. "You need to call Josie."

"Ah." Enfield looked down at the improvised table. Beneath his scars, his cheeks went red. "Is that the most urgent thing here?"

"You stood her up, then vanished for, like, weeks on end. Months even. I get why, but you guys had something good going on, and you can't leave her hanging. You owe her a call and an apology. Some chocolates too. Maybe flowers. In fact, definitely flowers."

"You're right." Enfield rubbed his eyes. "I'll get Taldiss to find me a new phone next time she's in town."

"Do you need Josie's number?" Fran pulled out her phone.

"No need. I memorized it, just in case."

"Aw." Fran smiled at him. "That's so sweet."

"It's certainly something." Enfield stood, picked up a crutch from the floor by his side of the table, and limped toward the door.

"Come on," he said. "The sooner we sort out the Source, the sooner I can treat dating like it's a real thing."

CHAPTER THIRTEEN

Elethin had expected the Roving Gaze to be some dark hole down a back alley, the sort of place where rats chewed on the legs of the bar stools and the floor was sticky with old beer. Instead, the place Kotia had set for their meetup was cheerful and brightly lit, with rainbow flags on the walls and a cocktail of the day spelled out in bright letters on a board above the bar. The street it was down was more of a side street than a back alley, in an area where the shops were pleasant rather than prestigious, the customers comfortable rather than wealthy. Not a place she would normally have bothered with, but not one she objected to.

Kotia was perched at one end of the bar, her wings hunched up around her shoulders, nursing a glass of lager. She looked around as Elethin approached and raised an eyebrow.

"I was starting to think you weren't coming."

"I considered it." Elethin took the seat next to her. "You didn't leave me with a lot of choices."

"That was the idea."

The barman wandered over. The stud in his upper lip shifted as he smiled.

"What can I get you?"

"I'll try the special," Elethin said. This looked like the sort of place where the staff was proud of their novelties, not resentful at having to make something fancy.

"Coming right up."

The barman took a shaker from under the bar and went to grab bottles off the shelf.

"What are we doing here?" Elethin asked, quiet enough for only Kotia to hear. "Get to the point quickly. If you don't, I'm leaving."

"We're going to rob a jewelry store."

"Sorry, not my skill set. You'd better find someone else."

"Don't worry, I've planned for your skill set. That's why you're here."

"I'm not a criminal."

"We met in prison."

"I'm not that sort of criminal."

"You're going to be."

"Really, you'd be better off with someone else. Someone with muscles and speed, perhaps someone with a getaway car. I'd only slow you down."

The barman set a glass down in front of Elethin. Under cover of reaching for her drink, she stretched out her fingers, preparing a spell.

Kotia shot out a hand and clamped Elethin's wrist. "If I see even a hint of a spell designed to change my mind, this conversation is over. And not in a way that ends well for you."

"You're threatening to hurt me in front of all these

people?" Elethin nodded at the barman and the mid-afternoon drinkers he was now serving.

"I've seen what you can do with broken glass, and I wouldn't risk it," Kotia said. "I also know things that could hurt your reputation, and you care about that a lot more."

Elethin brought her other hand around to lift the glass and take a sip. The cocktail tasted of almonds and cherries. "Seriously, I'm not the woman for this job."

"Seriously, you do it, or I spill what I know." Kotia let go of her wrist. "Your choice."

Elethin was too much of a professional to show a frown, but inside she was fuming. What choice did she have but to play along?

"I'll do it, but on one condition."

"You're in no position to make demands."

"You need me for whatever your plan is. That gives me some influence here."

This time it was Kotia's turn to pause and drink. Her frown showed. "What's the condition?"

"Once this is over, I get to cast a spell on you, one that will prevent you from ever talking about my time in prison."

"Why would I accept that?"

"You say you're offering your silence in return for my cooperation. All this does is formalize that deal, so I know you'll keep your word. Why would you say no if you're playing straight with me? And why would I ever help you if you aren't?"

Kotia's frown deepened, but she'd never been the most sophisticated of thinkers, and it was clear that she couldn't see a way out of this one. "All right. It's a deal."

They clinked glasses, and each took a drink.

"So, when are we relieving this poor shopkeeper of his jewels?" Elethin asked.

"Now." Kotia downed the rest of her lager and got down from her seat.

"What? You can't possibly expect me to—"

"I expect that if I let you leave, you'll immediately start looking for a way to charm your way out of this, maybe even a way to stitch me up. I'm not giving you that opportunity. Either you come now, or you get the consequences."

Elethin knocked back the rest of her cocktail. If she was going to do this, she at least wanted something to take off the edge. Sadly, not doing this didn't seem to be an option.

"We don't have a plan," she said, one last attempt at protest.

"I have a plan, and I'll tell it to you on the way." Kotia was heading for the door. "Now come."

Elethin summoned magic and waved her hands across her head and body. Her face transformed, her hair turned black, her skin darkened, and her ears gained the rounded tips of a human. The disguise wouldn't last long, but it might keep her out of trouble if Kotia's plan was as half-baked as she expected. As the magic settled, she followed Kotia out of the bar.

"The plan's simple," Kotia said as they walked down the back street. "I've disabled the alarm system, although they don't know it yet. We go in together as customers. There are only two staff members, one sales and one security. You use your charm or magic or whatever it takes to distract them. If you've got some way to stun them, even better. While they're off the ball, I grab the jewelry, and we run."

"That's your plan?" Elethin stared at her. "That's barely even a coherent thought."

"If you can come up with a better option before we get there, I'm all ears." Kotia pointed. "That's the place there, so you'd better think quick."

"I have no idea how to do this, I'm not a robber, but even I can see that this plan is garbage."

"You're about to be a robber. Maybe you can find some expertise then." Kotia approached the door of the jewelry store. "Ready?"

Elethin looked around. They still weren't on a very busy street, and only a few people were passing. The situation didn't look like it would get any better. "I'm as ready as I'm going to get."

"Then in we go."

They walked into the store side-by-side. As they entered, Elethin took hold of Kotia's arm, leaning toward her like they were a couple. Anything that might make them look more ordinary had to be good, and what could be more ordinary than buying jewelry for a loved one?

As Kotia had said, there were two staff members in the shop, a muscular Kilomea by the door and a smartly dressed elf behind the counter. The elf smiled at them and emerged from behind the counter, waving as she came.

"Hi, there," she said. "How can I help you?"

"We're looking for engagement rings, right, sweetie?" Elethin squeezed Kotia's arm.

"Yeah, sure, that's right." Kotia looked around the shop without the least shred of subtlety. Elethin was surveying the area too, but from the corner of her eye, while keeping her whole body turned toward the display in front of her.

"Did you just get engaged?" the sales elf asked. "That's so exciting!"

"It's all been super spontaneous," Elethin said. "We didn't have rings, and I have to admit, we don't exactly have the same tastes." She leaned forward conspiratorially. "I'm not even sure we'll go for rings, but we want something to mark the commitment, you know?"

"Oh, I totally do!" The elf smiled. "You've got to pick what's right for you, haven't you? Some people go for bracelets these days or even amulets."

"How about a watch?" Elethin asked. "Jo here really likes her watches, don't you honey?"

She squeezed Kotia's arm, and Kotia nodded. "Sure. Watches. Love them."

"Well, we've got some very nice ones near the back of the shop. Perhaps I could show you?"

"Actually, could you talk to me about these rings?" Elethin tapped a case in front of her. "Jo will want some time to herself to browse anyway, while I need someone to think aloud with."

The elf laughed. "Sure, I get it," she said. "Let me talk you through what we have here. There are some lovely options…"

She started talking about the rings in the case while Kotia detached herself from Elethin's grip and headed toward the watch display. The Kilomea security guard stayed stationary, looking alternately at them and the street.

"I like this one," Elethin said, pointing at one of the

rings, "but I'm not sure it would match my coloring." She turned to the Kilomea. "Your skin's closer in color to mine, could you come and hold it so I can see?"

"Not my job," the Kilomea said.

"It'll only take a moment, I promise."

"Gotta guard."

"Oh, well, that's a shame. I wouldn't want to buy something if I couldn't see how it will look from a short distance away." Elethin took a step back from the case. "Maybe I'll try somewhere else."

The sales elf's face stiffened as she looked at the price of the rings and felt her sales bonus fading away.

"Come here and help, Reda," she said. "Like the lady said, it'll only be a moment."

"Guarding," the Kilomea replied.

"Who's in charge while Charlie's out?" There was an edge to the elf's voice.

The Kilomea sighed and lumbered over to the display.

"Here." He held out his hand, palm open. "Rings."

In the corner of the room, Kotia reached for a stand of diamond-encrusted necklaces. She was going to make her move.

In a flash, Elethin summoned her magic. Inspired by things she'd seen Fran do, she closed her eyes and unleashed a blast of bright light that stunned the shop's staff.

"Now!" she shouted.

Kotia grabbed the necklaces and stuffed them into a bag. She swung her elbow back and smashed the glass of another display cabinet. An alarm started to blare.

"I thought you'd disabled the alarms," Elethin said.

"I thought I had." Kotia grabbed gold watches. "Too late now."

Reda the guard, still blinded by the light, grabbed for Elethin. She dodged aside and unleashed another flash to keep him stunned.

"Come on," she called over the alarm. "We have to get out of here."

"Not yet." Kotia was stuffing more jewelry into her bag.

A portal appeared in the middle of the shop, and two wizards stepped out. Both were wearing Silver Griffin amulets and carrying wands. The sound of breaking glass drew both of their attention as they appeared.

"Halt right there," one of them said as they pointed their wands at Kotia.

Elethin wanted to run while she had the chance, but then Kotia would still have a hold over her. Instead, she pointed at the curtains hanging across a door near the rear of the shop. They ripped off their rail and shot across the room, entangling one of the Griffins.

"What the…" The other one turned, and Elethin released a flash of light. He raised his wand to counterspell a moment too late and staggered back, temporarily blinded.

"Now will you come?" Elethin shouted.

Kotia vaulted across a display and ran for the door. Elethin followed her, glad that she'd worn shorter heels that day. The two of them dashed out of the store and down the street.

"Stop, thieves!" One of the Griffins stumbled out after them, waving his wand through a gap in the curtains wrapped around him. He shouted a spell and chains shot after the fleeing robbers. Kotia spread her wings and soared above while Elethin dodged aside, and the chains crashed uselessly against a wall.

The other Griffin staggered out of the store. The two of them sent a flurry of spells through the air. Elethin didn't stop to counter them, which would only have slowed her down. She kept running.

"Which way?" she called to Kotia.

"I don't know." Kotia was gliding eight feet above the sidewalk.

"You didn't plan an escape route?"

"No."

"This was not a plan."

"It worked, didn't it?"

Elethin glanced back. They'd rounded a corner, leaving the Griffins out of sight. Ahead, the streets became more crowded. She waved, dispelling the magic that had disguised her, returning to her normal appearance.

"You fly away," she said. "I'll blend in. We can both get clear."

"Good call." Kotia flapped her wings. "Thanks, El. Couldn't have done this without you."

She flew up and away.

"Remember," Elethin called after her, "you owe me a spell."

Kotia disappeared across the rooftops and Elethin into the bustling streets. Behind them, the Silver Griffins finally rounded the corner and stared around, frustrated.

"I hate policing this place," one of them muttered. "It's completely crazy."

"Could be worse," his partner replied. "It could be L.A."

CHAPTER FOURTEEN

Josie sat at a table in the window of the Blazing Bean, a cup of green tea in her hand. She'd arrived late, thanks to a meeting that ran over at work, but she wasn't the only one. She glanced at her phone, which told her that Enfield was twenty minutes overdue. If he stood her up again, there would be hell to pay.

She looked at the messages he'd sent. They were thoughtful, like everything he wrote, and apologetic, which was only fair in the circumstances. Still, she felt like something was missing, something held back. Enfield had always had his secrets—she was hardly an open book herself, given all the exclusive information she picked up at Philgard—but this felt different. Something was amiss. Something beyond the fact that he'd been out of contact for months.

The door of the coffee shop opened, and Josie looked up with a smile, but it was a pair of elderly dwarves coming in for afternoon tea and cake. She sank back into her seat. She hadn't realized how much she'd missed him until now, maybe hadn't let herself acknowledge it. She'd focused on how little there had been between them, only coffee and books.

She'd rationalized her feelings away as the frustration anyone would feel at being let down, at wasting their time. The truth was that she'd valued what had started between them, especially when work was taking over the rest of her life. Now that there was a chance to get it back, she was more eager for their long-delayed coffee date than she had been the first time around.

She drank her tea and checked her work emails on her phone. Twenty new messages in the past five minutes. No wonder it was hard to get things done when people were this demanding of her attention.

The door opened again, and she looked up. This time, it was a guy on crutches, his back hunched. He had his hood pulled up, half hiding his face, and the beginnings of a beard across his chin. She turned back to her phone as he headed for the counter.

One thing was notably absent from her inbox, and that was messages from the lunch club members. The coven was taking extra care about contact with each other while Julia put her plan into action. There were no texts or instant messages, absolutely no emails, and they kept any meetings small and discreet. It made organizing harder, but security was equally important right now. If Howard Phillips learned what was happening or any other senior staff worked it out, everything could fall apart.

She barely noticed the irregular footsteps approaching, accompanied by the thud of the crutch, until the guy in the hoodie stood across from her.

"Hi, Josie," a familiar voice said. "Sorry I'm late, this time and last time."

Now that he was facing her, with the hood pulled back a little, she finally recognized Enfield. It was a shock to see him like this, with all his weight on one leg and a crutch under that arm. The other crutch was tucked under his other arm, freeing a hand to hold a tray with coffee and cake.

"Oh my God!" She jumped to her feet. "What are you doing? I could've got that for you."

In the moment of shock, all she could think of to do was to grapple with the practicalities. She took the tray from him and set it down on the table, then turned one of the chairs to make it easier for him to sit.

"You don't have to—" he began.

"Yes, I do." She watched him ease into the seat, then sank into hers, watching his every move. "I've spent so much time being mad at you. I had no idea that… I mean, you said there'd been an accident, but I never dreamed it was anything this bad."

"You haven't seen the worst of it."

The way he said that sent a shiver down her spine. With one hand on either side of his head, he eased back his hood, exposing his whole face to the light.

On the left-hand side, the same side as his damaged leg, there were scars all down his face. They ran from under the new beard, up his cheek, and across where his hairline had been. The hair itself was now short and patchy as if it had been shaved off and was refusing to grow back. The scars seemed thickest in the gaps between clumps of hair, but she couldn't tell if that was real or a trick of her imagination.

"What happened?" she asked in a hoarse whisper.

"I fell off a mountain."

"That doesn't sound like a whole explanation."

"I can't give you the whole explanation, not without lying, and I feel like I owe you better than that. Sorry."

"You're sorry..." She shook her head. "Seriously Enfield, what's going on here?"

"I wish I could tell you. As soon as I can, I will. For now, 'fell off a mountain' will have to do." He pushed a slice of her favorite cake across the table. "If it's any comfort, I fell into water. This could be a lot worse."

"That's not very comforting."

"Then I'm sorry about that too."

She took a bite of the cake. It was delicious, and she felt bad for thinking that, given everything else. "I'm not convinced about the beard. I think you looked better without it."

"Not anymore." His voice was flat.

"Let me be the judge of that."

"Seriously, it's a mess under there." He ran a hand across his chin, wincing as his fingers traced the lumpen parts on the left side. "The beard will help me hide it since I'll probably stay scarred forever."

"And your legs?"

She immediately regretted asking for both their sakes. He winced at the words, and she realized that however bad things were, she could've hidden from it for a few more minutes. She could've let the two of them enjoy their coffee and cake before they faced the unpalatable truth.

Still, she had to use so much obfuscation at work, so much dancing around awkward truths to keep the business going that she didn't have time for it in the rest of her life. It wasn't better to get this done, but it was necessary.

"This one's mostly better." He patted his right leg. "The other one's taking longer. There's a good chance that I'll always have a limp."

"Will you be able to run again?" She pictured him in shorts and running shoes, the way his face had lit up at the thought of a good run.

"Maybe," he said. "But not as far, not as fast. Even if I don't end up with a limp, it's always going to be weaker than it was."

"I'm so sorry."

Enfield looked down at his coffee. Before the accident, he'd mostly drunk green tea. Apparently, his tastes had become darker and more bitter.

"It is what it is. Can't be undone. I'll do the exercises for my leg, apply the salves and the moisturizers to my face, try to minimize the damage. But I'm never going to be the person I was before."

"That's nonsense." Josie set her cup down sharply. "What happens to your body doesn't change who you are inside. You're still the same person."

"We don't exist outside our bodies. They house our minds, and we can't help changing when they change. If I can't do the things I used to do, how can I possibly be the same person?"

"You can still do plenty of those things, including all the ones that matter most to me. We can meet here and drink coffee and talk about books. That hasn't changed."

"Hasn't it?"

"Of course not. Tell me, what have you read recently?"

"Anything I could get my hands on." He tapped his left leg. "I've been lying around with a lot of time on my hands."

"So what was the best thing you read? Or the worst?"

"Someone found me a big pile of Dickens novels. That was certainly something." He took a sip of his coffee, and a glimpse of his old smile appeared. "Not all good or all bad, but all very much of its time."

"That's what I like about Dickens. Sure, there are eternal themes, but it evokes that era. What better way to look at the Victorian age than by watching someone dissect it?"

"Exactly. And reading about a great age of industrialization while living so close to Mana Valley, you can't help seeing the parallels. Makes me even warier about the role of business here."

"If it's any comfort, we hardly ever send urchins up chimneys anymore or make them operate cotton looms."

"I hear that good urchins are hard to get hold of."

"Exactly." Josie smiled. "I've missed this."

"Me too." Enfield's smile was there for a minute, but his frown returned. "It's good for lifting my spirits, but that's only a short-term thing. In the long term, I'm still adjusting to all of this."

He tapped his scarred cheek.

"You mean the limitations you're facing? Having less mobility?"

"That's part of it, but not all. Imagine looking in the

mirror every day, and the face you see isn't the one you're used to. Imagine it looks like this."

He turned his head to display the full extent of the scars. They were ugly, but Josie could still see the handsome face underneath and the good man she'd met.

"I think it's a lovely face still." She reached out to touch his cheek. Had she ever done that before, even when he wasn't scarred? He flinched away. Showing the scars was one thing. Letting her feel them was another.

"That's kind of you, but it's not a lovely face to me. It's a stranger, and I have to learn how to be that person."

"Maybe that's something I could help with. You could learn to be him around me."

Enfield looked at her, and there were tears at the corners of his eyes, but they never quite managed to escape. "I can't do that. You're one of the best people I've ever met, and I love spending time with you, but this is… Sorry if I'm being presumptuous, but I thought this might turn into a relationship."

"So did I. I still do."

Enfield shook his head. "Making a relationship work takes time and effort. It takes motivation and emotional energy, especially if you want to get it right. Good relationships don't magically happen just because you meet someone you like."

"I'm not a child, Enfield." She tensed, not only at what he'd said but at the whole of what he was saying. "I understand how relationships work."

"I didn't mean to…" He gritted his teeth, drew a deep breath, and sank back in his seat. "This is what I mean. Even a conversation like this, I don't have the strength for it. I'm exhausted. I'm always in pain. Just having a conversation about what to eat for lunch draws on reserves I need for other things."

"For your recovery?"

"That and something else, yes."

"Something else?" She clenched her hands on her knees. "So this isn't only about healing?"

"It's about how I got like this too, and that's not something I can ignore. I don't want to cut you out of my life, but with that, other people are depending on me, and I can't let them down."

"So you'll let me down?"

"I'm sorry." At least he had the courage to look her in the eye, to show that he cared. That made it worse somehow, seeing what she was losing. "For now, I can't do this. Perhaps once I've recovered, as much as I'm going to recover, once I have more energy, when I can give you the attention you deserve, maybe then..."

He let the words trail off and looked at her. That look was a question and a plea.

Josie looked back. She wanted to say no, that he couldn't drop this now and expect to pick it up later. She had a life of her own. She deserved a chance to move on.

Still, that life of hers was busy in its way, and the thought of going back to what they had was hard to resist, even if it was a distant promise.

"Maybe," she said. "If I'm still single. But I'm not sitting here waiting for you like some character from a Dickens story."

"Of course not." He smiled at her across his coffee cup. "The thought will keep me going."

She shook her head and gave a soft laugh. "What a stupid situation." She drained the last of her cup and stood. "I'm going for more tea. We're here now, so why not enjoy it one last time?"

"I'd like that. I'll have green tea, please."

CHAPTER FIFTEEN

Fran stood on the doorstep of the converted terrace house and pressed the button for apartment three. There was a distant buzzing sound, followed by a long silence. She pressed the buzzer again.

Next to her, a crow croaked and tapped its beak against the doorframe as if testing the wood's strength. Was it probing for weaknesses, like her father would do when facing a potential defensive point, or was it trying to get some morsel of food that she couldn't see? Knowing more about her feathered companions didn't make them any easier to understand.

She pressed the buzzer a third time and kept her thumb on the button until there was a *click*.

"Hello?" Cam's voice came down through crackly wires. "I didn't order anything, and if it's a delivery for one of the neighbors, I can't take it in right now."

"It's me, you idiot."

"Oh, Fran!" Cam laughed. "Sorry, wasn't expecting you."

"One of our meetings got canceled, so I thought I'd

come around to say hi." She blew out, and her breath frosted in front of her face. "Are you going to let me in? It's really cold out here."

"Sorry, yes, of course."

There was a different buzzing, then a *click*. Fran pushed on the door and it swung open. The crow fluttered onto her shoulder and the two of them headed upstairs.

When they reached the third floor, Fran brushed the crow off her shoulder.

"I want some time alone with my boyfriend," she explained.

The crow looked for a moment like it might protest, then thought better of it and perched on the banister instead, watching the stairs.

Fran found Cam's door closed but not locked. She opened it and walked into the small apartment. It was even more cluttered than usual, with plates piled up by the sink, takeout boxes in front of the TV, and books and papers on every other available surface. Fran stepped carefully over discarded shoes and around a stack of books to approach the small table where Cam was sitting, his laptop open and a heap of papers next to it.

"This looks intense." She bent to kiss him on the top of his head. He reached around to squeeze her hand, but his other hand kept typing, and he didn't look up from the screen.

"Deadline looming," he explained.

"I thought you still had a couple of months?"

"Professor Kendall says I need to give him two more chapters by the weekend if I want to stay registered and on track to submit. So two chapters it is…"

His typing slowed as he approached the end of a sentence. There was the final decisive tap of a period hammered into place. Then he turned to smile up at Fran.

"Hi, sweetheart. Sorry for the half-assed welcome. How are you doing?"

"Busy, but not as busy as you."

She sat on his lap and took a few minutes to get reacquainted. With so few free evenings and almost no weekends when they could both relax, a few spare seconds like this felt like a blessing.

"I could do with a coffee." Cam rubbed his eyes. "Would you like one?"

"Why don't I make it for you this time? As a way to make up for interrupting your work."

"I won't say no." Cam waved toward the kitchen. "Coffee's in the cupboard above the pot. Mugs are in there too, if there are any still clean."

As Fran got up, he turned back to his laptop and started typing again.

There weren't any clean mugs or space on the sideboard to put them down, so Fran filled the sink and did some washing up while she waited for the coffee to brew. By the time the pot was full and the kitchen full of that invigorating smell, she'd made a small patch of cleanliness but barely made a dent in the dishes compared with how many needed cleaning.

"What are you working on?" she asked as she set the coffee down next to Cam.

"Shifters in the Thirty Years' War. There's a theory that pack dynamics played a significant part in the allegiances of mercenary forces during some of the key campaigns.

Packs might have bridged the gap between armies and influenced what each one knew about the other because their concerns weren't the same as those of the commanders and nations."

"That sounds really interesting."

"Uh-huh." He kept typing away. "It is. I need to get this argument down while the pieces are still straight up here." He tapped the side of his head.

"You carry on then, and I'll tidy up a bit."

"Sure, okay."

She wasn't sure that he'd taken in what she was saying, he was so focused on his thoughts, and given *her* approach to work, she could hardly blame him. So she left him to his writing and returned to the sink with its towering stack of pans and dishes.

It took the best part of an hour to wash up, dry, and put away everything that had heaped up in the kitchen, then to rinse and sort all the takeout containers for recycling. Fran even found homes for the shoes and hoodies discarded in select parts of the apartment, but she drew the line at the basket of dirty laundry. She didn't dare touch anything that looked like a book or paperwork in case she messed with whatever system Cam was using to stitch his ideas and evidence together.

At last, she settled on the sofa with another cup of coffee.

Cam was cute when he was focused like this, his hair wildly disheveled from running his fingers through it, his glasses halfway down his nose. There was a gray smear on one cheek where he'd run a finger down an old book, then touched his face.

At last, he reached the end of a chapter and looked up with a smile.

"Sorry about that." He reached for the most recent coffee she'd brought him. "Given how little time I've got left, I can't afford to get distracted when I'm in the flow."

"I get it. It's great that you're so passionate about what you do."

"Still..." He glanced at the bottom of his screen, where the time showed. "I can spare ten minutes for you."

He came over to the sofa, cup in hand, and settled down with an arm around Fran. She leaned against his chest and smiled at the feeling of his warmth against her.

"A whole ten minutes," she said. "Aren't I lucky?"

"It's more than I've had for work recently." He pushed his glasses up and rubbed the bridge of his nose. "I've used as much annual leave as they'd let me, and now I'm frantically trading shifts with the others to maximize my study time. It's not ideal, but it'll have to do."

"Are you still earning enough to pay rent?"

"Rent and ramen noodles, plus a little over to cover my coffee bill. It's a good thing I don't have time to do anything fun right now because I couldn't afford it."

"I could help pay if you need me to."

"That's kind of you, but I've covered what I need, and it's only a few months. Then I can get back to proper hours at the Bean."

"And chasing prophecies."

"Very true." He gently brushed her hair with the tips of his fingers. "So, how's work going?"

"Crowded." Fran extended one arm. "There are so many people in the office now that we can't fit anymore. I'm back to working in my favorite coffee shop half the time, even though the cute barista isn't there anymore."

"I'm sure he'll be back."

"I hope so, but I might be out of the place by then. Gruffbar and Bart are talking about finding new office space."

"You'd give up on Worn Threads?"

"Or maybe use it alongside the new place. It depends on how much space we find."

"Wow, big moment."

"I know!"

"What is all this work that's filling the basement?"

"All sorts of things. The most exciting is that we're talking to developers about new software they could write for the FDS, not as part of our company, but on license. Some of them have really cool ideas, and it's going to be amazing to see the system pushed to its limits."

"Huh." Cam got a distant look in his eyes.

"Are you okay?" Fran asked.

"Yeah, it's something you said. It gave me an idea…" He jumped up from the sofa, almost spilling his remaining coffee, and hurried to the table. There, he grabbed a pen and a scrap of paper and scribbled down a note. "Got to write it down while it stays in my head."

He put the pen down, checked over the note, rested it against his screen, and returned to the sofa.

"Anything exciting?" Fran asked.

"It's too obscure to explain."

"That hasn't always stopped you in the past."

Cam laughed. "True, but this one is tough to explain and not worth the effort. Thanks, though, both for the inspiration and all the cleaning." He looked at the kitchen. "Oh wow, you really did do all the cleaning."

"If I'd tried to do all the cleaning, I'd still be roaming this place with a vacuum, a duster, and a trash bag."

"You did more than I've done in a month."

"That I believe. You're not normally like this, are you?"

He shook his head. "I like the place clean and tidy. It's just that right now, I have to let a lot of things pass. If I had a choice, I'd pick time with you over getting this place clean."

"If you want to spend time with me, then some basic cleaning will be needed." She sniffed. "When did you last change your t-shirt?"

"Best not to ask."

"Urgh!" She pushed away from him and curled up protectively in the far corner of the sofa. "I should have believed the people at school who told me that boys were gross."

"They were just jealous of our…" Cam frowned and took a deep breath. "No, actually, I take that back, I need a shower. But not until I've finished the next chapter."

"I admire your dedication."

Fran smiled, though behind it she was feeling a little sad. It was great to see him making so much progress on his thesis, but she missed spending time together. If he wanted to draft another chapter then that would be the whole of the rest of the day, and tomorrow was bound to be the same. Read, write, revise. That was Cam's life right now. Even cooking and cleaning only fitted in when they were desperately needed. It was selfish to want more of his time for herself when he was in the middle of this, but she couldn't help it. Besides, there were important things that the two of them were neglecting.

"Do you worry about what might happen with the prophecies while we're distracted?" she asked. "What Handar might do while we're not acting on that?"

"I guess." Cam frowned at his coffee. "I mean, that is a worrying thought, but I haven't had time for it. I'm too worried about whether I can hit this deadline."

"You can." Fran laid her hand on his knee. "I believe in you."

"Thanks." He took her hand in his. "I promise, once this is over, I'll have all the time in the world for you."

"Apart from the time you'll need for work, prophecy hunting, and finding an academic job once you're Doctor Cameron Kowal."

"Eh, academia can wait. You're what I need to make life happy and satisfying."

"Aw, that's so sweet." Fran kissed him. "But you still smell like a teenager's laundry basket."

She got off the sofa, took her cup to the sink, and rinsed it. "I'm going to leave you to it. The sooner you're finished, the sooner we can get back to tackling Handar and the prophecies together. Plus, then I can have my nice clean boyfriend back."

"Fair enough." Cam refilled his cup from the pot and took it to the table. "You want to meet up for dinner next week once I've sent off these chapters?"

"If you have time."

"I'll make time, I promise."

"All right, then. Just one evening." She kissed him, then headed for the door, navigating around the stacks of books and papers. "Have fun with your seventeenth-century shifters."

"Enjoy your overcrowded office."

"I will."

Fran walked out into the stairwell, and the crow fluttered up to meet her.

"Don't worry," she said, "you didn't miss out on much. Now come on, we might as well get back to work."

CHAPTER SIXTEEN

The one advantage of Cam being so busy was that Fran had more time available for other activities. While that mostly meant work, she could also head out into the hills a few days later to deal with another important part of her life. Traveling there by herself allowed her to practice the far stepping ability she'd inherited from Woodrow, sometimes using a single movement to carry her hundreds of feet up the trail.

"Watch this," she said to the pair of crows that had followed her and perched on a nearby branch.

Fran stretched out her foot and let the magic flow. The world became a blur around her, the forest hurtling past. When she put her foot down and raised her other leg, she was in a different place entirely. Unfortunately, that place was the middle of a prickly bush, whose spikes dug through her thick coat and jeans. Only a backpack full of technology kept her from getting spiked all over.

"Ouch!" Fran exclaimed as she pushed through the

branches and back to the path. "That's not what I was after."

The crows flew over and circled above her head, croaking with laughter.

"Yes, yes, very funny. I made a mistake. I bet you guys land on the wrong branches sometimes or get lost around the city."

The crows didn't seem to be listening. Something else had drawn their attention, and they were drifting toward the next valley over. If Fran had navigated correctly, a subject on which she had growing doubts, that would be the valley where the Evermores had their base in the abandoned mine.

It was tempting to take another swift step, but after the incident with the bush, Fran wanted time to consider what had gone wrong before she tried again. Instead, she ran along the trail through the woods, curious to see what had gotten the birds' attention.

As she approached a ridge, she heard a sound from up ahead. There were crashes and thuds, interspersed with people shouting and the low rumble of Evermore sound magic. The crows circled above the valley beyond the ridge, peering down at whatever was causing the noise.

Fran reached the ridge and peered over. To her relief, she was in the right place, but that relief was cut short by what else she saw.

Taldiss, Winslow, and a few other Evermores stood behind the barricades they'd been raising last time she visited, defenses improvised from parts of old buildings, mining debris, and felled trees. Light flashed, and noise roared as they launched magical attacks against the creatures charging at them.

Those creatures appeared to be made up entirely of stone. Not carved stone like a gargoyle or an animated statue, but the sort of rough, rounded rocks that appeared naturally all across the mountain sides. Some rock creatures were shaped like people, with two arms and two legs, although they varied in size from gnome height to twice that of the tallest elf. Others had four legs or more, moving across the broken ground of the old mining works like agile deer or prowling wolves.

Many of them charged at the barricade, but some stood farther back, lobbing rocks at the Evermores. One almost hit Winslow. Another was heading straight for Taldiss until she flung out a blast of sound so forceful that it flung the rock from its path, and it hit the barricade in front of her.

Fran didn't know anything about the rock creatures, but she could see that her friends were in trouble. The rock creatures outnumbered them, and they would soon be overwhelmed.

She gathered her power in her hands, forming a bright ball of light, and strode toward the creatures at the back, the ones that were throwing stones.

"Hey, you!" she shouted.

The creatures turned to her, and she flung a blast of light at them. It would've blinded and stunned most other beings, but the rock monsters, with their blank, eyeless faces, seemed unperturbed. They raised their stones and flung them at Fran, who dodged one, then another, before taking a desperate far step to avoid a boulder thrown by the biggest creature.

The far step carried her up the slope, above the monsters. As the boulder crashed down, they looked around in confusion.

"Over here," she shouted. Whatever else she did, drawing fire from the Evermores had to be useful.

The rock monsters picked up fresh stones and weighed them in their hands as if judging how they would throw them.

This time, Fran used sound instead of light. She called a rumbling wave into the ground beneath her feet and sent it down the slope, dislodging dirt, rocks, and debris. A landslide swept across the rock monsters, flinging them from their feet and entirely burying one.

Unfortunately, the landslide had left little ground beneath Fran's feet. The dirt beneath her gave way, and she fell, sliding down the slope on her ass.

"Incoming!" she cried.

One of the rock monsters was pulling itself to its feet. As Fran slid past it, she summoned a focused blast of sound and flung it at the creature. This time, the magic had an effect. The stony being clutched the sides of its head and sank to its knees.

With the last of her momentum, Fran jumped to her feet and ran toward the Evermores' defensive position. Although the Evermores had driven back some of the monsters, others were still going. Several had reached the barricades, which they were ripping down.

Fran held out her hand and called on another of the powers she'd inherited from Woodrow. A sledgehammer, its head reddened by a thin layer of rust, hurtled out of a heap of abandoned mining gear and into her hand. She wasn't used to wielding something so heavy, but her combat training paid off.

She gripped the shaft with both hands and swung it with all her might as she reached the rock creatures. Her blow hit the largest one in the back of the knee, and the rocks that made up its leg shifted out of place. It howled, a sound like stone scraping across stone, and fell.

Other creatures turned to face Fran. A blow from her sledgehammer knocked another monster back, but then stone arms grabbed her from behind, pinning her arms to her sides. The creature squeezed and Fran struggled to take a breath, never mind to break free.

There was a flash of light. A magically infused staff hit the monster that had hold of Fran. Its grip loosened and she squirmed free as another blow came in. Taldiss stood beside her, wielding the staff with speed and grace.

Together, the two of them battered at the creature. The blows of magical staff and mundane sledgehammer seemed to affect it equally. It staggered back, then turned and ran.

Overhead, one of the crows cried out in triumph. The whole attack had collapsed. Some rock creatures were running, while others dug their comrades out of the landslide, ready to carry them away.

As the last of them carried their injured comrades over the ridge and out of sight, one turned to look back. It let out a grating sound filled with defiance before disappearing from view.

Fran set down the sledgehammer and looked around. "Is everyone okay?"

A few of the Evermores had bruises and scrapes, but for the most part, they seemed to have emerged uninjured.

"We're going to have to rebuild this," Taldiss said bitterly, pointing at a part of the barricade the rock monsters had ripped open.

"True, but that's a small price to pay for safety," Winslow said. "Thank you Fran, for your help in achieving that."

"You know me, always happy to help you out." Then she looked away, embarrassed. "I mean, apart from all that time when I wasn't helping."

"That's behind us." Winslow held out a hand to help her over the barricade. "I assume you're here to help out some more by working with the Source."

"That's right." Fran followed him down the back of the barricade and toward the tunnel entrance. "Sorry I couldn't come more often, I know that moving the Source is important, but I have my work to consider."

"I understand. We pushed you too hard before so you left. I wouldn't want to make that happen again."

There had been far more to it than too much work, but she wasn't going to reopen those arguments. If she wanted to pursue her real goal, then she needed Winslow to accept her presence, and that meant playing nice.

"Hopefully, Enfield and I can work out something we missed before." She patted the hefty backpack she wore. "I've brought some new equipment that might help."

Winslow led her through the tunnels to the chamber where they kept the Source. The glow of its magic, combined with lights cast by the Evermores, illuminated the space so brightly that it banished the shadows from even the most distant corners of the artificial cave, carved out by miners decades before.

The Source itself stood in its containment unit in one corner of the room, a figure of pure energy, as blank-faced as the rock monsters. Enfield sat on a chair beside it, his leg stretched out in front of him, looking at the readouts from the sensors they'd set up around the unit.

"I'll leave you in Enfield's care," Winslow said. "If you need anything for your work, let me know." He lowered his voice. "Keep an eye on Enfield. It would be bad for him to push himself too hard in his condition."

The elder Evermore's footsteps faded down the tunnel, leaving Fran and Enfield alone.

"How are you doing?" She sat beside him.

"Slowly healing," Enfield said. "I've made some more potions that should speed up my recovery, but it's too late for them to be fully effective. Unfortunately, I was unconscious when I needed my own help."

"Josie told me about you two."

"Oh. That." Enfield sighed. "It's what I have to do."

"Are you sure? You two are so sweet together. Maybe it would help with all of this?"

"I'm sure." Enfield waved at the containment unit. "Can we focus on the work?"

"Sure." Fran opened her backpack. "I brought some new sets of sensors that Singar put together. These are to help us understand the energy fields, ready to move the Source, and not to help us understand what he's saying."

She gave a huge wink. Enfield laughed.

"Great subtlety. Winslow would never see through it."

"I know, right?" Fran laughed too. "Anyway, this is… Oh."

She held up the first piece of equipment. Its case had cracked, and so had the lenses set along one side. "That rock monster. When he was trying to crush me, he must have crushed these too."

She set the device down and pulled out others, laying them down on the stone floor. Every one showed signs of damage.

"Can you repair them?" Enfield asked.

"Maybe." Fran picked up one of the units. The tip of a small microphone fell out. "It depends on what parts we have here and how well I can understand Singar's work."

"That's better than nothing, which is what we currently have."

"Really?" Fran looked around at the rest of their equipment, rows of sensors plugged into a powerful laptop by tangles of interconnecting cables. "Surely we've got some useful data?"

"A little. I'm still struggling to find the patterns in how the Source responds to me. Isn't that right, buddy?"

He looked at the Source, which waved, its surface flickering as energy flows shifted.

"I'm sorry about all this." Fran walked over to the containment unit and pressed her hand against its magical field. The Source touched the same point, and she felt like she should've been able to sense its touch, but the unit's magic was too strong. She had made sure of that. "We're trying to learn about you, talk to you, so we can find a way to let you go safely. It's hard."

The Source pressed its head against the field, and the slump of its shoulders was full of sadness.

"We'll get there, I promise, right, Enfield?"

"Absolutely." He pushed himself up on his crutches and came over to stand beside her. "Whatever we say when Winslow's here, we're looking for a way to let you go. I hope you understand that." He shifted his weight, wincing as he did so. "I just wish we could understand you."

CHAPTER SEVENTEEN

Handar walked into a meeting room at Philgard Technologies and set a heavy box down on the table in the middle. Two more boxes were already sitting there, but now he had the full set, he could start unpacking them. He checked that the blinds were down on the room's glass walls and that its privacy spells were in place, then started to lay the prophecies out.

The door handle rattled, then someone knocked. Handar opened the door a crack and peered into the corridor.

"It's hard to attend a meeting when you lock me out of the room," Julia said.

"Sorry." Handar opened the door enough for her to come in, then closed it behind her. "I'm not taking any chances with this."

"Mysterious." Julia had her tablet in her hand. She peered into the boxes, then raised an eyebrow. "You've never struck me as a big reader. What's going on here?"

Handar started taking the books and papers out, setting

them in neat stacks according to where they'd come from and what he understood about them. They now included several notebooks of his, noting down every thought he'd had about the prophecies. Some of those thoughts seemed dumb when he read them back, others disappointingly mundane, but he didn't want to risk forgetting something that might help. It was hard enough for him to understand what any of this meant once, never mind to keep all those thoughts together in his head.

"You can't tell anyone about this," he said. "Not even the boss yet."

Julia looked even more surprised. "Are you plotting against him now?"

"'Course not. I'm not an idiot. I want to work this out first, then take it to him. I want to make sure it's useful before I waste his time."

"What is it that you're trying to work out?"

"The future."

"Ah, prophecies." Julia looked through one of the piles of papers. "You know that most prophecies turn out to be garbage, right? Aside from Tess, no one's reliable all the time, and a lot of what passes for prophecy is cryptic nonsense made up by frauds to grab people's money."

"I know that. I'm not an idiot."

"This one says otherwise." Julia held up a sheet of parchment. "Fake medieval. The ink's all wrong, and so are the spellings."

"Huh." Handar peered at the page. "You can work it out that quickly by looking at it?"

"By looking at it and applying years of experience, yes." Julia tossed that sheet on the floor. "You're clearly out of your depth here, Handar. Although it looks like you have found some interesting things…" She spread several more pages across the table and stared at them intently. "Where did these come from?"

"First two from the Dark Market. The others from a smuggler I knew in my adventuring days."

"You worked out that they were originally parts of a single document?"

"Yeah, well, they looked the same."

"I suppose that's true." She looked at him. "All right, you've surprised me. What is all this for?"

Handar frowned and rubbed a knuckle against the side of his head.

"Last year, the boss got hold of that prophecy, remember?"

"The Tess one, yes."

"Then he sent me to find more, but it didn't all work out."

"You got ambushed in a library."

Handar took the last few papers out of one of the boxes, then set the box down on the floor.

"I don't like losing," he said. "I wanted to find what I'd missed, to get it right. The boss said I didn't need to, but it's a matter of pride."

"I can understand that. No one's right all the time, not even him."

Handar shrugged. "Maybe he is, and I've been wasting my time. But I reckoned, if I could find something useful for the boss, I could make up for failing him before."

"So you started collecting prophecies and books about

them." Julia peered at one of the stacks. "And other people's research, by the looks of things."

"Whatever I could find."

"You stole these?" She pointed at the notes, not judgmental, merely curious.

"I had a conversation with the guy who made them. He agreed to share."

"I bet he did. What do you hope to get out of all of this?"

"To help the boss, of course. What else would it be for?"

Julia took a step back from the table, arms folded across her chest, one finger tapping on her arm.

"What indeed."

She walked around the table, looking at the stacks of paperwork, sometimes glancing through a book or document. She rearranged some of them, forming new piles. Handar felt nervous but excited. She was finding connections that he'd missed, wasn't she? This was going to work.

Julia suddenly looked up from one of the books. "Why am I here? You've been working on this for months, so why tell me now? Why tell anyone if you're still trying to keep it a secret?"

"'Cause I'm stuck. Like you said, this ain't my thing. I'm not good at it. Some of these, I can barely read half the words, never mind understand what they say. You're a witch and the smartest one I've met. You knew stuff about that first prophecy. You can work out how this stuff goes together, what it means."

"Perhaps, given time."

"You wanna help the boss, right?"

"Of course." Julia smiled at him. "What else could any of us want once we know the truth of his power?"

"Exactly. So..." Handar waved at the boxes. "How do we do this?"

"You're putting me in charge?"

"I guess." Handar shrugged. "I don't understand enough to know what we should do, so maybe you should be in charge."

"In that case, the first thing is to make sure we contain this. If we can use these prophecies, so can other people."

"Don't I know it. Had a couple of assholes break into my apartment, try to steal these for themselves."

"We'll find somewhere more secure here to store them, somewhere only you and I have the key to." She unlocked her tablet and tapped on the screen, looking for options in the office building's room list. "Do you know if there are duplicates of any of them?"

Handar shrugged. "They came from a lot of different people. I don't know what they did before they passed them on."

"Well, from now on, we don't give anyone else a chance to make copies. Prophecy is an arms race. The secrets of the future are only useful if no one else knows them."

Handar wondered if he should tell her about his copies, the photos he'd taken of every page of every document here, with Berra helping him out. Those were his backups. There was no risk they'd get into someone else's hands, and keeping that secret let him feel like he still had some control. Julia might take charge of the originals, but he'd have his backups if he needed them.

"No one else gets copies," he said. "Got it."

Julia was back to going through the documents. She mostly seemed to be keeping his system, putting documents back where she found them, except when there was another obvious connection. He liked that. It felt like she trusted him.

"This is good work for an amateur I don't mean that dismissively. You've achieved a lot."

"Thanks." He stood taller, back straight, grinning proudly. Maybe he hadn't been as lost in this as he feared. Still, he was glad he'd gotten her involved. She would work out what he'd missed, and they'd be able to help the boss.

Julia held up one of the scruffiest bits of paper, a large scrap taken from a piece of packaging, covered in his handwriting

"What's this one?" she asked.

Handar looked down at the table, embarrassed. "Just some scribbles. I was trying to work out more about an idea I had."

"Tell me about it."

"Really?"

"Really." Julia smiled, and her excitement spread to him. She put the paper down on the table and tapped it with a long fingernail. "It looks like it connects to a lot of these."

"It does." Handar ran the point of a claw around one part of the paper. "There was a lot of things talking about doors and gates. I thought that was all real at first, but then I learned that sometimes prophecy ain't like that. All them doors and gates, they could mean something else."

"Weakness." Julia tapped the middle of the paper. "That's what you think they represent?"

"Yeah. Then I thought about other things that could represent weakness, and I started listing them, so I could look for them in the other prophecies." He scratched his head. "Is that the right thing to do?"

"It's certainly an interesting approach." Julia looked down his list of words, then reached for another pile of prophecies. "Most professionals who work with prophecies prefer inductive to deductive reasoning since it reduces the risk of forcing your expectations on the facts. On the other hand, pattern recognition inevitably involves a certain element of deduction, bringing our existing frameworks to the evidence. After all, no one ever approaches the evidence with true neutrality."

"Er, so what's that mean?"

"I don't know yet." Julia unlocked her tablet and started making notes, her fingers darting across the touch screen. "You might be right, you might be wrong, but at the very least, you've given us a way to approach this."

"So I've done good?"

"Oh yes." Julia flipped a document page and ran a finger down the lines. She stopped and tapped a word with her finger. "That's the third reference to darkness I've found already and the second to nightmares. Were you specifically looking for prophecies on those themes?"

Handar shook his head. "Whatever I could find."

"Then I think there's another pattern here. I think Howard was right to be interested in the prophecies and wrong to stop focusing on them. It seems that someone foresaw his plans. If someone else had got to these before us, they could've used the prophecies against him, perhaps even redirected his power." She grabbed another document and started reading. "They could still do that."

"Not if they ain't got the prophecies, right?"

"Absolutely."

Handar grinned. He'd done the right thing. He'd collected things that were dangerous to Howard Phillips, the Darkness Between Dreams, and his plans for the world. That meant the boss was safer than before, that his plans could go ahead. Whatever Handar's past failures, they were behind him now. With Julia's help, he would ensure that the boss' plan worked.

"Should we tell him?" he asked. "I've been keeping it secret 'cause I wasn't sure I'd got something good yet, but if you've worked it out, it's time."

"Not yet." Julia laid a hand on his forearm. "We still don't know for certain what all of this leads to. I don't want to approach him with a theory that turns out to be wrong. Do you?"

"No." Handar shook his head. "Good thinking. So we keep working at it?"

"We do. I mean, I could pursue this on my own if you don't have the time anymore."

"I want to be part of it, to see where this goes. It's more satisfying than I thought, using my brain in a different way. I ain't good at it, but I'm enjoying it."

"Very well." Julia glanced at her watch. Her fingers went to the slender silver necklace she always wore. "Howard doesn't need me for the next three hours, and I'd like to get started on this. Could you fetch us a pair of secure laptops and some sticky notes to mark up the documents?"

"Sure. You want a coffee too? I need it sometimes when I'm trying to make sense of this."

"That would be fantastic, thank you."

Julia sat and pulled a pile of papers toward her. There

was a gleam in her eyes. Handar felt like he must look the same way, full of excitement at what lay ahead of them, at what they could achieve. On his way out of the room, he looked back. Julia leaned forward, smiling so wide she could almost have been laughing.

He stepped out of the room and let the door lock shut behind him. This was going to go well.

CHAPTER EIGHTEEN

Singar sat at a table in the Mana Wave Industries meeting room. Her appointment wasn't due for another few minutes, but she enjoyed the quiet that the magic around the area provided. With the rest of the office increasingly crowded, it was hard to hear herself think some days. No amount of noise-canceling headphones or loud punk music seemed to be able to drown out the chatter and bustle of the growing company. She couldn't work on her technology in here, away from her tools and components, but at least she could think about it.

There was a slight ripple in the air at the room's entrance as something disturbed the sound-baffling field. A moment later, Smokey jumped up onto the seat next to Singar. He sat with his head up and his tail hanging off the back of the seat, swishing slowly back and forth.

"You know there are no mice to catch here, right?" Singar tried to work out what the swaying tail meant.

"I'm not thinking about that sort of vermin," Smokey replied. "I've been dealing with the political kind."

"City council going well?"

Smokey's ears pressed down against the sides of his head.

"Election promises mean nothing to those people," he said. "I thought I could use them to get some things changed, but it turns out that the other councilors are so used to having their way, they don't see any reason why they have to do what they promised."

"Aren't they worried that they'll lose their next election to someone like you?"

"They think they can win anything with money, that my win was a fluke." Smokey grinned. "I look forward to proving them wrong. For now, though, I'm stuck trying to make even the smallest change."

"That would drive me crazy, seeing things done badly and not being able to fix it."

"It's driving me crazy, but I'm going to find a way through it. For now, this makes a nice change of pace." Smokey looked around the room. "I don't suppose you brought the list?"

Singar took a Manaphone out of her shirt pocket. It was a new shirt with an interesting printed pattern, more expensive than the secondhand flannel she usually wore. She wasn't sure if she liked it and felt a little uncomfortable with her unfamiliar look, but she had money now, and she was damned if she wasn't going to show it.

"Here." She opened a list of appointments on the phone. "Every one of them a developer with an idea to pitch at us."

"There are a lot of them," Smokey said.

"This is only today's batch. We've got more coming tomorrow and next week."

"Do we have to talk with all of—"

"Yep. Bart says that because we understand the tech, we've got to talk with them first to filter out the things that won't work or are too obvious and derivative. We make a shortlist. Then the business brains will team up with us to pick the ones we work with."

"Sounds like an excuse for Bart to avoid these interviews."

"Seriously, you think Bart would slack off?"

"I suppose not." Smokey brushed a paw across the fur of his cheek. "I'm getting jaded from all this time with politicians."

"How do you think I feel? I've got to work with a politician here all afternoon."

"Ha ha ha."

"Excuse me?" A young gnome, one of the new admin staff, had stuck her head through the silencing field and was looking nervously at them. "Are you ready for the first presentation?"

"Sure, send them in." Singar toyed with her whiskers. "I'm looking forward to seeing what they've got."

The admin gnome disappeared, and a moment later three dwarves walked into the meeting room, two of them wearing suits, the third in old-fashioned formal chainmail. They sat at the far end of the table, and one of them plugged a cable into his laptop. A screen on the wall blinked into life, and a slide appeared, showing a logo of two stylized axes across a keyboard.

"Good morning," the dwarf in chainmail said. "We're Clan Axfall Programming, and we would like to talk to you about what we can bring to the Fun Delivery System."

"Is it an ax?" Singar asked.

"Well, yes, but, um..." The dwarves looked nervously at each other, then the one in chainmail hit a key on the laptop, starting up a slide show. "Let us explain..."

What they'd come to explain, it turned out, was a game about a dwarf trying to make the perfect ax. Players would collect components from the world around them, based on what the FDS could detect in its surroundings, and use them in a crafting process. There were options for shared play, both offline and online, and for players to show their unique axes to the world.

"We should have had Gruffbar here for this," Smokey whispered at one point. "I have no idea how to judge an ax game."

"Me neither," Singar whispered back, "but if it only interests dwarves, it's probably not worth our time, right?"

The presentation included mockups of parts of the game but nothing that looked to Singar like gameplay footage.

"Have you written any of the code for this game?" she asked.

"Not yet," the chainmail dwarf said. "We didn't want to waste time if we didn't know whether you'd work with us."

"You thought proof of concept was a waste of time?"

"Um..." The dwarves looked at each other, and their cheeks went red underneath their beards.

"OK, thanks for talking to us." Smokey waved a paw toward the exit. "We'll be in touch. Or not."

Next came a lone witch. Instead of bringing a computer, she'd brought an FDS with its case cracked open and a tablet attached to the side.

"I hacked into your machine." She set it down on the table and put her hands on her hips. "Only way I could find out how it worked. You got a problem with that?"

"Should we?" Singar twitched her whiskers. "Seems like a good way to test what sort of people we are too."

"Well, yeah." The witch rubbed the back of her neck and looked at them a little less defiantly. "I've been places where I got kicked out for this sort of thing."

"Here, we're the sort of people who crack other machines for fun." Smokey twitched his tail. "So we're not angry, but we're not all that impressed either. Show us what your software does, and maybe that'll change."

"It's a game." The witch switched the machine on, and a variety of three-dimensional shapes appeared scattered across the table. "The design's abstract right now because I've not been working on appearances, but I think the fundamentals are strong and that we could skin it for a variety of different styles and settings."

For the next ten minutes, Singar and Smokey rearranged the shapes on the table, encouraged and sometimes guided by the witch.

"In the complete game, there'd be a tutorial for all this," she said. "You wouldn't need someone talking you through it."

"I'd hope so." Smokey swiped a block off the table, watched it vanish on the way to the floor, then turned his attention to her. "Which company do you represent?"

"I don't. I'm a freelancer."

"You developed all this on your own?"

"Yep."

"Even if we don't go ahead with your product, we might have a job for you here, right Singar?"

"With these skills?" Singar nodded. "Sure."

"I don't want a job. I like working freelance."

"Good attitude." Smokey returned to his seat. Next to him, Singar was making notes. "We'll think about what you've shown us and get in touch. In the meantime, feel free to keep hacking our products."

"Like you could stop me." With a triumphant smile, the witch picked up her FDS and walked out.

"She thinks she persuaded us, doesn't she?" Smokey asked.

"She's right. That was good."

"The others might be better."

"Then we'll have a really big shortlist." Singar raised her voice. "Next!"

"They can't hear you, remember. Silence spell."

"Oh yeah. Then let's hope that admin girl knows to keep sending them in."

The admin did know, and over the next few hours, Singar and Smokey met with several people pitching them software for the FDS. There were small companies and freelancers, like the first two appointments, and representatives from larger publishing companies. Sometimes those were PR and salespeople, full of hot air and empty promises. The better ones sent their teams of technicians, the people who understood their products and could talk through the technical details.

A lot of them had found ways to get their software onto an FDS, although some had mockups on simulators, and a few, like the dwarves, only had presentations, a point that counted against them where Singar was concerned. If she couldn't see the product in action, how could she know if it was real?

About half of the pitches were for games, like the first one that Mana Wave themselves had released. There were others too, some with musical or visual entertainments, ideas for magical three-dimensional movies and shows, and a few with apps that their creators thought might be useful to people who owned the FDS.

"You get that this is supposed to deliver fun, right?" Singar asked the third of the app guys. "Not a way to buy more groceries?"

"Sure, but a system can be practical as well as—"

"No thanks." Singar pointed at the door. "If you don't understand what we're doing here, you're not making the list."

Smokey watched that candidate leave, dejected.

"That was—"

"Don't bother saying harsh."

"I was going to say needed. I put up with enough nonsense on the city council. I'm not having my time wasted here."

"Wish we could take a break." Singar looked at their packed schedule. "I could do with a coffee."

"There's a pot in the staffroom."

"We have a staffroom now?"

"Of course."

"Well, I don't want staffroom coffee. I want Blazing Bean coffee and cake."

"Maybe the admin can go get it?"

"Are we allowed to use her for that?"

Smokey arched his back and stretched out his tail.

"Let's ask. I could do with a saucer of the good oat milk."

It turned out that the admin was not only willing but eager to go to the coffee shop, an excuse to get out from behind her desk and catch some fresh air. Singar's offer to buy her coffee and cake helped. One more interview later, their refreshments arrived, and Singar's spirits perked up thanks to caffeine and sugar.

"Bring on the next one," she announced, wiping crumbs from her whiskers. "Let's hope they're good."

By the end of the afternoon, they had a shortlist of companies and individuals whose software interested them.

"I thought it was all going to be licensing agreements," Smokey said, "but it's not going to be that simple, is it?"

"What do you mean?" Singer drained the last cold dregs of coffee from her cup.

"Some of the best ones, they've got solid concepts, but not the money or resources to make them real. Like that witch who came in second. No way she can build the whole game on her own, even if we offer her a licensing deal."

"So what can we do?"

"Fund some of them, maybe?" Smokey scratched himself behind the ear. "Pay them to develop the software in return for a bigger cut of its profits."

"That sounds like an issue for Bart and Gruffbar."

"Good. I've thought about this enough for today."

They left the meeting room and headed for the workshop, where they had their own workspaces. It was the end of the day, and many people had already gone home, but there was still plenty of bustle and chatter.

"You know what's amazing?" Singar asked. "How many people want to work with us now. All the job hunters turning up for interviews, all the companies coming to pitch us their programs. They're not only doing it because we're an option. They seem genuinely excited about us."

"We really are a big deal, aren't we?" Smokey hopped onto his seat.

"I got a new apartment last week, left the old neighborhood behind. I've always wanted it, always said I'd make it, but now we're here, it doesn't feel real."

"Don't worry. It could easily still fall apart." Smokey looked around. "That wasn't a very comforting thing to say, was it?"

"Maybe not, but I think it's what I needed." Singar started making notes on their shortlist, ready to send it to the rest of the Mana Wave board. "Got to have a reason to stay motivated."

CHAPTER NINETEEN

The Source sat in the middle of the cave, still held within its containment unit. Around it was a whole host of sensors. Some Fran had bought, some she had Singar make, and some she'd assembled herself. Several tracked the Source's movements, some watched its energy patterns, others listened to the sounds it made.

The most specialized sensors were the magically sensitive ones, and they were also the hardest to interpret. It was all very well to have a picture of what sort of magic had been radiating from the target at different times, but working out what that meant was a whole other matter.

Fran sat on a folding chair behind a table they'd set up close to the Source. The table was a solid old steel door meant to seal off a mine shaft in an emergency, balanced on two stacks of discarded bricks. Compared with all the shiny technology sitting on and around it, that table seemed like a throwback to a poorer time, something they should be able to replace. Still, it worked, and there was no urgency to get a proper table, so the computers the sensors connected to sat there, and Fran sat behind it, trying to discern patterns in the data they'd gathered.

"I really wish you could talk like us." Fran looked at the Source. "It would make everything so much easier. Or maybe if I could talk like you—if you talk at all. Something to let us share ideas."

She took her bag from under the table and unfastened her roller skates from the side. They were no use for traveling to and from the mine workings, but the floor in this cavern was flat enough for her to practice, and she needed something to clear her head.

She strapped the skates on and started doing circuits with her way lit by the Source's glow. Her path was a wide one, steering clear of the sensors to make sure that she didn't wreck any of them or get tangled in the cables. The ground was too uneven for fancy tricks, but staying upright on it, keeping her path as even as possible, provided enough of a challenge to engage her brain.

As she was on her seventh circuit of the room, Enfield hobbled in. He was down to a single crutch most of the time now, and though it hurt him to travel that way, his determination was impressive. The scars on his face were becoming less pronounced, and his returning hair hid some of them, but Fran accepted his diagnosis that his face would never fully heal. This was part of who he was now, and if he could accept that, so could everyone else.

"I brought fresh coffee." He set a pot down on the table next to the mugs they'd been using earlier in the day. "And a reminder from Winslow that we're to focus on returning the Source to its place on Earth, not get distracted with theorizing or looking for other outcomes."

"Do you think he knows?" Fran skated over, wheels clicking over bumps and dips in the floor.

"Knows what we're working on?" Enfield shook his head. "If he did, I think he'd confront us about it, try to make us stop. He knows what we're like, and he's trying to keep us traveling in his direction."

"Good luck to him." Fran poured herself a coffee. "By which I mean, he can take his attitude and go rot in a ditch."

Enfield laughed and took a seat. The relief on his face as he took the weight off his legs was obvious. He leaned the crutch against the table and reached for the coffee pot.

"It's not up to Blazing Bean standards." He poured himself a cup. "And we don't have a milk frother or sprinkles down here. Still, it should keep us going for a while."

"Thanks." Fran took the seat next to him. "I wish this was the Blazing Bean. I've hardly seen Cam at all in the past couple of months. Although even if we were there, he probably wouldn't be."

"Seems weird, going to that place without him. Are you all right with him spending all this time on research?"

"It'll be worth it in the end. I'm really proud of what he's doing. I just..." She sighed. "I wish it didn't take up so much of his time."

"If it gives you time for me and the Source, at least I get a bright side out of it." Enfield tapped one of their screens. "Take a look at this and see what you think."

The screen showed a pattern of magic on one side and a diagram of interlinked crystals on the other. She looked from one to the other, trying to work out what they were and how they were connected.

"This magic is familiar, but the crystals aren't. Why is that?"

"Because you recorded that pattern of magic yourself, last week."

"Cool! Yes, I see it now. That magic was coming off the Source when Winslow was in here, and the Source was getting agitated."

"Exactly. It's one of the few moments where we can clearly link a pattern in the magic to its cause."

"You think this was the Source's way of telling Winslow where he could stick his head?"

"Some sort of protest seems likely, either an argument or a powerful emotion, maybe even an attempt to disrupt the containment field. Comparing it with other patterns might help."

"So, what are the crystals for?" Fran's eyes went wide. "No, wait, I've got it. They turn magical light into other sorts of magic. If we pour pure Evermore energy through them, we'll make the same pattern as the Source did."

"Exactly." Enfield smiled. "It's not much, but it's a start."

"Awesome! High five!"

They slapped hands, then toasted each other with their coffee.

"That's some progress on communication, at least," Fran said. "Are we any closer to understanding his power? Without understanding, we can't replicate it, right?"

"Except that this is a form of replication. Maybe only a tiny part, but it's something. We've been treating communication and replication as two separate problems, jumping back and forth between them, but what if they're the same? What if one leads to the other?"

"Ooh, ooh, yes, of course!" Fran bounced in her seat with excitement. "If he's communicating with his energy, then replying means putting out energy like his, which is exactly what we need to replace him in the kemana network back home."

"Which means that we can finally free him."

A crackling sound drew their attention to the containment unit. The Source was leaning hard against the field, pouring his energy into it, and where the two forces met, sparks flew. Those sparks stayed inside the unit, unable to break through its barriers, but still, it was an intimidating sight.

Fran got out of her seat and skated over to the unit, moving carefully so she didn't disrupt their sensors.

"Make sure you're recording this," she called to Enfield.

"Always."

She pressed her hand against the field, close to where the Source had his. The energy of the unit fizzed and tingled against her skin. The Source, seeing her hand so close to his, moved his hand over so their palms pressed together, with only that thin layer of magic between them.

"You understood what we were saying, didn't you?" she asked.

For a moment, the Source's hand glowed brighter.

"You know that we're trying to get you out."

Again, that flash of brightness.

"Could you use this to communicate with us, this thing that you're doing now?"

The Source's hand flickered, and it jerked away from the field. Something there hadn't worked right.

"Sorry," Fran said. "This must be so frustrating. I have

no idea how I'd feel if I was cooped up like you and if the only people who might get me out were the same ones who trapped me there."

The Source flung itself against the field and Fran jerked back. The wheels of her skates tangled with wires on the floor and she fell, crushing a sensor beneath her.

"That's not helping," she snapped, then softened her tone. "I suppose that's not your fault."

There was a *thud* of Enfield's crutch on the rock floor and his uneven, shuffling footsteps. He stopped close to her, looking straight at the Source.

"On the mountain, you reached out for me, remember?" He held out his hand. "I was so busy trying to survive, I didn't think about the rest of it, but looking back, your magic felt a lot like mine. Like Evermore magic. Do you have the same magic as us?"

The Source stretched out its hand, which flashed twice.

"Is that a no or another yes?" Enfield frowned. "Or something more complicated. Maybe you can make your magic like ours, but it doesn't have to be that way. Is that it?"

This time the hand flashed once.

"It is, isn't it?" Enfield hobbled excitedly back to the table and typed something into the computer. "All the sensors are on. Can you make the power in your hand like it was that day? I know how it felt, how it looked, but I want to see what the magic was."

The Source didn't move, but the glow of its skin went through subtle changes. It became a little less bright than it had been, perhaps because the urgency born of frustration and desperation had gone away, or perhaps for some completely unrelated reason that Fran couldn't understand. That was the problem with all of this. It was so incomprehensible.

"Look," Enfield said softly.

Fran went over and looked at the screen. The magic pattern was very similar to the one they'd been looking at a few minutes before.

"It's imitating Evermore magic," she said.

"Or the Evermores copied a form of its magic. Either way, that's something we can understand."

"Ooh, ooh, I just remembered something." Fran's fingers danced across the keyboard as she went rooting through weeks worth of data files. "Look at this one."

It was a reading of the Source's magic from one of their previous working sessions.

"I don't get it," Enfield said. "This looks nothing like the Evermore power."

"No, but see this pattern here? That's what would happen if you made something like Evermore powers for heat instead of light. And this one..." She opened another set of data. "Nuclear radiation."

"Really?" Enfield peered at the data. "Do magic users summon radiation?"

"Not often, but I watched this video once about the theory of how they could be combined. It's possible. It's just not a good idea for most people. For a being of pure energy that can soak up anything the world throws at it, it's probably fine. Not much risk of cancer when you're the source of all magic in the world."

Enfield looked at the images on her screen, then at his.

"You're right," he whispered. "There's a pattern. It's been right in front of us this whole time."

"And now we know, maybe we can replicate that pattern. We can make a device that puts out magic like the Source does."

"Sure, but can we make a device that puts out as much magic as the Source? Because if not, we still can't power the kemanas."

"One step at a time." Fran skated back to the containment unit. "You can wait a while if you have to, right? After all, you were trapped for twenty-six thousand years. A few more weeks won't matter next to that."

The Source scraped its fingertips down the inside of the magical field. Sparks poured down its arm, all colored an angry red, and it growled.

"Okay, maybe you can't wait." Fran hurried back to the table. "We're working as fast as we can, right Enfield?"

"That's right."

"Working on what?" Winslow had appeared in the doorway and stood looking at them, one eyebrow raised.

"On how to move the Source back to Earth, of course," Fran said. Lying didn't come easy, especially when she had to convince someone as experienced and smart as Winslow, but there was so much at stake here.

"Good." Winslow looked from her to the Source and back again. "I would hate for you to get distracted." He looked meaningfully at Enfield. "Either of you."

CHAPTER TWENTY

This time, Elethin put on a disguise before she met with Kotia. Part of the disguise was mundane, putting on clothes that she would never normally wear: loose jeans, a rough woolen sweater, and a padded black coat, along with scuffed up sneakers from a thrift store. She used her magic too, changing her face, her hair, and her complexion. Her pointed elf ears again turned into the rounded tips of a human. If she could've changed her height, she would have, but it was much harder to make an illusion like that convincing when you had to interact with the world.

They met in a different bar. This one was much more like what she had expected the first time, a dingy dive with a sticky floor and suspicious stains on the baize of its pool tables. The barman was in his fifties and should have cut his hair short instead of trying to use it to cover his bald patch. His prematurely wrinkled face crumpled further as he hunched over the beer taps.

"What d'you want?" he asked.

"Beer," Elethin said. "Whatever's cheap."

The barman poured her a glass of lager and took payment.

"Ain't seen you here before," he said.

"Hopefully you won't again." Elethin tasted her drink. It was every bit as bad as she expected. "I'm only here to meet a friend."

She walked over to a corner table where Kotia was sitting, hunched over a drink of her own, her wings tucked in tight behind her. She looked up at Elethin and raised an eyebrow.

"Whatever you're selling, I'm not interested."

"It's me." Elethin took a seat next to Kotia, so she could talk quietly. "You think I'd come here looking like myself?"

"Shit, El." Kotia laughed. "Why don't you do stuff like this all the time? Imagine what you could get away with."

"My illusions are too vulnerable, too easily disrupted. I wouldn't want to risk getting caught wearing one if I didn't have to."

"You don't have to now. I was hoping you'd bring your pretty self along to help with the sale."

Kotia patted the bag on the seat next to her, which clinked.

"You'll have my words. That should be enough." Elethin looked at the bag. "Are you carrying all that jewelry around in there?"

"Of course. I've got to show it to the potential buyers."

Elethin shook her head. "No wonder you ended up in jail."

"You were there too, remember? If either of us was so very smart, we wouldn't know each other."

"I'd be happy with that."

"Then help me out now, like we agreed, and we can arrange for you to never see me again."

"Happy day."

At that moment, five magicals walked into the bar. The leader was a wizard in a loosely cut suit and a brightly patterned shirt, twirling his wand between his fingers. The others looked human enough that they could've been wizards too, but there was a hunched wariness that made Elethin think they must be shifters. They wore suits similar to their boss but with tamer shirts.

Kotia whistled and waved. The wizard nodded at her, then at the barman, who had started rapidly pouring drinks. By the time the new arrivals slouched across the room to Kotia and Elethin's table, their drinks were waiting for them: four glasses of cheap lager for the shifters, a bottle of second-rate whiskey for their boss, and three glasses to go with it.

The wizard sat opposite Kotia and ran an inquiring gaze across Elethin. She'd toned her looks down enough to draw less attention than usual, but his look still left her feeling unclean.

"This your help, Kotia?" he asked. "She doesn't look like much."

"Jacob, this is El," Kotia said. "El, Jacob."

"Good to meet you, El." Jacob poured whiskey into the three glasses. "It's important to know who you're dealing with."

"I get that." What Elethin didn't get was why Kotia had used her real name, or at least part of it. Was she being dumb or trying to keep things awkward for Elethin, to remind her of how she was trapped in this?

"You've got the goods?" Jacob nodded at the bag. "Show me."

"In a moment." Kotia licked her lips. "First, I want to make sure that the other bidder's here."

"Other bidder?" Jacob narrowed his eyes and put the stopper back in the whiskey bottle. "I asked you to get something for me. Where do bidders come into it?"

"I've got to make sure that I get appropriately paid for my work. It shouldn't be a problem. You were going to pay me fairly, right?"

"You're on fucking thin ice," Jacob growled.

Kotia shrugged. "We've all got to play the hand we're dealt."

Jacob's shifter guards turned as someone else walked into the bar. A pair of dwarves, three gnomes, and a Willen stared across the room at their table.

"Kotia," one of the dwarves growled, "what are they doing here?"

"Same as you," she said. "Making a deal."

One of the shifters hissed something Elethin couldn't hear and prowled toward the new arrivals.

"Yeah, well, your brother deserved it," the Willen responded and drew a knife. Next to him, one of the gnomes summoned magic between her fingers.

The barman sank out of sight behind his bar.

"You stupid cow," Jacob said, glaring at Kotia.

He grabbed the whiskey bottle by its neck, smashed it against the table, and held the jagged end out like a weapon. At that moment, the new arrivals charged, some swinging fists and weapons, others flinging spells. Jacob's guards shifted into wolves and leaped to meet them.

Elethin ducked beneath the table as the two sides clashed. She wished she'd worn her spell-silk to have some protection, but an Okorafor and LeGuin blouse was far too refined for a place like this. Whiskey dripped down her neck as Kotia moved the table to fit down there with her.

"I can't believe you dragged me into this," Elethin snapped as the room filled with sounds of violence.

"Me?" Kotia laughed. "You messed up plenty of people on the inside."

"When they pushed me to it. Nobody forced this on you."

"They didn't need to. I'm making opportunities."

"You're making a mess of both our lives."

"Guess you'd better help me clear it up then." Kotia grinned.

Elethin wanted to curse, but she wouldn't waste her breath on Kotia.

The table lurched as someone slammed into it. Elethin scrambled clear a moment before it collapsed beneath the weight of a dwarf and the shifter he was fighting. As she ran across the room, staying low and trying to reach the shelter of the bar, a stray spell skimmed her. Icy cold brushed her arm, frost running to her fingertips. More importantly, that magic disrupted the illusion disguising her. The face she'd put on flickered and faded away.

Now she did curse.

The fight was all across the bar, shifters and shorter magicals battling each other with fists, claws, spells, weapons, and broken furniture. A wolf howled in pain as the Willen slashed it with a knife. Another of the wolves had hold of a gnome in its teeth and was slamming her against the wall. Jacob was in a spell battle with two of his opponents, flinging magic and counterspells back and forth, the air thick with wasted power.

Elethin considered the risks of staying versus those of trying to get out. In the end, what decided it was her frustration. She'd spent years waiting in prison, her whole life dictated by other people, her movements at their mercy. She wasn't going to be vulnerable like that again.

She reached behind the bar and grabbed a glass in each hand. Standing, she took a split second to pick her targets, then flung the glasses at the magicals most in her way. One glass shattered on the hard head of a dwarf, while the other glanced off the side of a shifter's furred face. Both were thrown off balance by the unexpected impacts, giving their opponents a chance. As the dwarf went down beneath a mass of teeth and claws, and a spell hit the shifter, she ran past.

One of the gnomes stepped in her way. "Where are you going?" she snarled, hefting a chair leg in her right hand, its end viciously splintered.

"Out," Elethin said.

"Oh no. No one leaves until we get the gems."

"Really?"

Elethin raised her hand and summoned a flash of light. The gnome flung up defensive magic to stop it from blinding her, but the movement put her hand in the way of her view. At that moment, Elethin kicked her hard between the legs. The soft old thrift store sneakers didn't have the same impact as the tip of her good shoes would have, but it was enough. The gnome curled over, groaning.

Elethin dashed out the door and up the stairs to the street, leaving the chaos of the gang fight behind her.

In the street, she straightened her clothes, pulled out her phone, and called for a cab. For two nervous minutes she stood waiting, glancing back down the stairs in case anyone came after her. Then an eagle-borne taxi landed, and she jumped into the basket.

The giant eagle tapped an electronic device on the side of the basket.

"Where to?" a recorded voice asked.

Home would've been the most obvious answer, somewhere safe she could recover from all of this. Still, that meant hiding from her problems, not fixing them. She needed a way to sort this out. Instead, she gave the address of Gruffbar's apartment block.

It took half an hour to cross the city. Flying taxis weren't cheap, but she could afford them now. She could afford so many nice things she wanted, and she could lose them all so easily. If the Silver Griffins caught a hint of criminality in her life, it would be straight back to Trevilsom, and no chance of time off for good behavior this go around. Centuries of prison, terrible clothes, terrible food, and terrible people, of having no control over her own life. She couldn't bear the thought of it.

The eagle set its basket down on the roof of Gruffbar's building. Elethin paid, then found the stairs down. There was always a way down from the roofs in Mana Valley. Too many people flew for designers not to plan for it.

When she reached Gruffbar's apartment, the sound of the TV was emerging through the door. She knocked, and he opened the door, looking at her in surprise.

"Two visits in one lifetime," he said. "By my beard, I am honored."

"Are you going to let me in?"

"Do I have to?"

She sighed. She didn't have the energy for another fight, even a verbal one.

"Could I please come in?"

"Well, when you put it like that…"

He stepped back and let her in, then closed and locked the door. His shotgun ax leaned against the frame, where he could reach it to deal with intruders.

"Nice look," he said. "Been slumming it?"

"You could say that." Elethin kicked off the tattered shoes and sank onto the sofa, curling her legs beneath her. "I don't suppose I could have a drink?"

"I've got whiskey, but it smells like you've tried that already."

"Whiskey would be good. I'm sure it's better than what's on me."

He sniffed. "Reckon you're right."

He poured two generous measures of amber spirits into glasses and handed one to her, then settled into a padded armchair. He pressed a button on a remote and the TV switched off.

"What brings you here this time?" he asked.

Elethin looked around the apartment. Its decoration was still minimal, with no sign of the wealth they were starting to accrue. Did he prefer it this way? Had he not had time to shop? Was all his money pouring down a drain of debt? She doubted it was the last option. Loath as she was to admit it, Gruffbar seemed to have his life more in order than she did.

"You got out of a life of crime, right?" she said.

"I did."

"It doesn't come back to haunt you?"

"A few people have tried to drag me back in. I've learned to set my boundaries to stop them. It's not easy, but it works."

Elethin took a sip of her whiskey. It was better than the stuff Jacob had bought and infinitely better than the cheap lager. It was tempting to knock it all back in hopes of numbing herself, but that wasn't a solution. When she woke up in the morning, someone else would still have a hold over her, and she'd be no closer to real freedom.

"You know how much I hate to ask for anything from you," she said, "but I need help to get clear of that life before it sucks me back in for good."

CHAPTER TWENTY-ONE

The storage room was a cold, windowless place in the basement of Philgard Technologies' main office. Its concrete walls added to the sense of being somewhere bleak and desolate, a bunker to ride out an apocalyptic war or the secret basement of a serial killer. Those walls also provided security, a way to keep out intruders and anyone wanting to see what was inside. That made it the perfect place for Handar and Julia to keep the prophecies.

"Here." Julia handed him a sheet she'd been writing on. "That goes in the red section."

Handar took the paper and stuck it to the wall, in an area marked off with red tape. There were sections in other colors too. Each section was a theme of topics covered in the texts. It had become easier to refer to them as blue, red, or green rather than, for example, "the section covering nightmares, dreams, and things that come out of them, and possibly some meta-coverage on how prophecies work, but we might be wrong about that."

They'd decided early on not to stick the original documents to the walls. It wasn't a matter of principle, protecting precious historical documents unharmed for future generations. If their plan worked, Handar reckoned future generations would have far bigger concerns than old papers.

Instead, their motives were pragmatic. Parchment didn't hang up so well, tearing pages from books was awkward, and sometimes they needed to see both sides at once. So instead of sticking up the originals, they wrote out relevant parts or summaries of what the prophecies said, then stuck them to the wall of the secure room.

"It's starting to look like a crazy guy's apartment in here," Handar said. "One of those conspiracy nuts who think the world's out to get them, stringing together newspaper articles and mad ramblings."

"Maybe we are crazy," Julia said. "We're certainly involved in a conspiracy."

"I guess." Handar stroked one of his tusks. "I just always thought of myself as a plain-speaking guy. I might not tell the truth, but I don't get into all this tangled stuff."

"Then you shouldn't have started chasing down esoteric knowledge. It all leads here in the end."

She took another sheet to the green section, rearranged the pieces, and attached it to the wall. "If this is about weaknesses, it's a particular sort. Weaknesses of the mind and weak places in the magic that holds the world together."

"Are those the same thing?"

"No, but they could become related. A powerful magic user who lost their sanity could easily become a weak spot in the fabric of reality, their power rewriting the world around them."

"You think that's gonna happen? Some big wizard's gonna go crazy and help the boss unleash his nightmare realm?"

"It's possible, but that's not what I was getting at. I'm still looking for the patterns."

She went to one of the other sections, then back to green, and scribbled something down on a sheet of paper on the table. That was something else that they'd agreed on early in this process—to keep the work physical instead of digital. If they put it on a computer, a tablet, or a phone, it could get hacked or accidentally shared. If it was all on paper, all in this one room, it was secure.

Handar couldn't remember if he'd always been this paranoid or if working in security had made him this way. It didn't matter. If it meant that he did the job well, that was all that counted.

"What you got there?" he asked.

"A ritual," Julia said. "There are parts of the prophecies that point at particular strands of magic, ways of rearranging the world. I don't think they're an instruction manual, but I'm using them to put the pieces together. That way, perhaps I can do whatever this is talking about."

She gestured at the papers on the walls.

"Is that a good idea?" Handar asked. "I thought the boss was going to unleash all this power. The prophecies was just saying when, where, and what'll happen."

"He might need some help. Especially if someone else has seen these prophecies and plans to stop him."

Handar thought of the two magicals who'd been in his

apartment. They thought they were so smart, stealing his work, but whatever their agenda was, they weren't going to get their way. He was going to make sure that the boss won out.

"Good thinking. Is there something I can look for in the documents to help you work out this ritual?"

Julia tapped a finger against the table and looked thoughtfully at her notes.

"I don't mean to be rude, but explaining it to you would take longer than it's worth. These pieces aren't clearly marked. It's only because of all my magical experience that I can see how they might be useful together."

"That ain't rude. It's realistic. I wouldn't pick you for a wrestling match. You shouldn't pick me for a magical puzzle."

"Exactly. Besides, I think what I need now is to try this out."

"Really?" Handar looked at the notes on her piece of paper. It seemed like a disconnected jumble of signs and letters to him, but then he wasn't a witch. "You've found it all?"

"Probably not, but I've found enough to make something coherent. Testing it out and seeing the results will help me understand what I'm looking for next."

"What will it do?"

"I don't exactly know, but if we're right about the symbolism of the prophecies, it will help me to identify someone's weaknesses or possibly to use them."

"You got someone you wanna learn about in mind?"

"I have, but you don't need to know who yet." She

opened a bag in the corner of the room and took out a piece of chalk. "Let's do this."

Handar pushed the table back against the wall, making space for Julia to draw a circle on the floor, its perimeter marked with runes and other magical symbols. She set up a bowl of smoldering incense in the center, not the stuff that made temples smell good, but something that stank of sulfur and rot.

"Don't suppose we can get some fresh air in?" Handar gagged at the smell.

"You want to open the door?"

"You must have an air freshener spell."

"I don't want any extraneous magic interfering with what I'm working on. It's all quite delicate and uncertain."

"Better get on with it then before I upchuck."

Julia waved her wand, and the smoke from incense formed a ring floating above the chalk circle. As it twisted and turned in time with her chanting, it took on the forms of the runes on the floor.

Darkness crept across the room. The bulb hanging from the ceiling didn't look any dimmer, but it was as if the light from it got sucked away, drawn to somewhere else before it could reach Handar. He tensed, as he always did when something changed in the world. Better to be ready for trouble that never came than to be caught by surprise.

The growing darkness wasn't only an absence of light. It was a thing in itself, something that grew and intensified, especially in the center of the room. Within the circle, a black disk was forming. Handar stared at it, and his perception shifted. The magic wasn't making something in the air. It was opening a hole, a gap in the world through which he could see somewhere else, somewhere dark and ominous with occasional flickers of red light.

With a growl, something stepped out of that circle. It stood on four legs, each ending in irregular, jagged claws. Dark fur hung from an arched body. Saliva dripped from between needle-sharp teeth and bubbled as it hit the concrete floor.

The creature looked at Julia and opened its mouth. She stepped back and raised her wand. Her eyes were wide, face pale.

"This ain't what you were after, is it?" Handar asked.

"I—"

The beast lunged at Julia. She managed to get off a spell, which knocked the creature aside, and it slammed into the wall. Papers full of prophecy came tumbling down around it as it turned and raised a claw.

Two folding chairs sat next to the table. Handar grabbed one of them and crossed the room in three swift strides. The creature turned its head as he approached, and he swung the chair straight at its face. Needle teeth went flying and the chair buckled under the impact, but the creature stood its ground. As Handar pulled the chair back for another blow, the creature lashed out, knocking the chair from his hands.

Handar swung a punch. He caught the beast in the jaw. A fragment of broken tooth dug into his hand, but the creature jerked back, and that made it worth the pain. Before he could get another blow in, a swipe from a paw knocked him flying. He slammed into the far wall and slid to the floor.

Julia had shrunk back into a corner and was waving her

wand, frantically flinging magic at the dark circle still floating in the middle of the room. "Keep that thing busy. I'll try to get rid of it."

"Keep it busy?" Handar pushed himself up into a crouch. "You've got to be—"

The creature slammed into him, knocking him against the wall. The back of his head hit the concrete, and the world started to spin. He punched at the creature's face, but it dodged aside and hit him with a claw, ripping his suit and carving three nasty scratches down his chest.

Handar flung another punch, but this one was a distraction. As the creature dodged, he kicked, knocking one of its legs out from under it. The beast stumbled, collided with the table, and more papers fell on the floor. With a roar, Handar charged at it, using his fists to hammer at its flank.

The beast roared back and twisted around, its spine curving in impossible ways. A clawed paw gouged deep wounds in Handar's leg, and he fell, cursing and writhing.

The creature stood over him, legs planted on either side of his chest, and lowered its head slowly toward his throat. Its breath was hot and stinking, its eyes filled with madness. Handar grabbed that head and tried to turn it aside, but the creature was powerful and determined, and the burning of acid spit across Handar's skin made his arms tremble.

"I'm running out of busy," he said. "You'd better have a way to get rid of it."

"I'm trying." Julia had stepped up to the circle. She chanted and shaped the ring of smoke with her fingers.

The hole in the world shifted and flickered. "Now it's ready."

"Ready?" Handar tried to wriggle clear, but the beast had him trapped.

"The way is open. We need to get that thing through."

"You want what, for me to carry it there?" He pressed his hands harder against the beast's face, trying to keep its mouth from his throat. Broken needle teeth tore at his fingers.

Julia waved her wand and shouted. The pressure on Handar lifted as the creature floated into the air, legs flailing.

"Quick," Julia gasped, "do something. I can't keep my hold for long on a monster like this."

Hander got to his feet, ignoring a dozen points of pain. He brought his hands together, then swung them around. A single joined fist slammed into the beast with all his strength. The blow sent it flying through the air into the darkness in the center of the room. It passed through the hole in the world and vanished.

Julia waved her wand. The smoke dispersed, the hole disappeared, and the darkness left the room. She let out a long breath.

"Sorry about that," she said. "It didn't work out like I expected it to."

"What was that thing?" Handar asked, staring at the space where the monster had vanished.

"My guess is that it's some sort of nightmare creature."

"Like from where the boss calls home?"

"Or somewhere like it, yes."

"How'd we summon that?"

Julia pointed at the papers that were still hanging from the wall.

"A matter of misinterpretation," she said. "That talk about doors and gates wasn't a metaphor. It was a reality. These prophecies, this magic, are all about opening portals, or something like them, to let other forces into our world."

"Like the boss is planning to do?"

"Exactly."

"So we can help him?" That would make the confrontation with the nightmare beast worthwhile, injuries and all if it let Handar do his job.

"Absolutely," Julia said. "Although I still need time to work out how. Don't mention anything to him yet. Whatever magic we come up with, it should be a surprise."

CHAPTER TWENTY-TWO

Fran, Bart, and Smokey got off a lizard-drawn bus on a street full of office blocks. This wasn't the very heart of Mana Valley, where the biggest corporations had the shiniest offices, but it wasn't all that far from it. The sidewalks were full of magicals hurrying from one place to another, some of them talking, others checking their phones. Many had the harried look of people who were already late for something important.

Fran picked Smokey up so he had a better view of their surroundings. That wasn't something he would've let her do when they first worked together, but now he accepted occasional gestures like that. It made her smile to think that he trusted her. It also made her smile to feel the cat's soft fur. Some things never stopped being nice.

"This is different from the last place," Smokey said, neck stretched so he could look around. "A lot fewer rocks for starters."

"I wanted to show you some different options," Bart said.

"It was different, but while I like a place with a supply of mice, I'm not sure an office in a cave is the way to go."

"It would've had novelty," Fran said. "Added to our quirky, fun-loving image that Elethin's always talking about."

"It's not as distinctive as you might think." Bart set off down the street, and Fran followed, still carrying Smokey. "A lot of dwarf and gnome businesses set up their offices in cave systems. It gives them a traditional feel that can be reassuring for their clients and home-like for staff."

"So you and Gruffbar would like it?" Fran asked. "That's got to be a tick in the pluses column, right?"

"If I'm honest, it's not for me. I think it's important for the business world to move with the times. As I said, I also think it's important for you to see what options we have, and this is another of them."

Bart pointed across the road to an office block with a "for rent" sign out front. The building was relatively modern, mostly concrete and glass, and ten floors tall.

"That's more like it." Smokey jumped down from Fran's arms and prowled over to a crossing point. "Would we take a couple of floors?"

"I thought we could rent the whole building." Bart pressed a button on a post by the crosswalk. In a box at the top of the post, a glowing red imp looked down and stuck up a thumb at him.

"All of it?" Fran asked, mouth hanging open.

"Think how crowded we are right now in the office. Then there's the admin staff we currently have working in back rooms at the factories and the admin, technical, and creative teams we want to recruit over the next year. If we're going to keep expanding, we need a building this big."

"But… but…" Excitement and uncertainty battled for control of Fran's vocal cords.

On the top of the pole, the imp facing them turned green, while others farther up the box turned red, signaling vehicles to stop. Fran, Smokey, and Bart hurried across the street.

"Can we afford all this?" Fran looked up at the building, which seemed more imposing up close.

"If the IPO goes well, yes," Bart said.

"How big an 'if' is that?"

"It's the 'if' that our whole company depends on."

"What can we do to make sure it goes well?"

"At this point, not a lot. Keep the business running smoothly, keep up your press appearances, and the rest is in the hands of the investors."

It was a scary thought that their fates depended on strangers and their money, but Fran knew that it was one she had to get used to. In the meantime, there was no harm in planning for what they might do when the money came in.

If the money came in.

"Hello there." A dwarf estate agent waited for them at the building's entrance, wearing a sharp suit with a tablet in his hand. "You must be Mr. Trumbling and Ms. Berryman."

He shook their hands. There was a hiss by their feet.

"This is our other colleague, Smokey," Bart said.

If the estate agent was surprised to be in a conversation

with a cat, he didn't show it. "Pleased to meet you too. Please, if you could all follow me…"

He used a small crystal to release the locks on the building's magical security system and led them inside. Fran looked around in wide-eyed excitement at an echoing lobby with a marble-topped reception desk and a row of elevators behind its security barriers.

"These aren't active at the moment." The agent pushed through one of the waist-high security gates. "If you take the building, we can have them set to a security system that suits you, whether magical or technological, with appropriate passes for staff and visitors." He pressed a button, and the doors of one of the elevators opened with a chime. "Shall we?"

They all got in, the doors closed, and the elevator rose.

"The building's elevators have enough capacity to serve all ten floors during full occupancy," the estate agent said. "If you fill the place up, you might get a bit of a queue in the mornings, but nothing that will delay people getting to work."

Fran looked at the numbered buttons for different floors, with little rings of light around them. Elevator buttons had never really caught her attention before, but today they seemed exciting.

"These could be our elevators," she said. "Imagine having an office big enough to need elevators!"

The estate agent laughed. "You must be in quite a hole right now if you don't have this."

"It's a lovely place," Fran said defensively. "It's just… It's getting crowded."

"Ah, of course."

"Our company didn't exist two years ago," Bart explained.

"And you can afford this place already?"

"Possibly."

"Wow. I should talk to my financial adviser about investing in you guys."

"Please do," Fran said. "We really want more investors, right Bart?"

The elevator bell chimed again, and the doors opened.

"I thought we should start at the top," the estate agent said, his voice echoing back from the empty space ahead of them. "You get the best view from up here."

Fran stepped out of the elevator and looked around. She could see the whole of the top floor of the building, from one side to the other. There were no walls, no doors, no desks or chairs or meeting rooms, only an empty expanse of concrete floor, glass walls, and mottled ceiling tiles.

"It's a bit barren," she said. "I guess we can put some carpets in, but won't it get noisy with everybody in one big room?"

Bart exchanged a look with the estate agent. "She's new to this," he explained.

"I guessed."

Bart took Fran by the arm and led her over to the window. She expected him to point out something in the view, but instead, he turned her so the floor stretched out before her.

"If we move in, it won't stay like this. We'll arrange to have walls put in, to make meeting rooms and offices and whatever else we need. Then we'll get it decorated and carpeted, wired up, and connected before we bring in the furniture. You have to picture it a little differently if you want to know what we're getting into."

"They'll put in extra walls for us?" Fran was amazed.

"Of course." The estate agent beamed at them from behind his beard. "We would never expect anyone to occupy this place as-is. This is merely a canvas on which you can paint your design. By keeping it blank, we maximize flexibility."

"Did you hear that, Smokey?" she said. "We can design it however we want."

"Then let's make an office as it should be," Smokey said. "One where any magical can operate the doors, no matter their size or shape. Somewhere with ramps instead of stairs and with bathrooms designed for those of us who don't have two legs."

"Can you do that sort of thing?" Fran asked.

The estate agent stroked his beard and looked around. "My company works with some very talented architects. We've done work in the past improving accessibility. I don't see why we couldn't take it further. Of course, it will be easier in a blank space like this, but it might still take time and be expensive."

"That's okay. We're willing to pay extra to get things right." Fran glanced at Bart. "I mean if our chief of finance agrees to it…"

"It sounds good to me," Bart said. "I'm tired of having to stretch to reach the taps."

Fran walked around the office, trying to work out what it would look like once they moved in. She could imagine a hundred different versions, and because this was her imagination, most of them featured bright colors and shiny things. She knew that the reality would be a compromise, something that would suit other people as well, but for a moment, it was fun to imagine an office designed for a company staffed entirely by Frans.

"What else do we want from an office?" she called. "Like, blue-sky thinking, if money was no object, how would we have this place?"

Smokey scampered over, tail in the air.

"I'd want nap baskets," he said. "Scratching posts in the meeting rooms. Maybe a treat dispenser."

"Good water coolers," Bart called. "Comfortable chairs. Adjustable desks."

"Boring!" Smokey replied.

"But fundamental. What's the point in having a flashy office if you won't be comfortable in your seat or if you'll have to crane your neck to see the monitor properly?"

"That's… All right, that's smart. I would like a better desk setup."

"Ooh, how about a pool table?" Fran said. "And a games machine. And some big comfy couches."

"This is starting to sound more like a youth club than a workplace."

Fran shrugged. "We're all going to need breaks between working on designs. Why not make a place for them?"

"Could we put in a bar?" Smokey asked. "That seems like something Gruffbar would like."

"Whatever you want, my company has the contacts," the estate agent said. "Of course, you're welcome to go through your suppliers, but we can arrange certain discounts and help to coordinate it all."

"For a fee, I assume," Smokey said.

"Of course. This is business, after all."

Fran gazed out of the window. This was so much more than business for her. It was the fulfillment of a dream she'd had for so long she couldn't remember its beginning. It was the logical next step in all the past year's hard work. It was the reward they would receive for so many of their achievements.

A bat-borne taxi flew past the window through the graying sky of dusk, and she smiled as she watched the bats' wings frantically flapping.

"I think we should take this one," she said.

"I can arrange to get the paperwork to you tomorrow." The estate agent rubbed his hands together.

"I'd like to see that paperwork," Bart said, "but I'm afraid that we can't sign anything yet. Not until after our IPO. Then we'll know if we have the funds we need."

"Oh." Fran sagged as her dreams of a glittery office with a view of the city, an adjustable chair, and a candy dispenser slipped out of her reach. Then she brightened. "I'm sure it will go great, and we'll be straight back here to get our new office set up, won't we, Bart?"

"It's starting to look that way." He smiled at her, then turned to the estate agent. "Though we still need to negotiate rent."

"Of course."

The two of them turned away, talking in very serious tones.

Fran took out her phone. She wanted to get a photo of the view to show Josie. When she looked at the screen, she saw several missed calls and an urgent message from Agent Baldwin of the FBI.

"Flaw with containment units," the message said. "Fix needed ASAP. Call me now."

Fran's heart sank. The containment units were one of Mana Wave's two big products. If there was a problem with them, and if it got into the news, it could seriously damage their image, not to mention their IPO. She dialed Singar's number as she hurried toward the elevator.

"Hi, Sin. It looks like we might have a problem. Meet me at the office as soon as you can."

CHAPTER TWENTY-THREE

For the next two days, Fran threw herself into the FBI issue, meeting with Baldwin, looking at broken components, trying to work out what was going wrong. The problem with having a larger company was that there were more things to do, more commitments she couldn't get out of. Fixing the unit was important, but so was everything else. Which was why, on Friday night, she set aside her screwdrivers and solder and headed for a videogames arcade.

"Normally I love this place," she said to Gruffbar as she waited for people to finish coming in. "But I'm so nervous about the containment unit. All I want is to get back to the workshop."

"A change of scenery will do you good," Gruffbar said. "Help clear your mind. Plus Singar's still working on it, right?"

"Yes, but she should be here too."

"When even you don't want to be here?"

"You know what I mean."

Fran looked around the room. There were some people she recognized: staff from Mana Wave, tech and business journalists, some faces she couldn't quite place. There were also a lot of strangers, more than she'd anticipated, cramming themselves in between the old games machines. One face was noticeably absent.

"Maybe your boyfriend can calm you down," Gruffbar said. "Once he turns up."

"I'm not sure he's coming."

"Really? He'd miss out on this?"

"I don't think he's in the mood for a free bar and nibbles right now."

"I meant this big moment for your company."

Fran looked down at the floor. If she was honest with herself, she hadn't believed that Cam would miss it either, even though he'd warned her that he was getting perilously close to the deadline for his thesis. She'd assumed that he would find the time for this somehow. Apparently she'd assumed wrong.

"Sorry," Gruffbar said. "I've hit a nerve."

Fran shrugged listlessly.

"It's okay."

"It clearly isn't. Is Cam being a jerk? Because if he is, I can go around and have a word." Gruffbar cracked his knuckles. "Maybe take Singar too. She's got a Taser, you know."

"That's very… I want to say it's sweet of you, but I'm not sure that's the tone you're going for. Anyway, there's no need. Cam isn't being a jerk. He's very busy writing his thesis."

"He has to do that now?"

"He delayed it for a long time while doing other things."

"Hm. Sounds like a problem of his making."

"They were important things."

"Like what, brewing coffee?"

Fran wondered if she should take this opportunity and tell Gruffbar about what she and Cam were looking into, about the years he'd spent gathering signs and prophecies and analyzing how they fitted together, looking for a threat that was coming to Mana Valley. But they hadn't agreed to tell anyone else yet, and she wasn't sure she could get the story quite right, especially when she only had a minute before the rest of the evening began.

"I'll tell you another time." She knew as she said it how lame it sounded.

Fortunately, there wasn't enough time left to worry about it. Elethin hurried over, managing to look elegant in jeans and a Mana Wave t-shirt, the outfit that all of their crew were wearing this evening. Even some of the audience wore the t-shirts. Did that mean they had fans or had Elethin hired some extras to fill the place up? It wasn't impossible, but was it necessary?

"It's time, Fran," Elethin said.

Fran drew a deep breath and thought about happy things. Her favorite games. Cute bunny rabbits. Sugary drinks with silver sprinkles on the top. A smile crawled up her face as she walked toward the low stage they'd set up at one end of the room.

"You've got this," Gruffbar said.

"I've got this."

Amid a fanfare of computer game music, Fran jumped

up onto the stage, waving to the crowd, many of whom were applauding.

"Hi, everyone!" she called.

The applause increased. Cameras flashed. Magical recording devices darted through the air, looking for the best angles to view her and her audience.

"Hi! Hi. Um, could you maybe tone it down?" She laughed. "Not that I don't appreciate all this, but you might want to hear what I have to say."

The applause turned to laughter, which faded into silence. The music died away, and Fran stood alone in front of a crowd of people, all of whom wanted to hear about her latest project. It was as scary as it was exciting.

"If you're here, I don't need to tell you about the Fun Delivery System or how we only had one game to launch the system with. That's a big limitation, and it's been wonderful to see how many people put their faith in Mana Wave's technology despite that. We told you there was more to come, and you believed us. Now it's time to show you that you were right to trust us."

Behind her, an FDS started its projection program, sending out illusions of animated characters and game pieces on the stage around Fran, as well as swirling patterns in the air.

"We've been talking to a host of talented designers and programmers," she continued. "People with great ideas for what the FDS can do. We've picked out the best projects that they had, and over the next year, we'll be working with them to bring those games and entertainments to life. There are slow, thoughtful puzzles, high-speed chases, fighting games, and a short film that will be the first fully three-dimensional magically projected movie in two worlds. To start it all off, tonight, I want to show you this..."

A pair of motorbikes appeared on the stage, magically projected by the machine.

"Who wants to race me?" Fran grinned.

A lot of the fans stuck up their hands, and Fran was tempted to bring one of them up, but Elethin had been clear in her instructions. Instead, Fran looked at the journalists to see who had volunteered. Getting one of them involved would likely mean a better review from that journalist and more coverage from their colleagues.

"Hey, look!" she exclaimed. "Don Karelsky is here! Don, why don't you come on up?"

A wizard in a pinstripe suit and red tie came onto the stage. He waved to the audience. This was part of what made Don a good choice. He knew how to perform for the cameras.

"Here you go." Fran gestured to one of the bikes. "You take blue. I'll take red."

"Can I sit on this thing?" Don raised an eyebrow.

"It's not quite that solid, but if you sling a leg over, the projection will shape itself around you."

Fran mounted her illusory bike, which promptly shrank to fit her size, and Don did the same. Around them, projections of trees and hedgerows appeared.

"Where would you like to race?" Fran asked. "The countryside? The big city?" Neon signs and tower blocks replaced the trees. "Maybe the Arctic?" Now they were surrounded by ice.

"Have you got a beach?" Don asked. "I love the sunshine."

"Of course."

A beach appeared beneath the bikes, with palm trees to one side and the sea to the other. The animations weren't very detailed, but their presence projected into the room, more than making up for that. Fran heard the crowd's excitement.

"Turn the right handlebar to accelerate, left to brake, both to turn," she said. "Are you ready?"

"Sure, let's do this."

Numbers appeared in the air between them, counting down. When they hit zero, music started. Fran turned her accelerator, and the projected scenery shot past on her side of the room. A moment later, Don caught on and started his bike. His scenery started moving as he rushed to catch up with her.

Fran knew she wasn't moving, but she couldn't get over how real it felt. The simplified, projected scenery flew past like she was racing, images becoming a blur. Even as she subtly eased off the speed to let Don overtake her, she felt the exhilaration of it. The thrill of something that she, Singar, Smokey, and their recruits had created.

Don crossed the finish line three seconds ahead of Fran to applause from around the room. She shook his hand and turned to face the crowd.

"Of course, it doesn't have to be bikes." She snapped her fingers. Waist-high dragons replaced the bikes. "Who wants to ride?"

For the next few hours, Fran worked the room, talking to journalists and fans, while the lucky ones got to try out the new racing game. It was easy to get enthusiastic when she talked about something so fun. It made the conversations enjoyable, especially when she discussed details with the more technologically literate reporters.

Elethin had told her to smile and laugh, but that instruction wasn't necessary for the team except for Gruffbar. How could they not be enjoying themselves?

"When will this game be available?" one of the journalists asked. "What's your release date?"

"Today," Fran said.

"Today?" The journalist blinked. "What about prerelease publicity? What about building up hype?"

"We don't need those things. The game speaks for itself."

Plus, Elethin had calculated that just this once, existing interest in Mana Wave's next step would allow the sudden launch to be a dramatic, attention-grabbing novelty rather than a poorly planned flop. Responses from everyone involved seemed to prove Elethin right.

Still, beneath .the smiles and excitement, part of Fran felt blue. She couldn't quite summon her usual levels of energy, even when the press conference descended into a free-for-all of drinking and playing on the games machines.

She sidled up to Elethin. "Can I go home now?"

Elethin looked at her with concern. "Are you all right, Fran?"

"Just tired."

Elethin looked around the room, then back at Fran, doing the careful calculus of publicity. At last, she nodded.

"Go on. They've seen your face, heard your speech, and

asked you their inane questions. Your work here is over, and I can tidy up at the end. Or rather, I can supervise the tidying up."

"Thanks, Elethin." Fran hugged her. "You did great."

Fran grabbed her coat and backpack and headed out the door.

Having used tiredness as an excuse to leave, she knew that she ought to head home and sleep. But it wasn't a big detour to walk past Cam's building, and she found her feet leading her that way.

She'd promised herself that she wouldn't disturb him if he was asleep, but the light was on in his window, so she pressed the buzzer.

"It's me," she mumbled into the intercom.

"Come on up."

Cam met her in the doorway. There were bags under his eyes, and his hair was sticking up everywhere.

"Is everything okay?" he asked. "I thought it was your big launch event tonight?"

"It was, but you weren't there, and I missed you."

"I'm sorry. I would have come if I could, but I didn't have time."

"You never have time at the moment."

"I know. I'm sorry." He hugged her. "It'll be over soon, and I'll have all the time in the world for you."

"How do I know that? What if you keep on writing and writing?"

Cam took a step back and looked at her, hands resting on her arms.

"I promise, it won't always be like this. In a month, either I'll be finished, or I'll have missed the deadline, and it'll be too late for me to write anything. That's why I have to push so hard now because my time's nearly up."

"I guess."

"I thought we talked about this?"

"We did. It's just that there's a difference between saying I won't see much of you and living through the reality of it."

They hugged again.

"It's hard at the moment," she mumbled into his sweater. "We've got this big release, and the IPO, and thinking about an office, so there's no spare space in my head, and the containment units are going wrong, and that could wreck everything, and I don't know if I can cope with it all."

"Of course, you can." Cam squeezed her tight. "You're Fran Berryman. You're the smartest, most creative, most passionate woman I know. You're not just going to cope. You're going to excel."

"I am?" Fran asked in a small voice.

"You are." Cam looked at his laptop, then back at her. "I've nearly reached a good place to stop, and I need some sleep. Why don't you stay over? I'll make you breakfast before I start working again."

"I like breakfast."

"And I like you. Give me ten minutes. Then we can get to bed..."

CHAPTER TWENTY-FOUR

A pebble slid out from under Enfield as he emerged from the mine's mouth. His foot shifted, he stumbled, and for a moment he felt as if his weight was about to carry him to the ground. He clung to his crutch, fighting to stay upright despite the throbbing in his leg and how the crutch dug into his armpit.

"I can do this," he muttered, shifting his weight onto his good leg. "Good" was relative, of course. That leg still had some stiffness too, but it worked, and the other one was getting there. He hoped to switch the crutch out for a walking stick soon. Whether he ever got past that point to walk without aid was another matter.

He hobbled across the broken ground in front of the entrance. It was difficult going, but it was worth it to get some fresh air and daylight. He'd been spending too much time cooped up in the tunnels, whether resting, doing exercises, or studying the Source. He needed to get out into the world more, to clear his mind and his lungs.

"Here he comes," Taldiss called from her position

behind the barricade. "The broken hero returns to the light."

"I'm certainly broken." Enfield lurched toward her with uneven steps.

"Yeah, right." Taldiss snorted. "You'll be better soon enough."

"There's better, and there's best. I'll never be that again."

"You were never that before, not while I was around."

Enfield laughed. "You might be better at climbing and tracking, but I was a faster runner than you."

"I was working on that."

"How, by getting springs put into your legs?"

"Rockets. Although it's hard to get hold of a surgeon up here for such delicate work."

"Hard to get hold of anything." Enfield got up onto the platform beside her and leaned against the barricade. "I don't suppose you're going into town for supplies soon?"

"Depends on the whims of Winslow. Why, what do you want?"

"I was wondering if—" A movement on the ridge above caught Enfield's eye. "Did you see that?"

"See what?"

"That!" He pointed at the ridge. A rock had come loose and was rolling down. Except that it wasn't only one rock, it was a dozen of them moving together, and another set had started rolling down behind them.

"They're back." Taldiss whistled sharply and filled her voice with magic to help it carry. "Hey, anyone who can hear me, get out of the tunnels and over here right now!"

The first set of boulders had reached the bottom of the slope. Its roll turned into a forward dive as the amorphous blob of stone became a human-like figure. The rocks behind it took on a four-legged animal shape and headed for the walls, while others followed.

"Hold here," Taldiss said. "I'll go cut them off."

She dashed along the defensive line, running to head off the first of the rock monsters. Enfield gripped his crutch and made to go after her, but a stab of pain in his leg froze him in place. By the time he focused again, he could see that it was too late, that the monsters were nearly there. He could also see that others were heading for the low point in the defenses where he stood. Someone had to hold the line.

The first of the monsters reached the barricades where Taldiss had arrived. She sent out a huge wave of sound magic, which flung one of them back and knocked the other to its knees. Enfield knew from experience that a move like that would have drained a lot of her power, but it should buy time for the other Evermores to get there, and he could hear their voices emerging from the tunnel.

They weren't here yet, though. He was, and ready to face the oncoming creatures. One was charging straight at his part of the barricade, and he stunned it with a concentrated blast of sound. Another jumped, four-legged, toward the barricade. Enfield swung his crutch, channeling his magic through it like a weapon. It hit the rock monster in the head, knocking it off course and down to the ground outside the barrier.

Other Evermores emerged from the tunnel mouth and sprinted toward the defenses. More rock monsters were coming, pouring down from the ridge above. Enfield wanted to run to intercept the nearest ones, but he could see that he wouldn't get to the right place in time.

"There!" he shouted, pointing at a spot on the barricade. "And there, quick!"

Evermores rushed to where he directed them.

Taldiss had run along the defensive line to intercept another of the monsters as it crossed the wall. She grabbed hold of it and swung herself up onto its shoulders, then pressed her hands to the sides of its head. The monster swung a fist at her. She ducked but managed to cling on, legs clamped tight around the creature's body.

Then she channeled her magic into its head. The whole of that stone shook, cracks started to appear, and pieces fell off. The monster staggered back across the barricade, stumbling like a drunk. Taldiss leaped clear and let it run away.

Enfield gripped his crutch, filling it with power, ready to face whatever monster came at him next. The results were disappointing, even frustrating. Instead of charging at him, the monsters moved around, heading for empty points on the defenses. The other Evermores could get there fast enough to intercept, but Enfield was on his own. He desperately wanted to be part of the fight, to contribute to their shared defense, but what could he do?

"Taldiss, over there!" he shouted, pointing at a monster she'd missed.

"Got it."

She ran along the barricade, grabbed a stick along the way, infused it with her magic, and swung it around as she reached the oncoming monster. The first blow stopped it from advancing over the defenses, and a second sent it staggering back.

"Someone to the left," Enfield shouted.

While the Evermores were busy on the right, a group of rock monsters had been coming quietly down the other side, not rushing but steadily advancing, waiting for their moment. They almost had it, but thanks to Enfield, the Evermores were there before them. Several blasts of sound together pushed the creatures back. A narrow beam of light gouged a blackened scar into one's head, but that didn't bring it down.

Enfield gripped his clutch tight as if by readying himself he could bring the fighting closer.

"They're trying to break through the old coal store," he shouted, pointing at a brick building the Evermores had incorporated into the defenses. One of the larger rock monsters was punching its outer wall, sending up dust clouds, and some of the bricks were starting to break loose.

Once again, the Evermores followed Enfield's lead, rushing to the building. Taldiss scrambled onto the roof and started beating the monster on the head, while some Evermores went in to shore up the house, and others launched magic at the attackers.

One of the smaller monsters tapped the large one on the hip, and it started to back off. Taldiss swung her improvised staff, glowing with power. There was an explosion of light and splintered wood, and the monster stumbled, then fell, its face scorched black.

Almost immediately, other rock monsters were around it. None of them was as large, but with several working together they lifted their prone companion and carried it away while the rest kept up the attack. Among those carrying the injured monster, there was a low sound, rhythmic and persistent, like the grinding of rocks against one another.

Looking around, Enfield realized that this wasn't the only place where the rock monsters were carrying off their wounded or the first time he'd seen them act like this. They weren't senseless brutes. They were a community, perhaps a pack. They were capable of caring for their injured. They were communicating, using those singsong grinding sounds to talk.

Brutal as it was, their behavior gave the Evermores something to work with.

"Take them down in different places," Enfield shouted. "Give them plenty of distractions dealing with the injured."

The Evermores split up and spread out along the line. On their own, it was sometimes hard to hurt the monsters, but when they did, they saw the results. Uninjured rock monsters went to help the injured ones away, further weakening the attack.

"Look out," Enfield shouted. "They're sending in another big attack on the right. They've put the toughest at the front again. Take them down, and we'll be safe."

Taldiss led a small band of Evermores across the open ground, to the right of their defenses. Before the first monsters reached the barricades, the Evermores flung blasts of sound and magically infused missiles at them. Taldiss filled a rock with power and threw it. The flash and *thud* of its impact were like a grenade going off in the face of one of the creatures, and it fell back, knocking another over.

One still reached the walls, only to be knocked back by blows from two magically empowered staffs at once. By then, they'd injured enough of the monsters to keep their companions busy, and the attack collapsed amid more of the grinding, groaning noises the monsters made.

Enfield surveyed the ground beyond the barricades. There was movement, but it was mostly up the ridge, monsters retreating rather than attacking.

"We're clear," he called.

At that moment, Winslow emerged from the mine entrance.

"Good work, everyone," he called as he approached the defenses. "I'm sorry that I wasn't here sooner."

"We didn't need you, chief," Taldiss called. "Enfield sorted us out, right, Enfield?"

Enfield shook his head. "I'd rather have been in the fighting, but that's a thing of the past." He waved his crutch. One end had twisted from an impact against the rocks.

"Don't worry." Winslow laid a hand on Enfield's shoulder. "I'm sure you'll be recklessly throwing yourself into danger soon enough. Just give it more time."

"I've given it time," Enfield said.

"Not by Evermore standards. Remember, you have millennia ahead of you. There's no reason to resent a few months lost."

There was every reason. Those months seemed to last for years as Enfield sat around, unable to do things that mattered to him, like running or hiking or defending his friends.

Except he'd found a way to defend them this time: not directly through action, but indirectly, by guiding others. His forced stillness had given him a chance to observe their opponents, spot the attacks, and work out the patterns. It wasn't the part he wanted to play, but it was a lot better than nothing.

"They're more sophisticated than we thought," he said. "They're talking to each other, planning and directing their attacks, discussing how to help the injured."

"I fear you might be reading too much into animal noises," Winslow said. "They attack us ceaselessly, without reason, throwing themselves away to fight us. That doesn't speak of sophistication."

"They must have a reason. We simply don't know it yet."

"Instinct is enough for wild beasts."

Enfield wanted to snap that Winslow had said things like this about the Source and been proved wrong. Most of the Evermores still believed Winslow, and Enfield was trying to convince their leader that he'd accepted his view. He couldn't use that argument here.

Besides, he knew that his response was driven as much by pain and frustration as by reason. He shouldn't be lashing out at Winslow, even if he disagreed. If the Evermores had missed something about the rock monsters' behavior, they would work it out in time. For now, what mattered was that they were safe and that their current home was once again secure.

That and the tiredness that swept over Enfield any time he exerted himself.

"I need to rest." He pushed himself up on his damaged crutch.

"A wise idea," Winslow said. "Perhaps later we can discuss your progress in studying the Source."

"Of course."

Enfield hobbled toward the mine entrance, his head hanging. Then a voice rose behind him.

"Here's to Enfield," Taldiss cried. "We'd have been stuffed without him."

"Hooray for Enfield!" the Evermores shouted together.

Enfield smiled and stood straighter as he headed for his bed.

CHAPTER TWENTY-FIVE

Howard Phillips stepped out of the back of the black SUV into the night-darkened street in front of the gates to the graveyard. In his hand was a briefcase.

"Sure you don't want me to come with you, boss?" Handar called from the vehicle's window.

"No need." Phillips pulled a key from his pocket. "I'll call you when I need you."

Handar looked around. "What if someone—"

"I said no need." Phillips waved a dismissive hand. "Go. I don't want that car out here drawing attention."

Handar drove away, leaving Phillips alone in the flickering light of a magical street lamp. The darkness beyond the gate didn't bother Phillips. He could see well enough in even the deepest night. The trembling in his body didn't come from stress, fear, or anxiety. It came from anticipation. Soon, his time would come.

He unlocked the gate, walked through, and locked it again behind him before heading off down a path between the rows of gravestones. The darkness closed in around him, and he embraced it. He was at his best at night.

He felt the sleepers in the city around him, many of them lost to dreams, some to nightmares. Those were the ones that empowered him, their dread, their tension, their horror becoming a palpable force, something he could draw from the world, which could power his magic—no better time for what he needed to do.

The grave he'd picked out was near the center of the cemetery. It was marked by an elaborate statue of a robed dwarf, as befitted one of the city's founders, one of the magicals who had been foundational in inspiring the dreams of others and in setting up the institutions that became nightmares to so many. A nexus within Mana Valley.

Phillips set the suitcase down on a nearby grave and took out the equipment he'd prepared. With sulfurous dust, he sketched a circle around the grave, with magical signs at its cardinal points. The incense he set smoldering by the feet of the statue, next to a large crystal that cast a blood-red glow on the stonework around it. Then he took off his clothes, carefully draping his suit over a headstone to stop it from getting creased. Naked in the moonlight, he reached behind his neck and unfastened his skin suit.

The skin split and fell away. The Darkness Between Dreams squirmed out, a thing of glistening blackness, writhing tentacles, and twitching stalks with bulbous eyes at their ends. It draped the skin suit across another stone and approached the chosen grave.

Slowly, solemnly, the Darkness Between Dreams started to chant the words of the ritual it had planned, one of the last pieces it needed to complete its great scheme. With this night's work, all of the groundwork would be in place. The strands would be woven, the magic prepared. All that would remain was the final ritual, to pull the power together, rip a hole in reality, and unleash the nightmare realm. The Darkness smiled at the thought, revealing terrible teeth.

As it chanted, it thrust its tentacles into the ground and flung dirt from the grave. It dug strongly but carefully, hurling the earth far away so it didn't disrupt the circle. Every detail mattered here, as it did with so much of the Darkness' planning. The success of the greatest powers could hang on the slenderest threads.

It reached the coffin, which was old enough to have started to decay but not old enough to have disintegrated yet. Prizing the lid open was easy, a brief scream of rust-tinged nails being wrenched free, a splintering *crack,* and the upper half came off. The Darkness took hold of it with three tentacles and flung it away, a grotesque Frisbee that spun through the night, trailing dirt, then clattered off a grave.

The Darkness reached into the coffin. Each tentacle drew out a cluster of bones, leaving behind only shreds of half-disintegrated clothes and grave dust. Power flowed through the bones, the Darkness, and the graveyard's dirt as it withdrew from the hole.

It walked around the circle, laying the bones out next to magical signs that thrummed with power. Dark magic spilled into the grave, filling the space where the body had been. In that magic were images of tragedy and trauma, monsters and mayhem, flashes of heartbreak and grief. Everything that gave the Darkness life.

It waved its tentacles, chanting faster, weaving the magic in the air around it. Strands of power twisted around each other and became a net connecting every sleeping mind in Mana Valley.

In the distance, through the gravestones, a light moved. The Darkness glanced at it. Probably someone passing outside the graveyard, on their way home from a party or late-night work. Perhaps they too would join the dreaming soon.

The bones rose from the ground, and their power flowed from them, the strength of history, tradition, and expectation of this founding figure himself. One by one, they crumbled into dust as the spell drew their very essence from them.

The light was coming closer. The Darkness frowned. No one else was supposed to be in the graveyard at night. It had made arrangements to ensure that the groundskeeper would stay otherwise occupied, and the security guards would look the other way. Why was someone coming now?

Teenagers perhaps, proving their daring by coming here after dark, breaking so many taboos. The interruption was annoying, but perhaps they could be made useful, sacrifices for the cause, more fear for the spell. No one was more nervous than a young magical trying to prove how brave they were.

Then the light brightened, a floating orb hanging in the air. Several of the Darkness' eyes turned away on their stalks rather than face that fearsome glow.

"Silver Griffins," a voice called. "I don't know who you are or what you are, but put all your limbs in the air right now."

This went beyond annoying. This was inconvenient. The Silver Griffins might manage to disrupt the ritual. They might summon others or tell them what they'd seen. That couldn't be allowed.

The ritual had connected the Darkness to the graveyard itself. As it raised its tentacles slowly into the air, it reached out with its mind, found the iron fence, and redirected some of its power there. Its chant changed and a barrier of magic flowed from the fence, rising to join in a dome over the graveyard, one that would stop any messages from getting out. Cellphone, spell, or winged messenger, it didn't matter. As long as that held, these Silver Griffins wouldn't be calling for help.

"Stop the chanting right now."

The Silver Griffins, a wizard and a witch, stepped into the light from their magical orb. They were both pointing their wands at the Darkness. If the witch looked unsettled at what she was facing, the wizard looked outraged as he gazed across the grave and the floating bones.

"I said stop the chanting," the witch said. "Put those bones down right now."

The Darkness had played along for long enough. It flicked a tentacle and a spell shot toward the witch. She was fast. Her wand sparked, and a counterspell obliterated his magic. Still, he had many tentacles and an abundance of power. He flung more spells at her, and though she countered as many as she could, her wand could only be in one place at a time. She staggered back as a spell hit her and sank to her knees, wailing in horror at the terrible visions filling her mind.

With a *clink* of metal links, heavy chains flew through the air and wrapped themselves around the Darkness.

"I don't care what you are." The wizard pointed his wand across the grave. "I'm stopping this right now."

"Really?" The Darkness's voice was somewhere between a gurgle and a screech. Just hearing it made the wizard turn pale. "You think you can stop me?"

Tentacles rippled and the chains rusted, crumbled, and fell to the ground in a shower of brown flakes.

The wizard flung another spell, then another. The Darkness countered one, caught the other, and let the freeze run up a tentacle, forming a coat of ice. The wizard was experimenting, trying different spells to see what would work, what the Darkness couldn't counter.

It was as admirable as it was inconvenient. Every moment of distraction was a moment in which the ritual's power faded. The risk increased that the whole thing would fail and the Darkness would have to start all over again, would have to pick out a new grave for a new way of orienting the power.

It flexed its frozen tentacle. The ice shattered and fell sparkling to the ground. The Darkness incorporated that magic, turning it back against the wizard. Ice ran from the ground across his feet, and up his legs.

"What the..." The wizard waved his wand as he frantically tried to counter the magic that threatened to freeze him in place.

"You..." The witch rose unsteadily to her feet and pointed her wand at the Darkness. "How did you know?"

Now it was impressed. Few had the strength to overcome a nightmare once it released those images in their mind. This was a magical with real strength of will. Such a shame that she'd wasted her talents on the Griffins.

"I didn't know," it said. "I didn't need to. You betray yourself. Your horrors are always there, in your mind, waiting to seize hold. All I have to do is let them out."

The witch waved her wand. Another spell flew at the Darkness, who easily dispelled it. That distraction kept the Darkness from seeing the next spell coming. Thoughts became muddled, and its tentacles drooped as a stun spell hit.

"Come on, Jeff." The witch strode around the grave and pointed her wand at her partner, who was now entirely frozen in place. "I'll get you out. Then we'll deal with this thing."

Her spell, which would stun some magicals for hours, lasted only moments on the Darkness. It shook off the bewilderment and raised its tentacles. That stunned moment had ruined its remaining concentration and severed the last strand holding the ritual together. All that work wasted…but some of the power remained.

"You'll deal with nothing." The Darkness spread its tentacles wide. The dark magic in the grave briefly became a portal, long enough for one creature to come through.

A nightmare hound leaped out of the grave and fell on the witch. She tried to bring her wand around, but claws knocked it from her grasp. She tried to punch the hound, only for it to catch her fist between jagged teeth. The frozen wizard could only watch in horror as the hound tossed the witch into the grave and jumped down on top of her.

"Don't worry." The Darkness walked around the grave. "I'm not going to leave you here on your own."

It pressed a tentacle against the wizard's frozen back and pushed. He toppled, statue stiff, and tumbled into the grave. The hound howled in renewed excitement as it started clawing and biting its second victim.

The Darkness looked around. The circle of sulfurous dust had become scuffed in the fighting, and the glowing crystal had gone dim. Worst of all, the scuffle had used up this grave's power. Yes, it would have a new sort of power soon and a suitably nightmarish one, given the atrocities the hound was committing. But it wasn't the type of power the Darkness needed.

It would have to pick a new grave, a second-best grave, to start again. It would have to call Handar to bring fresh ingredients. This was inconvenient, and the Darkness didn't like that. As Howard Phillips, it wasn't used to anyone in Mana Valley daring to inconvenience it.

The Darkness walked over to the gravestone where it had hung its suit. With a slender tentacle, it drew a phone from the jacket pocket. It would call Handar in a moment, but first, something else. It called a number, and, after a few rings, a croaky voice answered.

"Why are you calling me now?" they grumbled. "Don't you know it's the middle of the night?"

"Councilor Blessby, this is Howard Phillips."

"Oh." The voice on the other end of the line suddenly grew alert. "I'm terribly sorry, Howard, I didn't realize that—"

"You were supposed to make some arrangements for me tonight to ensure that the authorities steered clear of certain parts of town."

"I did, honestly, Howard."

"Then why was I disturbed by a pair of Silver Griffins?"

"I have no idea. They must have disobeyed orders. I swear, it won't ever happen again."

"It had better not. What's the point in owning a city councilor if they let things like this happen?"

The Darkness Between Dreams ended the call and put the phone away after venting its frustrations. Then it turned slowly on the spot, surveying the surrounding graves. Perhaps tonight could be redeemed if it found a suitable grave quickly.

From the grave that was already open, sounds of chewing emerged.

CHAPTER TWENTY-SIX

"Aren't your crows coming with us?" Smokey asked as he, Fran, and Singar stepped out of a portal.

"Not this time." Fran closed the magical mirror she'd used to summon the portal and put it away in her backpack. "I don't want to risk leaving them behind. Besides, if I need one, I can find a crow around here."

"Can we get this over and done with?" Singar said. "The whole thing leaves a bad smell in my snout."

"We've worked with the FBI before," Fran said as they set off down a dirt road between rocky hills, following the instructions she'd received. Both she and Singar had backpacks full of equipment, and the webbing Smokey wore around his feline body had tools strapped all over it.

"I didn't like it much then, either," Singar said. "Too much like working with the Griffins. Then we needed whatever work we could get. Now we've got the FDS."

"One day, hopefully, we can put all our focus into things like that. For now, we need to keep selling the containment unit to stop us from going, like, completely broke while we play around with cool new toys. Selling the containment unit also means getting broken units to work."

"I know. I just don't like it."

Around a bend in the road was a cluster of black off-road vehicles with tinted glass. A group of witches and wizards had gathered between them—Agent Baldwin's magical FBI team.

"Good to see you, Ms. Berryman." Baldwin was dressed in a well-cut black suit and matching tie, as always. As he greeted them, he took off his sunglasses. "And the rest of your team."

"Thank you for letting us come along on your raid, Agent Baldwin." Fran shook his hand. "Seeing you use the containment unit in action is our best chance to diagnose what exactly is going wrong."

"You couldn't get that from the broken ones we sent?"

"They helped, but faults are a process, not only a result."

"Well then, you'd better put these on." Baldwin handed Fran a black body armor jacket with "CONSULTANT" printed on the back. There was a smaller one for Singar. "Sorry, I couldn't find one sized for a cat."

"I don't plan on getting involved in the action," Smokey said.

"In my experience, no plan survives contact with a magical drug gang, but we'll do our best to keep you safe. You folks stay back, keep your heads down, and everything should be fine."

Jacketed up and still carrying their equipment, the Mana Wave team followed the FBI agents as they made their way on foot through the barren, rocky hills. It was a half-hour walk from the vehicles to their target site, dry and dusty the whole way.

"If you don't want the criminals to hear cars coming, can't you use a portal to transport straight in?" Fran asked.

"That works fine with conventional gangs, but against these magicked-up mobs, it's as likely to trigger an alarm or defenses as it is to give us an edge." Baldwin ran a hand over his closely cropped hair, black shot through with gray. "Sometimes the old ways are the best."

Past a certain point, everyone fell silent, and the agents used hand signals to communicate. They split into groups, some rushing off to flank the site, while Fran and her companions followed Baldwin on the direct approach.

They stopped behind a cluster of low, scrubby bushes in a dip between two small hills. Peering through, they saw a set of trailers around a shack built out of corrugated metal. Smoke was streaming from a pair of chimneys on top of the shack. The whole place reeked of bad magic.

Outside the shack were an elf and a witch wearing hazmat suits with the masks pulled back, each smoking a cigarette. Nearby, a shifter and what looked like an ordinary human leaned against motorbikes. They both had guns. Other figures were moving between the trailers, but Fran couldn't make them out properly.

Baldwin pressed a finger to a small headphone he was wearing, nodded, and whispered a reply. He drew his wand.

"We're about to go," he said quietly. "Once it starts, you folks are welcome to come out of cover but stay back from the fighting, understand?"

"Suits me," Smokey said.

"That's fine." Fran took sensors out of her bag. "We should be able to get most of the readings we need from a distance."

Baldwin turned, tapped his earpiece again, and spoke quietly.

"All teams, wands and weapons loose. We are go."

Then he crept out from behind the bush. A couple of agents followed him. They all had containment units hanging from quick-release straps over their shoulders, covered in dark cotton so their mirrored bases wouldn't catch the sunlight.

Fran's attention stayed torn between setting up equipment and watching the beginning of the raid. In broken glances, she saw Baldwin and his crew advancing toward the trailers. The guards by the motorbikes looked up in alarm at a shout from the far side of the site. The elf in the hazmat suit spun in panic and spotted Baldwin's group. The elf shouted, and everything went mad.

Suddenly, the air was full of flying spells and the sound of gunfire. Somebody screamed. Somebody else cursed at the top of their lungs. The shack's door burst open, and a gnome in a hazmat suit ran out, saw what was going on, and ran back in.

The calm of the agents was amazing to see. As bullets flew their way, they picked up speed, running steadily toward their opponents. Baldwin and one of those following him used defensive spells to keep them safe, while the third agent used her magic to take down the criminals. One of the guards dropped, frozen stiff, and an exploding bike flung another one to the ground.

The gnome burst out of the trailer again and flung

something the size of a soup can. It landed close to Baldwin and exploded, tossing him and his agents to the ground in a burst of light and smoke. As they staggered to their feet, there was a second explosion, this time magical, which threw them over again and filled the air with flashing lights.

There was fighting all around. The windows of one of the trailers shattered. With a *clang*, another one crashed onto its side. Gangsters and agents ran back and forth, shooting spells and bullets. Two of them were rolling around on the ground, punching and kicking each other.

Fran reached for her dummy wand. If Baldwin and his people were in trouble, surely she should help?

"Not our fight." Singar rested a hand on her arm. "Don't risk yourself."

"But we have to help."

"That's your logic? We'll help more in the long term by watching, monitoring, and working out what's wrong with the containment units. That way, they won't have surprise escapes by the bad guys."

"I suppose."

Fran saw that Singar was right. It just didn't feel that way.

Baldwin pushed himself back to his feet and pulled the covering off his containment unit. As the gnome tried to run past him toward a row of bikes, Baldwin skimmed the unit across the ground, giving it extra propulsion with a blast of magic, and triggered its containment field. Rods shot up from the mirror base, and magic crackled between them. For a moment, a magical glow caught the gnome. Then something sparked at the edge of the base. There was a colored flash, a *bang,* and a trickle of purple smoke as the gnome broke free and kept running for the bikes.

"Did we get that?" Fran asked.

"Got thaumic radiation readings," Singar said, looking up from one of the monitoring devices.

"I've got mundane audio and visuals," Smokey said, paws resting on a specially adapted camera.

"And I was scanning for spell matrices." Fran waved something like a tablet with carved crystals on the end. "Looks like we've got everything we need."

"I'd like a closer look at that unit as soon as I can," Singar said. "Examine the damage and any residuals that might get lost."

"I'm sure that as soon as they've captured everyone, we can…" Fran looked up at the sound of an engine. "Uh-oh."

A motorbike was roaring toward them, the gnome in the hazmat suit on the back, pushing the gas for all it was worth. He still had his mask on, and something glowed in a satchel by his side.

"He's heading straight for this gap," Fran said. "What should we do?"

Singar pulled a containment unit from a bag and flung it on the ground. "More field testing."

As the bike raced toward them, Fran flung a blast of light at the gnome, but either the suit protected him from its effects, or he preferred to ride on blindly rather than face the FBI because he was still heading straight for them. She tried a wave of sound, and the bike shook like it was riding through an earthquake, but the gnome kept it steady, and now he'd almost reached them.

Fran flung herself aside, and the others did the same. As

the bike reached where they'd been standing, Singar hit a switch on a control she was holding. Their containment unit sprang into action, its magic grabbing hold of the gnome as he rode past. He was snatched off the back of the bike and into the magical field. The bike roared on for a moment longer, riderless, then crashed into a heap of rocks.

"Got him." Singar grinned.

"Thought you didn't like helping the law?" Smokey asked, emerging from under a bush.

"I like rising to a challenge."

"Um, guys..." Fran pointed at the containment unit's base, which was starting to smoke and spit sparks. "What's causing that?"

Smokey looked at the unit, then at the gnome's satchel, which had fallen off right next to the unit. Something inside had an unpleasant glow. Grabbing its strap between his teeth, Smokey ran off with it in the direction of the raid. The unit stopped sparking.

"That worked," Fran called.

Smokey stopped running, dropped the satchel, and took a step back. "I don't like the feel of this thing."

The fighting was almost over. Baldwin and his team had gathered the encampment's occupants. Some were in containment units, but others were only in handcuffs, and the FBI agents watched those warily. Baldwin walked over to the Mana Wave team, picking up the satchel on the way. He opened it and nodded.

"Magical drugs. Some of these are really nasty. Glad we were able to cut off the flow." He nodded at Fran. "Thanks for your help, ma'am."

"It was mostly Singar," she said.

"Your unit seems to be working." Baldwin glanced back. "Two of ours failed. Don't suppose you've worked out why yet?"

"I've got an idea, but I need to check it."

Fran walked from her hiding place out into the fight's aftermath. The air was full of strange chemical smells and the tingle of spent magic. She walked over to the containment unit they'd seen fail, which was still lying where it had been used, a haze of smoke hanging over it.

"Do you have those readings?" she asked the others, who had followed her with the equipment. They brought up their data while Fran crouched beside the broken unit, examining it.

"What do you think?" Singar asked. "Faulty part?"

Fran shook her head. "Interference. We tested this thing to death in controlled environments, but out in the field, there are lots of other spells and magical effects that can interfere with its power."

"I don't buy it. We did field tests."

"Those were with custom-made models, where we were meticulous about getting the details perfect." Fran lifted the unit so they could see the wiring and mystical components under the mirror. "Look at those connections."

Singar looked, frowned, twitched her whiskers, then snorted.

"You're right. The design's fine, but the quality from the factory has gone downhill. A unit like this would work in controlled environments, and a proper unit would work in a situation like this..." She waved at the chaos of their surroundings. "The faulty tech can't hold up to a real test."

"Is it fixable?" Agent Baldwin looked down at them. "These are a great tool when they work. I'd hate to give them up, but we need kit we can rely on when lives are on the line."

"It's fixable," Fran said. "We don't need to change the design, only bring in tighter quality control at our factory."

"Make that factories," Smokey amended. "Might as well apply this lesson to the FDS before something goes wrong with that."

"We'll take this back to show people." Fran put the broken unit in her backpack. "Please send back all the units you have. We'll check them over and replace any connections that aren't up to standards, free of charge, of course."

"Sounds good." Baldwin nodded at the unit holding the gnome whose escape they'd thwarted. "Might need to hang on to a few of them for now, though. Don't want to let our new friends get away."

CHAPTER TWENTY-SEVEN

Elethin drummed her fingers on the table, glanced at the bar's door, then down at the time on her phone. "What if she doesn't turn up?"

"Then this plan won't work," Gruffbar said, "and you'll spend the rest of your life chasing around on your friend Kotia's half-assed criminal capers."

"One, she is not my friend, and two, that is not very reassuring."

"I wasn't trying to reassure you, not when I can enjoy watching you squirm instead." Gruffbar sipped his ale and grinned.

"You're the worst." She sank into her seat.

"Yet you came to me for help."

"I needed a plan."

"You got one."

"One that won't work if Singar is much later."

As if on cue, the door to the bar opened, and Singar walked in. She shook the rain from her whiskers and strolled over to them. "Where's my drink?" She placed her bag on the table and took a seat.

"You weren't here." Elethin sniffed. "In fact, I was starting to wonder if you would turn up at all."

"Nice attitude. Where's the gratitude for the Willen who's come to save your skinny behind?"

"I'm most frightfully sorry. Should I write you a little thank you note on some gift stationery?"

"I could've stayed on Earth with Fran and those FBI guys instead of hurrying back here. It wasn't raining in New Mexico or whatever they called that place."

"At least this rain means a thaw," Gruffbar said. "Winter's nearly over."

"I haven't made a single snow rat yet. What a waste."

"Could we focus on the issue at hand?" Elethin snapped. "I have a very important fraud to commit, and you two jokers aren't helping."

"Actually, I am." Singar took three FDS devices out of her backpack. "Here's the answer to all your needs."

"You're kidding me?" Elethin shook her head. "I know what our system can do, and it won't do what we need today." She sank her head into her hands. "I'm going to be stuck with that idiot Kotia forever."

"These aren't ordinary units." Singar pointed at where she'd cracked the cases open. "I've made modifications, and Smokey wrote the software we need. We strap one to me, one to Gruffbar, and plant one where you're meeting. Once the three get into proximity, the program will start, and we're good from there."

"Plant it where I'm meeting?" Elethin picked up one of the bright orange boxes. "How am I supposed to do that?"

"That's for you to work out." Gruffbar downed the last of his beer, picked up an FDS, and headed for the door. Singar followed him. "See you soon."

Elethin was left alone in the bar, nursing a white wine spritzer and an orange plastic box full of electronics. She sighed and picked up a backpack that she'd bought from a discount store, chosen to go with the casual clothes she'd put on to look less like her usual self, in case that was any help.

She switched the FDS on, put it into the bag, tightened a few straps, then used a pointed nail file to bore a cluster of small holes through the material over where the unit's projector technology sat. That would at least let her carry it close. She hoped the device didn't move too much in the bag.

With a grimace of disdain, she pulled on a baseball cap, strapped on the backpack, and headed out.

The rain poured down outside, a whole ocean seeming to tumble out of the sky, every drop a fraction above freezing. They immediately soaked into her oversized hoodie and baggy jeans. The clothes not only lacked style but were unable to protect her from the elements. Just great. At least the cap kept the rain out of her eyes.

She walked down the road, trying and failing to avoid puddles, took a series of turns down increasingly narrow side streets, and stopped at an empty, litter-strewn junction between an abandoned factory and a deserted warehouse.

She took off her bag and looked inside. The FDS had shifted, which made her part of the plan no use. At least she was the first one here, so she had a chance to remedy that.

She took out the FDS and balanced it on a pair of bricks, leaning against a wall close to the junction. That should keep it from being ruined by one of the rising puddles. She hoped the case could keep out the rain long enough for the device to do its job.

Then she tore the backpack and scuffed it in the dirt, turning it into another mangled bit of detritus like so many in the street before draping it over the FDS with a strategically placed hole for projection. That would have to do.

She was just in time. With a flap of wings, Kotia landed beside her, carrying a clinking knapsack.

"I can't believe you've still got those," Elethin said. "How did you get out of the last fight with them?"

"I have my ways." Kotia winked. "Now I have you here as backup and can finally sell them. Remember, if anything goes sideways, fling up a bunch of flashing lights and shit like that. I'll get out, and you can run or fight, whatever you like."

"Definitely not fight."

"You've changed since prison."

"I wish you had."

The was a hiss of tires through water and the distinct chugging sound of a steam engine. An armored steam wagon, its hood reinforced and windows one-way glass, drew up to the junction.

"You introduce me to all the nicest people," Elethin said.

The back doors of the steam wagon opened. Four burly Kilomea stepped out and looked around, surveying the scene. Then a smaller figure emerged. She had the features of a Kilomea but was half the height of her bodyguards. Her shoulders were stooped, her arms thin, and her skin wrinkled. A pair of long tusks ran from the corners of her mouth, up her cheeks, almost to her eyes. One of the guards opened an umbrella and held it over her, keeping off the rain.

"Kotia," the wizened creature said.

"Mother Harball." Kotia bowed her head respectfully. "Thank you for meeting with me."

"I was curious. You caused some chaos between my rivals."

"Think of that as an audition. A chance to prove what I can do."

Elethin didn't know whether to laugh or applaud how Kotia was spinning her inept attempt at a simple sale into part of some grander scheme. The Arpak certainly had no shame.

"So what, now you want into my crew?" Harball croaked. "You think a little thing like that earns you respect?"

"Not yet," Kotia said. "While I have your attention, I've got something you might like to buy. Something valuable and untraceable if it's handled right."

"I like untraceable. Show me."

Kotia pulled a gem-encrusted necklace from the backpack.

"The whole stash is like this. Valuable to the right person, but I'd rather have cash."

"Of course, you would."

Harball nodded at one of her guards, who walked over. He pulled a jeweler's lens from his pocket and pressed it into his eye, the device looking tiny in among that ugly flesh, then peered at the gems.

"Wait." One of the other guards pointed. "Someone's coming."

Two figures approached from different sides of the junction. They'd gotten close before anyone heard them through the drumming rain. One was a dwarf with bright red hair and a bandana wrapped across the bottom half of his face.

The other appeared to be a gnome, but it was hard to tell when heavy leathers and a biker's helmet with the visor down covered them. The gnome's face was invisible, but the dwarf had a mad gleam in his eyes. Each held a pair of machine pistols, one in each hand.

"None of you bastards reach for a weapon," the dwarf growled, "or I'll spray you with more than rain."

Mother Harball scowled. "You dare to cross me?" she croaked. "Do you know who I am?"

"I've got an idea, yeah."

"You're still doing this?"

"We are."

Kotia was quivering with fear while Elethin stood beside her, her back rigid with tension, her hands sliding up her sleeves. The guards didn't move, but they watched the newcomers carefully.

"So what is this?" Harball asked. "You here for those gems or me? Robbery or assassination?"

"Depends on what'll make us the most money." The dwarf ran his eyes across the whole group, then brought his attention back to Mother Harball. "Maybe a kidnapping's in order. What do you think?"

"Who sent you?" Harball asked. "Bet I can pay you better than they do."

"Money isn't everything."

"Depends on how much money you've got."

"Enough of this shit." In a single fluid motion, Elethin drew a needle-like knife from her sleeve and flung it at the dwarf. It hit him in the side of the neck, and he sank to his knees. One of his guns clattered to the ground, but he kept hold of the other. His hand swayed, and bullets sprayed wildly around the junction.

"Dung fuckers!" the gnome screamed and opened fire.

One of Harball's guards lifted her and jumped into the back of the steam wagon, sheltering his boss with his body as he went. Rather than try to fight two lunatics with automatic weapons, the others leaped in after him. The door slammed closed, the wagon lurched, and it shot down the street, straight toward the gnome.

"I'm out of here," Kotia cried, spreading her wings.

"Oh no you don't." Elethin grabbed one of her wings and flung her down in a puddle, then planted a foot on her back. Kotia looked up in wide-eyed fear as Elethin drew more knives from her sleeves.

The gnome jumped out of the way as the steam wagon hurtled toward him. He fired wildly at it as it passed but missed, bullets instead cracking off a wall.

Elethin flung two more of her knives. They hit the gnome in the chest, and he fell flat on the ground, guns falling silent.

"Don't move," Elethin hissed into Kotia's ear. Then she stalked across the street to where the dwarf was kneeling. He raised his gun and pulled the trigger, but the hammer *clicked* down on an empty chamber, the ammunition spent.

"Get...you..." he groaned.

"I can't let that happen." Elethin pulled the knife from his neck and plunged it into his chest. He fell over and lay still.

The wagon was gone, the attackers down. The only sound was the rain. Elethin prowled back to where Kotia lay whimpering in a puddle.

"You were right," Elethin said. "I have changed since prison. I have even less patience for people who mess with my life."

Another knife appeared in her hand, and she crouched over Kotia, the blade's tip an inch from the Arpak's eye.

"We're done," Elethin said. "I need to ensure your silence. So, either accept the spell that will stop you talking about my past, or..." She looked pointedly at the knife. "What's it going to be?"

"The spell," Kotia moaned. "Please, the spell."

"Good choice. Now give me your hand."

With their palms pressed together, the two magicals recited the spell. In places, the words were the same from both of them. In others they differed as Kotia bound herself to silence, and Elethin set out the terms of the secrecy. Magic emerged, silver and shining, between them, then flowed down Kotia's throat and disappeared.

"There," Elethin said once the magic finished. She pocketed her knife and helped Kotia to her feet, pleasantly smiling as if they'd met for a drink. "Now tell me, what was I doing when we first met?"

Kotia opened her mouth to speak. Something bulged in

her throat and choked off the words before they could begin.

"Looks like it worked." Elethin picked up the bag of stolen jewelry. "I think I'll keep these too. Now go away and stay away unless you want to meet these again."

With a flick of the wrist, one last knife was between her fingers. She flung it past Kotia, and it buried itself in the masonry between two bricks.

"Y-y-yes El!"

Kotia flapped her wings and took off. Elethin watched until she'd vanished from sight, then walked over to the hidden FDS and switched it off. The air flickered, and the knife in the wall disappeared, as did the marks where bullets had hit.

A moment later, the dead gnome was replaced by Singar, with no helmet, guns, or biker leathers, pulling herself out of a puddle. The dead dwarf became Gruffbar, with no sign of a knife in his neck. Each of them unstrapped an FDS from their back.

"You owe us big time." Singar wrung puddle water from her shirt. "I feel like I'm never going to get dry."

"Wish we'd done it on a sunny day," Gruffbar said. "At least it worked. I don't see Kotia messing with you again."

"I can't believe you pulled that off in front of Mother Harball, of all people. Did you know it was going to be her?"

Elethin shook her head. "Is she a big deal in the criminal community?"

Singar nodded. "No one you want to cross."

"Then it's a good thing she's got no reason to think we did."

Gruffbar peered into the knapsack and whistled. "What are you planning to do with all this?"

"Return it anonymously, I suppose." Elethin sighed. "There are some lovely pieces in there, but I really would like to put my life of crime behind me."

Singar picked up the FDS from the side of the alley. "You know what I think?"

"That it's a good thing those bodyguards weren't better armed?"

"That too. Mostly what I think is that we should make a noir-style crime game for the system. Action, intrigue, and mystery in darkened back streets." She looked up at the still-streaming sky. "The illusion of rain could make it really atmospheric."

CHAPTER TWENTY-EIGHT

Fran stood in the New Mexico desert, leaning against her rental car, a new all-terrain vehicle with an electric engine. Agent Baldwin had offered to lend her a car for a few days while she stayed on Earth, but she'd declined. She didn't want to drive around in an FBI vehicle in case the agency tracked it and learned something they shouldn't.

The air above the creosote bushes glowed, and a portal appeared. Enfield stepped through, leaning on his walking stick and wearing a heavy backpack.

"Are you all right with that?" Fran hurried forward.

"I'm fine," Enfield said. "The extra weight's not a problem as long as I'm on my good leg."

"You know that you need both legs to walk, right?"

"I said I'm fine. Is this for us?" He nodded at the car.

Fran opened the trunk, and Enfield placed his bag inside, next to the backpack she'd brought with her. Some of the same sensors they'd used to observe the containment units would make themselves useful again. There was also a second bag that she'd gone back to Mana Wave Industries for, a large, heavy bag.

"I still can't get used to you with a beard," she said as she got into the driver's seat.

"You don't like it?" He strapped in beside her.

"I don't dislike it, just trying to adjust. It's like when they change the recipe of your favorite soda, you know? It might even taste better, but before you can work that out, you've got to get used to the old flavor going away."

"It's okay. My chin is still here."

"How am I supposed to know that, hm?" She put the car into gear, and they headed out across the desert. "What did you tell Winslow about where you're going?"

"I didn't, flat out refused to tell him. I dropped enough hints for the others to think I'm meeting up with Josie. By the time Winslow gets that information, he'll feel like he's been smart and found the solution, so he won't go digging any deeper."

"That's cunning. Hey, you could always go and meet with Josie afterward..."

"Sorry, Fran, but you know where I stand on that."

"I do, but it seems such a waste."

"Enough about that. Tell me how the raid went."

They drove for twenty minutes, following a route that Fran had worked out as much through magic as through the power of the car's satnav. That brought them to a valley where centuries of erosion had carved strange pillars, their peaks like conical wizards' hats. At the entrance to the valley, they parked and got out their equipment.

"I've done a lot of big things recently," Fran said. "This feels as if it could be, like, the biggest one yet."

"If it works, it could change the world."

"I know! That's so totally awesome."

Buoyed by that thought, Fran led Enfield down the valley, which she had scouted out the previous day. Like then, they passed a few depressed magicals heading back the way they were coming from.

"It's still not working properly," a witch said sadly as she passed. "You might as well turn around and save yourselves the trip."

"We're good," Fran replied. "But thanks for the advice."

Halfway down the valley, there was a bowl in the ground, as wide as the valley itself and as deep as Enfield was tall. In its center stood a crystal pillar shaped like the valley's strange stones. It glowed with a flickering light, and with it came an equally erratic flow of magical power.

It was sad to see a kemana in such a state, but from what Fran could gather from the news, it wasn't unusual. All over Earth, the kemanas were dwindling, magical power fading with them. Slowly but surely, wonder was seeping from the world.

A few magicals sat around the bowl's edges, staring at the crystal. None of them paid any attention to Fran and Enfield as they approached the crystal, opened their bags, and started assembling a complex magitech device.

"Are you sure this will do?" Fran said. "I mean, will testing it here show what would happen if we plug into the whole network from where you usually keep the Source?"

"It won't be quite the same," Enfield said. "The magic won't be able to spread from here to any other kemanas. We should still see what would happen at individual sites as the power and signal spread."

"Awesome." Fran grinned. "I'm so psyched to see if this works."

"You and me both, but I might not have used those exact words."

It took time to assemble the device they'd been building. They'd had to disassemble it to make it portable, and connecting the pieces was a complex business. Still, it was only a fraction of the time it had taken to build the device in the first place, working with what they'd learned from observing the Source, analyzing its energy signature, and looking for ways to replicate it.

The tipping point had been working out that the Evermores' power was only one branch of what the Source could do. That had given them a pattern to work from, one they were familiar with as part of their powers. Once they had that and the converters Fran had made to provide Evermore-style power for her company's batteries, the design quickly came together. Now, they had to hope it was the right design.

By the time they finished assembling the device, some of the local magicals had come closer.

"What is that?" asked an elderly gnome.

"Stand back, and you'll get to see," Fran said.

Already nervous, the locals promptly stepped well back, returning to the edge of the kemana, and stood staring down at the device.

It was one of the stranger-looking machines Fran had built, an array of lenses and prisms held together on a collapsible aluminum frame. Cables led to crystals at key points in the structure, and they'd strung runes written on plastic cards all over the outside. Completely extended, it was eight feet tall and four feet wide, and while much of that space was hollow, every empty inch of it counted toward their calculations.

Attached to one side was the largest battery Fran had built so far. Just pressing her hand against its side, she could feel the raw magical power it contained. The factory foreman had raised all sorts of questions when she'd brought it down to charge, but the advantage of being the boss was that you didn't have to provide answers.

Fran plugged in the last cable, adjusted one of the prisms, then looked at Enfield. "Ready?"

"Ready."

He retreated to the kemana's edge. The slope up was steeper at the top, and he reluctantly accepted an offer of help from one of the locals when it became too difficult to ascend using his walking stick. Once he was clear, Fran followed, trailing a set of wires behind her. At the top of the slope, she sat next to Enfield and placed a control box in his lap.

"You should start it," she said.

"You built it."

"With you. It wouldn't have been possible if you hadn't learned about the Source through…" Her voice trailed off, and she forced her gaze away from his damaged leg. "I mean, if not for your insights."

"If this is the price I pay for saving the world, I can live with that." Enfield tapped his thigh. "What we're doing now could make it all more bearable."

"All the more reason why you should press the button." Fran nudged him. "Go on. You know you want to."

Enfield smiled. "I suppose I do."

He flipped a switch on the control box, then another. A button lit up.

"Here we go."

Enfield pressed the button.

For a long moment, all that happened was a soft humming sound. Then that sound grew louder, shaking the ground beneath them. Small rocks bounced around in the dirt, and some locals looked alarmed.

The shaking faded away, and the humming receded as light started shining through the strange device down by the kemana crystal. Not only light but magical power streamed from the crystals through the lenses and prisms, being twisted, knotted, refracted, reshaped, fractured, and combined in new forms until it became a single bright beam shining into the crystal.

The kemana crystal, glowing so faintly and flickeringly, slowly and steadily brightened until the whole valley basked in its light.

"It's working." Fran gripped Enfield's arm.

"It really is."

One of the locals, a witch, walked hesitantly down the slope until she was right by the crystal. She spread her arms wide and closed her eyes.

"It's happening," she called. "The power, I can feel it returning, coming back to the kemana, coming back to me."

More of them hurried down to stand beside her.

"She's right," a gnome cried, laughing in delight. "The magic is back."

The locals gathered around the crystal, reinvigorated by its power. Then, as the initial moment of awe passed, some of them turned to look in wonder at Fran and Enfield.

"You did this, didn't you?" one asked. "How did you do this?"

"It won't last," Fran called. "Not yet. I'm sorry."

"But you did it?"

"Yes, we did."

The locals huddled closer, basking in the magic, while Fran and Enfield used their sensors to take readings for later.

"This is so cool," Fran said. "It's like nothing I've ever done before. It's something that's making these people so happy. It's…"

"It's about to break down." Enfield pointed at the smoke streaming from one of the lenses. "We should power it down."

Fran flipped a switch on the control box. Nothing happened. She flipped another.

"I don't think we can turn it off," she said. "The magic has a will of its own."

"Looks like that will might be self-destructive."

More of the lenses and prisms were smoking and cracking. The closest locals backed away as a cable fell loose and melted on the ground.

"Everyone get away from it," Fran called. "Quick!"

The locals scattered as runic cards burst into flames, and a prism exploded, showering the area with shards of glass. Fran closed her eyes, unable to bear the thought of watching her device explode. Everything was bright through her eyelids.

Then the ground shook. The brightness receded, and a humming filled the air. At last, it all faded away.

Fran opened her eyes. The generator device stood by the kemana crystal, damaged but not destroyed. The crystal had returned to its former faltering glow.

"Thank goodness for that," she said. "We won't have to rebuild it from scratch."

Fran and Enfield went back down to the kemana's center and disassembled the generator. They put all the pieces, damaged or not, back into their bags. Everything would be useful in understanding what had and hadn't worked and why.

"Now what?" Enfield asked.

"Now we scale it up," Fran said. "It's going to be hard work to make something like this on a scale that can provide a long-term power source. Even if your home can magnify its power and spread it through the network, we need something that will last and with enough power to get things started. This was great for ten minutes in one kemana, but it's not a fix for the whole world."

"Still, the idea we had worked, right?"

"Oh, yes." Fran grinned as she put the last of the crystals away. "Do you think we should tell Winslow yet? I really want to see the look on his face when we tell him that he was wrong, that we don't have to keep the Source trapped forever."

"Not yet. Not until we've built something that can power the whole kemana network. Winslow will find any excuse to say no to things that aren't his idea. We can't leave him any gaps to work with."

They headed up the slope, taking their bags with them.

The locals helped them get their bags over the edge of the bowl and helped Enfield clamber out.

"Will you be back?" one of the locals asked.

"We might not, but the power will be soon." Fran squeezed the woman's shoulder. "Trust me. It's going to be great."

"Who are you people?" someone else asked.

"Us? We're just a pair of inventors, looking to make the world a better place."

CHAPTER TWENTY-NINE

As Josie rummaged around in her desk for a pen, a pair of books hidden in the back drew her attention. They were both used copies of the same old fantasy novel, one that she'd mentioned to Enfield and that had interested him. She'd spotted them in a secondhand store and bought them on a whim, planning to surprise him the next time they were looking for something to read together. Then he'd gone quiet, and she'd pushed the books out of sight, unwilling to let them go but not wanting the daily reminder of his absence. She'd almost forgotten them.

She took the books out and flattened the battered corner of a cover. She'd loved this book when she was younger, and she'd looked forward to learning what Enfield thought of it. She'd hoped that he would love it, but even if he didn't, they would get an interesting conversation out of it. In some ways, it would've been a test, a way to see how closely their tastes aligned and perhaps how they coped with a difficult difference.

Now, the books were a bitter reminder of what might

have been. Josie wanted to drop them into the trash basket, but that would be a waste of good reading material and perhaps rob someone else of the chance to discover this wonder in a secondhand store.

Instead, she got up, walked the three steps to the coat stand in the corner of her office, and put the books in her bag. She would return them to the shop the next time she was passing. Maybe she'd pick up something better instead.

There was a knock on the office door. Josie kept it open when she wasn't in meetings or on calls as a way to be accessible to the teams she was running, but her staff still knew to knock before walking straight in. A pale gnome with wavy black hair stood in the doorway with a tablet in his hand.

"Hi, Ted." Josie waved him in. "What can I do for you?"

Ted passed her the tablet so she could see the data on its screen.

"We've got the feedback from the focus groups for the new time management app," he said. "It's not great."

Josie looked at the headline figures, then skimmed through the quotes below, comments people had made about the app when given a chance to work with it. "At least it's better than the last iteration. I hoped we'd fixed some of these issues."

"I think there was a fight between the team designing the interface and the ones working on the scheduling system. Things didn't get coordinated properly."

Josie pressed a hand to her brow. Sometimes this place was so exhausting. They could achieve so much if they got organized and worked together properly, yet people kept getting into these conflicts. She understood why it was happening, but that didn't make fighting the fires less frustrating.

"Give me a minute." She typed out a rapid email, only a few sentences, checked it for errors, and hit send. "There. I've told the heads of both teams that you're now in charge of getting these issues fixed. Either they do what you tell them, or they'll answer to me for it."

"Me?" Ted's eyebrows shot up. "Isn't that a bit above my pay grade?"

"Not for much longer. I'll contact HR after lunch and tell them to start the promotion paperwork."

"Really?"

"Ted, we've had our issues in the past, but you get things done, and right now that's what I need. I love working here, I love what I do, but this place is driving me nuts. Some changes are coming, I'm sure, but until then, I need people around who can help me cut through the nonsense. So, do you want a promotion or not?"

"I mean, yes, of course."

"Good." She finally found a pen and scribbled a note to remind her of what she'd promised. "Now, I have to get out to a lunch meeting, so unless there's anything else..."

"No, that's it. Enjoy your lunch."

Ted took his tablet and hurried out. Josie grabbed her coat and bag and headed out after him, locking her office behind her.

One short elevator trip and two taxi rides later, she was in a high-end coffee shop on the other side of the business district, sitting with Julia Lacy and Sylvia Dodd.

"Sorry I'm late," Josie said. "Traffic on the second ride was a nightmare."

"It's fine," Julia said. "Better safe than sorry. We don't want anyone from Philgard to know about these meetings."

"How is it all going?"

"Well, I think. I've managed to redirect several of the people searching for approvals or opinions from Howard so they go to me or one of the coven. Together with a few procedural changes, that's given us more control over the day-to-day running of the business. It's letting people get used to our authority."

"I hoped that might bring more order, but things seem as conflicted as ever."

"We'll get there. It takes time to change the whole culture of an organization." Julia turned to Sylvia. "How are your meetings going?"

"I've met with the rest of the coven individually or in pairs, like you asked," Sylvia said. "It makes coordination slower, but there's no data trail, and I think we've avoided being seen. Even if someone spots one of these meetings, I can say that I'm catching up with old friends."

"How are the others doing?"

"Getting there. We're facing the most resistance in information systems. You know what a bro zone that team can be."

Julia rolled her eyes. "The land of jock nerds. I'm familiar with its bad habits and worse attitudes."

"We've managed to get some transfers in place from healthier departments and told them to keep their heads down. When the time comes, they'll know the teams, and they'll be ready to be moved up to team leads."

Not for the first time, Josie was impressed by the slick professionalism of their slowly building coup. Everything was done within the business' rules, carefully putting the pieces into place without ruffling feathers. No one outside their clique seemed to have the slightest clue that anything was amiss. If someone had seen the pattern, they kept quiet about it.

"I've picked out a couple of candidates," Josie said. "People who can replace the managers we want to get rid of once Howard's sidelined. I've given them tasks to test them out, and so far they're doing well."

She thought of Ted, managing the tensions between two teams, and his colleague Debby, who had unexpectedly found herself in charge of a big design project. There was real potential there.

"You've got a good eye for talent," Sylvia said. "Have you considered a career in HR?"

"I like working on products too much. Besides, I think we have someone ready to take over that department." Josie winked at Sylvia, who laughed.

"I should hope so, after all the work I've put in."

The conversation briefly subsided while a waiter brought their coffee and sandwiches. Julia dropped a good tip onto his empty tray and waved him away with a smile on his face.

"It helps that Howard isn't paying attention," Josie said. "No one's seen him roaming the building in weeks. Did you arrange that?"

Julia shook her head and finished chewing on a mouthful of her cheese baguette.

"He has a project to distract him," she said. "Not my doing, but good timing for us."

"Is he finally raising an army of zombie office staff?" Sylvia grinned. "You could save a fortune on health costs."

"Not quite."

"A new product?" Josie was curious about what the real answer might be.

"Another takeover of one of our competitors?" Sylvia asked.

"Neither of those."

"Then what?"

"Don't worry about it."

Josie sat back and toyed with her coffee cup. She trusted Julia to judge what they needed to know, but still, she would've been more comfortable with more information, with more clues about where the boss' attention was while they plotted against him. It didn't help that she felt vulnerable after Enfield and Julia's dismissive tone had hit a raw nerve.

"Don't give me that." Sylvia leaned forward, staring at Julia. "We're all in this together. We need to know what's happening."

It was a relief to Josie to hear someone else express what she hadn't, to have a chance to learn more without upsetting her relationship with Julia.

"Really, we don't need to get into that."

"I don't believe it." Sylvia sat back, arms crossed. "Even now, you're keeping his secrets for him? What the hell, Julia?"

For a long moment, they sat in silence with Julia staring at her coffee cup and the others staring at her.

"Can I get you ladies anything?" the waiter asked, approaching the table again. His face fell as he caught Sylvia's withering gaze. "I'll come back later."

"You do that."

He hurried off, leaving them alone again.

"You're right," Julia said. "That was low of me. You're both taking a risk by joining me in this endeavor, and you deserve to have your questions answered."

"Good, and..." Sylvia leaned forward again, and Julia did the same, full of eager energy.

"Howard has a private magical project he's working on," Julia said. "I won't go into the details for various reasons, not least that I don't know them all. The important thing is that it will give him more magical power."

"Why couldn't you tell us that?"

"Because I was still working out what to do about it. I didn't want to get anyone's hopes up, but I think it might offer us an opportunity."

"What sort of opportunity?"

"The opportunity to take that power for ourselves."

"How?"

Julia unlocked the screen of her phone and brought up a photo. It was of a basement room, its walls covered with sheets of paper, old books, and manuscripts lying amid a scatter of notes on a table in the middle.

"Handar brought me some papers he'd been collecting," she said. "Papers that he thought could be useful to Howard. I've kept them from the man himself while I have a chance to go through them.

"They're not exactly about Howard's project, but they relate to it closely enough. I've been working on a ritual that we could use to divert the power as he summons it, to take it for ourselves."

"For ourselves?" This wasn't what Josie had expected. They were crossing from a plan to improve a business into something stranger and more unsettling.

"Mostly for Philgard," Josie said. "It turns out that Howard has been turning the whole business into a conduit for this power. That's part of why he's kept things so chaotic, so the negative emotions can fuel his magic."

"Asshole," Sylvia growled.

It was a lot to take in. Josie's hero, Howard Phillips, had been deliberately causing all the problems she'd faced so he could feed his magic with other people's angst. Still, it made sense of how Philgard worked in a way that nothing else had.

"We're going to end this, right?" she asked.

"Of course," Julia said. "We'll channel the power back into the business, use it on rites that help people work together, enchant our technology, and make our buildings better places to work. We'll replace his anarchy with harmony. The magic will also empower our managers so they can use it to run things more smoothly. Of course, we'll need some of it to keep these spells running so Philgard can achieve its full potential."

It was hard to argue with the logic of empowering themselves when she put it like that.

"This is a big step." Julia looked intently at the other two. "It's more than we talked about before. I won't pretend it doesn't cross a line. If you want out, I won't stop you, and I won't blame you. Just, please, don't tell Howard.

Let the rest of us continue, so the madness in this business can end."

Sylvia looked at Julia, judging, considering.

Josie sat back, and her hand settled on her bag. She felt the shape of books in there, the books that she'd meant to share with Enfield. If she couldn't be happy in her private life, she could at least be satisfied with her work. She could rise to the challenge given here. She could fill her time with something that wasn't him.

"I'm in," she said. "To the end."

"Fuck it." Sylvia waved dismissively. "I'm not going to let the new girl outshine me. I'm in too."

"I'm so glad to hear it," Julia said. "Perhaps you could help me explain this to the others? We'll need all the witches we can trust if this is going to work."

CHAPTER THIRTY

Two rows of containment units sat at the end of the factory, waiting to be boxed up and sent to Earth. One row was the used units sent back by the FBI, old components ripped out and replaced. The other row was new units built with recalibrated machinery to improved specifications. Fran and Singar walked along the rows, inspecting every unit, while the factory foreman watched them nervously.

"Our quality assurance team would be happy to do this," he said. "They know how the tech works. They understand the new standards. Honestly, we could have got it right before if we'd known what was needed."

"I know." Fran offered him a sympathetic smile. "It's not that we don't trust anyone here. This contract is too important for us not to give it the personal touch."

"Speak for yourself." Singar turned over a unit to examine its workings. "After what we saw in New Mexico, I don't trust anyone here to get this right."

The foreman clutched his clipboard tight and watched Singar, brow furrowed.

"Ignore her," Fran said. "She's grumpy because—"

"I'm grumpy because this should've been right the first time, and some overgrown ape messed it up. Dung and dust, how hard can it be to take pride in your work?"

Singar flipped the unit back over and moved to the next one. Around them, the roar of machinery ground on as the factory produced more units like these.

"They look good so far." Fran hoped to bring some relief to the poor foreman. "Right, Sin?"

"So, far, sure..." Singar squinted at a mirror base, then flipped it over. "I'll be happy when we've checked the whole lot." She looked up and switched to a different frown. "What's he doing here?"

Fran looked around to see Cam approaching down the length of the factory. He waved. A flutter of excitement rose in her chest, immediately followed by a wave of dread. What could have brought him here in the middle of the day? It had to be something bad, didn't it? Otherwise, he would still be busy writing, like he'd been doing every day for what felt like forever.

"What's wrong?" She rushed over to him.

"Nothing."

"Then what are you doing here?"

"Bart said this was where I'd find you."

"But your thesis..."

"Is finally finished and submitted about an hour ago."

"Really?"

"Really."

"Yay!" She flung her arms around him. "Congratulations!"

She kissed him hard, both their hearts racing in the moment of excitement. It took a while to bring her attention back to where she was, and when she did, she saw Singar and the foreman leaning together, laughing as they looked at her.

"What?" she asked, but she knew, and she didn't care.

"I know you're busy too," Cam said, "but I wondered if I could persuade you to come out with me now and celebrate?"

"Of course! This is far too important a moment to miss." Fran looked at Singar. "I mean, maybe after we've finished this."

"I've got it." Singar waved a clawed hand. "You two go celebrate."

"Really?"

"Really. Anything to get those gormless grins out of my face."

"Thanks, Sin, you're the best."

"Yeah, right."

Singar turned back to her work while Fran took Cam's hand and they ran together out of the factory.

"Where are we going?" she asked breathlessly.

"A surprise," he replied. "You've put up with so much from me. I thought you deserved something special."

The basket of a flying taxi was waiting for them by the factory gates, a giant eagle perched on the fence. They climbed into the basket. The eagle took hold of the handle between its claws, and, with a beat of its wings, they swept into the icy air.

Fran noticed something in the bottom of the basket. "Ooh, what's this?"

"What does it look like?"

"A picnic basket, but it's a bit cold for eating outdoors."

"All part of the surprise."

"Speaking of which, can we stop at my apartment on the way? I've got a surprise for you too."

Cam gave the eagle fresh directions, and it changed course. A few minutes later, they set down on the patch of grass next to Fran's building. She hurried inside, and when she emerged a few minutes later, there was an extra bulge in her bag.

Fifteen minutes later, they approached a tower close to the river. It was old and broad, built of stone rather than the glass and concrete used in so many of Mana Valley's shining office blocks. The top spread wide, like a mushroom cap extending from its stalk. Greenery covered it.

"Wow," Fran said as they flew closer. "Look at that! The palm trees and flowers, how are they growing in this cold?"

The eagle set down on a platform sticking out from the tower. Cam paid, and he and Fran got out, taking the picnic basket with them.

At the end of the platform, a gnome in a uniform with shiny buttons sat behind a counter. Behind him, the air around the plant-covered rooftop shimmered.

"Tickets, please." The gnome held out his hand, and Cam handed over two slips of thin cardboard. "Thank you. In you go."

They walked past the gnome and through a magical field. Immediately, the air changed, becoming warm and humid, more like a jungle than a windswept winter city.

"Phew!" Fran peeled off her jacket and hoodie. Cam, sweat beading his brow, did the same.

"Like it?" he asked.

"I love it! What is this place?"

"It's a botanical garden run by the university. Anybody can buy tickets to visit if they want to, but the keepers don't advertise it. I think they prefer to keep the place quiet."

"So, how did you hear about it?"

"Same way as usual. A customer at the coffee shop."

"The coffee shop you've hardly been to in months?"

"I heard about this a while back. I've been saving it for a special occasion."

They strolled along a winding path between clusters of verdant plants. Huge leaves hung over them, casting the path into shade. Fran, who had been relishing any sign of sunlight through the winter months, suddenly didn't mind it vanishing. This place was more than warm and bright enough.

Cam led her to an isolated glade, a small grass-floored clearing with no one else in sight. The only movement was the closing of a small carnivorous plant trying to catch a fly. The jungle around them was full of bright blooms in every color of the rainbow.

"This is amazing," Fran said as she helped Cam lay out a picnic blanket. "Did I say that already?"

"Something like it, but please keep going. I like to know that you're enjoying yourself."

"What's this in the basket? Caramel cake, cheese puffs, orange soda, those fancy chocolates from the store near Josie's office... Cam, these are my favorite things!"

"That's the idea." He lay back on the blanket and let her continue with her excited unpacking. "I've been a lousy boyfriend the last few months. We agreed to it, but still, it didn't feel good. This is my attempt to make up for it."

Fran turned to him, clutching a bottle of her favorite soda.

"It's more than an attempt. You've, like, totally succeeded." She kissed him briefly, then turned back to the food. "What do you want?"

They ate and drank, talked and laughed, truly relaxing together for the first time in too long. There was so much to catch him up on, from what she'd done at work to a cute puppy she'd seen in the street. Cam had things to tell her too, about how the thesis had worked out and his supervisor's surprise when he finally turned it in. Fran couldn't remember the last time she'd been so happy. When she'd eaten as much as she could manage, she turned to her bag.

"Time for my surprise." She took a package out and handed it to Cam. "Here. Congratulations."

He accepted the package and unwrapped it, revealing a hardback book, its blue cover worn at the edges and faded with age. Cam turned it carefully, opened the front cover, and looked at the title page.

"Tolweck's *Magical History of the European Wars*." Cam looked up at Fran with a smile. "Did you know that this is the first recognized work in my field of study?"

"You're not the only one who's done some research." She beamed. "It seemed like the most appropriate present."

He peered closely, a finger hovering an inch above the fine print. His eyes went wide.

"Fran, is this... Is this a first edition?"

"Only the best for my boy." She wrapped an arm around him and snuggled against his side. "Why don't you read me a story?"

Cam carefully closed the book and sat staring at its cover.

"Fran," he said, his voice tight. "How much did you spend on this?"

"I can't tell you that. It's a present."

"Fran, I know how much these things go for. This must have cost ten times more than this whole date."

"I guess, maybe."

"It wasn't a cheap date."

"I never said it was. I just..." Fran looked up at him. His brow was wrinkled. "I wanted to do something nice."

Cam sighed and set the book down carefully on the picnic basket.

"I'm sorry, Fran, but you've given me a book worth more than anything else I own, and you're treating it so casually."

"It's okay. I can afford it."

"That's great, but I can't. I couldn't afford it if I saved up my wages for years."

"After this, you'll get a proper job, an academic one, right?" Fran sat up and looked at him. "Why does that matter anyway? It's a present. It's about getting you something you wouldn't get for yourself."

Cam got to his feet, too agitated to sit still. "How can I ever repay you for something like this?"

"You don't repay me. It's a present."

"That works great when we can give each other

presents of similar value, but I can't get you anything like this."

"Once you get a new job..."

"You'll still be earning ten times what I do! Fran, senior academics don't earn the sort of money that lets you casually give away first editions of Tolweck, and I'll be a junior academic on the very lowest rung. Your tech business money is so far beyond me."

"So?"

"So? So how can things ever be equal between us? You'll be buying flashy gadgets, new fashions, tickets to the best gigs, and I'll be offering you soda pop and cheesy puffs."

"I like soda pop and cheesy puffs."

"Are you trying to miss the point?" He stood with his hands on his hips, frowning at her. It was saddening, unsettling, and exactly the opposite of what she'd wanted, what she'd expected.

She got to her feet and took his hand. "I'm sorry. I didn't mean to make you uncomfortable."

"I know." He leaned his forehead against hers. "How can this work between us if things are so unequal?"

"The way I see it, things are equal in every way that matters. We both love each other, right?"

He smiled at those words, and she smiled too, so wide it nearly hurt.

"I guess we do," he said.

"We're both pursuing our dreams, going for the jobs that will make us happy and satisfied, that will let us be the best at things we're passionate about. Isn't that right?"

"It is."

"There we go. We're equal in the really important things, the ones that give life meaning. It's sad that the world won't pay you as well for your work as it pays for what I do, but we can't change that. What we can do is support each other as best we can with what we get. Maybe that means, for now, I pay for the expensive things, but you'll still find ways to make our lives wonderful in your thoughtful way.

"When I'm exhausted by my work and about to fall apart, you'll hold me together and keep me calm, as I'd do for you. Maybe one day, I'll get distracted and ruin my business just as you become important, and you can pay for everything. What's important is that we have each other, and we have lives that satisfy us."

Cam pushed back a strand of hair from her cheek. "How did you get so wise?" he asked quietly. "And so compassionate?"

"I just want everyone in the world to enjoy themselves. The rest flows from there."

"I'm so glad I found you."

"I'm glad too. My business is amazing, but you're still the best thing in my world."

Their lips touched, and for a long time, they forgot the picnic.

CHAPTER THIRTY-ONE

Across the cavern floor, the light flickered. Enfield looked up to see the Source looking back at him inside the containment unit.

Enfield had gotten good at judging these situations. Although the Source had no eyes, he could tell by its stance when it was looking at him and when it was simply facing in his direction. There was an alertness to the creature, a certain tilt of its head that gave it away.

Or maybe it was all in Enfield's imagination. Maybe he'd spent so long down here that he was starting to imagine things.

The Source wasn't his only company. Fran came sometimes, and the other Evermores increasingly came to him for conversations or advice, but still, he wasn't getting out and about like he used to do when his legs were healthy. Sitting in one room for days on end was bound to affect a person's mind.

"I still can't talk about this." Enfield pointed at the components spread across the table in front of him. "I'm sure you understand. Walls have ears. But I think you'll like what we're making."

When he'd started work on components for the improved magical generator, he'd been worried that Winslow might spot what he was doing, and he'd done his best to hide its parts. Over time, he'd realized that Winslow had no clue what he was looking at where technology was concerned. Tell him that this was for the sensors and moving the Source, and the Evermore leader would believe it. Enfield was free to disobey Winslow right under his nose, as long as he didn't say it aloud.

The Source raised an arm and pointed toward the door.

"Sorry, I can't let you out yet," Enfield said. "Someday, hopefully, but not yet."

The Source pointed again, pressing a finger against the magical field until it crackled and sparked.

Enfield looked out the door. There was nothing to see, only a cold stone mine shaft. Now that he was paying attention, he caught a sound. More than one. The distant crash of heavy things slamming into each other. Shouts of alarm. The deep, muffled rhythm of Evermore sound magic in use far away.

"Not again." Enfield got to his feet, grabbed his walking stick, and headed for the door. The sounds became louder and more distinct as he strode along the mine shaft, heading for the daylight at the far end. The air got colder away from the heating the Evermores had installed in parts of the old mine complex, but he ignored that. There were more urgent issues.

There was fine rain in the air outside the mine, so fine that it was almost a mist. It darkened the stones and dripped from the brickwork of the old industrial buildings, filling the world with its gray gloom.

That wasn't the only gray descending upon the Evermores' hideout. Rock monsters were assaulting the barricades again. This time, some of them had tucked themselves into balls for others to roll them down the slope, to crash into the defenses. Part of the barricade had almost broken down, and one of the old buildings was cracked open, tiles sliding from collapsed roof beams.

The Evermores held their ground, as always, working under Winslow's command. They flung magic, both light and sound, and hit the monsters when they got close. Still, a blow from a staff couldn't stop a heavy rock from rolling into its target, and when the creature unfolded itself to climb back up the slope, it was already too late.

Enfield hobbled over to take his place at the barricade, close to Taldiss.

"This is the worst one yet." She flicked the ends of her dark hair from her eyes. "Not a heavy attack, but persistent. Sooner or later, they'll break through, and I wouldn't bet on later."

A rock monster crashed into the barrier in front of them, making it shake. Then the creature unfolded its limbs and got to its feet.

"Why are you doing this?" Enfield shouted at it.

"No point asking that," Taldiss said. "These things clearly aren't smart."

"How do we know that? It's not like we've tried to have a conversation."

"It's a bit late now."

"Do you have a better plan?" Taldiss looked at him,

mouth open like she had an idea but couldn't work out the words for it. Then she shook her head. "Fine, you're right. What have we got to lose?"

Another rock monster rolled into the wall close to them with a crash. As it started getting to its feet, Enfield and Taldiss both shouted at it.

"Hey, what do you want?"

For a moment, the creature looked at them. Then it trudged back up the slope.

The rocks kept crashing against the Evermores' defenses. Walls cracked. Barricades fell. Volleys of magic failed to hold the attackers back, and desperate construction work couldn't repair the damage as fast as it happened. Slowly but surely, the rocks were winning.

Enfield and Taldiss kept shouting whenever a rock came near. At last, one of the smaller ones stopped and looked at them, its head tipped to one side. For a moment, Enfield thought they got through to it. Then it turned and trudged back up the hill.

"We're wasting our breath," Taldiss muttered.

Enfield, his leg aching from standing in the cold and wet so long, winced as he flexed his muscles.

"We've got to breathe anyway. Why not use it on this?"

Another ball of rock, the biggest yet, hit the center of the walls, shaking the defenses so hard that it flung Winslow into the dirt. That ball of rock unraveled into two big monsters, who took a step back and stood staring at the Evermores. In the silence that followed, a smaller monster strode down the hill and stopped facing Enfield and Taldiss.

"What is it doing?" Winslow picked himself up out of the mud and came over to stand by them.

"I think it wants to talk." Taldiss brushed back the damp hair now plastered to her forehead.

"Hi." Enfield waved. "Is that why you're here, to talk?"

The creature made a noise like rocks tumbling down a mountainside.

"Wish we had a dictionary for this." Enfield scratched his head. "I don't suppose there's any point asking you to speak more clearly?"

The creature spoke again, slower, and this time Enfield thought he heard something like familiar words.

"I almost understood that." He looked straight at the monster. "Could you say it again, please?"

"Why did you attack us?" This time, the words were clear.

"You attacked us," Enfield said.

"We tried to follow the way. You attacked us."

"The way?"

"The way into the tunnels. To follow it."

Enfield looked at Taldiss. "You were here for the first fight, right?"

"Yes."

"How exactly did it start?"

"We were out here, and a couple of these things came thumping toward the tunnel mouth. We tried to tell them to stop, but they didn't listen, so we defended ourselves and the way into our home."

"Defended yourselves by throwing spells at them?"

"How else?"

Enfield turned back to the rock creature.

"My name is Enfield. What is yours?"

"In the old speech of our people, I am Cracked Pebble on a Windswept Mountain."

"Can I call you Cracked Pebble?"

"It will do."

"I think there's been a misunderstanding, Cracked Pebble. We're living here, and when your people came, we thought you were attacking us. We defended ourselves."

"We live here."

An awkward silence fell. There was a clatter as a tile fell in one of the damaged buildings.

"You don't live here," Winslow said. "The place was empty when we arrived and for weeks after."

"We live here, and we live there." Cracked Pebble pointed up the nearest mountain. "In between, we move with the seasons."

"You're nomadic?"

Cracked Pebble tipped his head to one side and rubbed a rock hand across his chin, making a scraping sound.

"This word, yes. We are nomadic. Live in the high places and the low places. Our way carries us to our low place. We were going there when you attacked us."

The Evermores looked at each other.

"We're sorry," Enfield said. "We didn't think anyone else was living here. We've been attacked before by others, and it seemed like someone was attacking us again. We only tried to defend ourselves."

"You hurt us."

"We're sorry. You hurt some of us too."

Cracked Pebble turned and made a rumbling sound, low and penetrating, that swept across the valley and up the ridge. The other rock creatures strode down and gathered facing the Evermores.

"Is this about to kick off again?" Taldiss whispered, gripping a staff tight, magic in her hands.

"I don't think so," Enfield whispered back. "At least, I hope not."

Cracked Pebble pointed at Winslow.

"You are the leader?"

"That is correct," Winslow replied.

"You are in our low home. All of you."

"It is our home now."

"It is still our winter home."

Another awkward silence.

"Would you be willing to share?" Winslow asked.

"Yes," Cracked Pebble replied. "Why would we not?"

"Because it's your home. Because you were here first."

"It does not matter who was here first. It is our home. It is your home. If we do not fight, then we share."

"I feel like I'm missing something," Taldiss whispered.

"I think I get it," Enfield whispered back. "They don't view places possessively like we do. They're used to being there impermanently, to sharing their space with other creatures on the mountain. Maybe one group is there in summer and another in winter. Maybe it's more complex than that. But you can't get possessive if you're not always there to possess the thing."

"You can get defensive when newcomers attack you."

"Exactly. And you can feel it's your right to go where you've been going for years, for example, down into that mine."

While they whispered to each other, Winslow had

continued his conversation with Cracked Pebble. Now he turned to face the Evermores.

"It is agreed," he said. "We will share our space rather than keep fighting. It will take time to work out the details, as the two sides learn how each other lives, how we use this space, but if we can safely do so, we will live together until it's time for us to return home." He looked pointedly at Enfield. "Hopefully that will be soon."

The Evermores dismantled the barricades, and the rock people walked in, across the open ground, and into the mine's darkness.

"Well done, Enfield," Taldiss said loudly. "You got us out of a fight we couldn't win."

Other Evermores cheered for him.

"Well done, indeed," Winslow said. "You did well by starting that conversation."

"Thank you." Enfield shifted his weight to stop his good leg cramping up. "I wish I'd thought of it sooner."

"What now?" One of the Evermores asked, looking at Enfield.

"Yeah," someone else called. "How do we work out a way to share with creatures who could crush us by sitting down?"

More questions came, all directed at Enfield, who struggled to take them all in. The cold, the damp, and the ache were distracting him.

"We watch them," Winslow interjected, frowning. "We let them watch us. We speak slowly, and we listen carefully. I will assign someone to collect all of our observations and share new knowledge so we don't miss anything, and I will talk with Cracked Pebble to set out any rules we need. Understood?"

There were nods and sounds of assent.

"Good. Then please, head into the mine and get to know our new friends."

The Evermores headed eagerly into the darkness, leaving Winslow and Enfield alone on the broken defenses.

"You did well today," Winslow said, "but your ideas won't always work. Remember to talk to me first next time."

"I just thought that—"

"Remember who has the experience here, who is in charge."

"Yes, Winslow. Of course."

"We don't want the others to get confused about that. If leadership is unclear, actions become confused, and we become less effective."

"Very well. I'll try to talk to you next time."

"Don't try. Just do it." Winslow walked slowly through the rain toward the mine entrance. "Come, we should get to know the newcomers."

"Of course. I'll be there in a moment once I've warmed up my leg."

Once Winslow was gone, Enfield took a moment to look around the valley at the detritus of the fighting he'd ended. He'd done a good thing, and he was proud of it, so why did he feel like a naughty child who'd been told off?

He shrugged. His body was painful enough without letting tricks of the mind discomfort him too. Walking stick tapping on the rocky ground, he headed into the mine.

CHAPTER THIRTY-TWO

"I'm a little confused," Bart said, looking around the store. "This doesn't seem like a place where investors spend their time. Is an event here the best final push before our IPO?"

It was an entertainment store, one of two big multi-department ones in Mana Valley. This department was for video games and the systems to play them. There were also two departments for books, one for films and TV, one for recorded music, one for instruments, and several sections for crafts. This place catered to almost every source of entertainment a magical could imagine.

"Oh, Bart." Elethin shook her head. "If we want to impress potential investors, there's no point in appealing to them directly."

"Really?"

"Not right now. We've already done that part. They know about the IPO. They know all the arguments for buying our shares. What we have to do now is prove to them that those arguments hold up, that we're good value for money."

"How does any of this help with that?"

Across the store, on a raised platform, half a dozen people were sitting in comfortable chairs around a low table, all with game controllers in their hands. In the middle of the table sat an FDS, projecting their latest prototype game, an adventure story in which the players had to fight opponents and solve puzzles to get from level to level.

Fran was one of the players, excitedly grinning as she directed a troll around the table. Next to her was Cam, controlling a small wyvern, and three random customers picked out of the crowd to play this one level. Around the platform, other keen fans were waiting, hoping they'd get picked to play next.

While FDS fans were eager to try the new game, it was the sixth player who'd drawn in the crowds. Controlling the sword-wielding princess character was Heidi Trill, the golden-feathered Arpak who played Encanterel in *Orchard of Stars*. Half of the crowd might be dedicated gamers, but the other half were soap opera fans, watching wide-eyed as their favorite actress played games only a few feet from them. One of the other players was so distracted by her presence that he barely took part in the game.

Heidi squealed in excitement, the sound magnified by the store's speaker system.

"I've got the gem!" she exclaimed. "What do I do now?"

"That cave!" Cam called. "Take it there, quick, before the bad wizards get you."

Heidi's avatar raced across the table and dove into an illusion of a hole in the tabletop. With a flash, the words

"LEVEL COMPLETE" appeared in the air. The players sat back, and the crowd applauded.

"All right, who's next?" Fran asked as store staff ushered the volunteer players off the stage. Hands shot up in the front row.

"You see this?" Elethin said to Bart. "This is hype, and it's reaching a market that doesn't normally care about games. This time tomorrow, the *Orchard* message boards will be full of pictures of this event. Fans will rush out to buy FDSs and pre-order the game to play the same character Heidi did, so they can feel that little bit closer to her.

"Meanwhile, the gamers will place their pre-orders because the game looks cool. That in turn will get stories about us in the press: about this event, how fun it was, what clever marketing it was, how great the game looks, or how terrible it looks. There'll be hype. There'll be backlash. There'll be a backlash against the backlash. We will be everywhere. When the investors see this level of press attention…"

"Then the investors will leap on the IPO." Bart nodded. "Because instead of telling them that we're worthy of attention, we've shown it."

"Exactly." Elethin patted him on the head. "See, you can learn."

In her heels, Elethin was twice Bart's height, yet somehow she'd found a way to make him feel even smaller.

"For a woman whose job is to make us likable, you can be mean."

"Sorry." She shook her head. "I've had to lay off being rude to Gruffbar for a while. I suppose I'm letting it out on you."

"Apology accepted. Tell me, are we doing the same thing at the other store?"

"Oh, yes. Right now, Singar and Smokey are playing with one of the show's male leads, while Gruffbar manages another crowd like this one."

"Singar and Smokey? Are they really the people to make us likable?"

"Smokey has novelty value and the potential to become some sort of cute cat meme. Singar plays the hard case, but she can be funny when she's being a bitch, which is the perfect mode for gaming. Remember, we're after attention."

"Then why aren't you up there? Whatever your faults, you're the most glamorous face of our company."

"That's sweet of you to say, and it's why I'm not there. One thing we can't do if we want to run more events like this is to outshine the stars. That's why I had Smokey rig this game for the day."

"Rig it?"

"Oh, yes. Our actor friends are playing on an easier difficulty setting than the rest. They'll look like total winners, which will mean they go away and talk about how great the game is to all their fans."

"Isn't that cheating?"

Elethin laughed.

"All PR is cheating. If we followed the real logic of the market, all the consumers would know about products would be bare facts and reviews by neutral observers. My job is to cheat the system until we get the best sales and the biggest investors, and right now, I'm a good cheat."

There was another cheer as Heidi completed a tricky puzzle.

"One more level to go." Elethin glanced at her watch. "Come on, let's get closer so we can help manage the crowd when this finishes."

"You mean so you can fangirl at Heidi?"

"What can I say? I'm cheating the system to my advantage too."

They made their way around the crowd and got to the front with help from one of the store's burlier employees. Excitement grew around the table as the players worked together on the most complicated and exciting level of this demo.

"I've got the key!" one of the audience volunteers exclaimed, leaning in her seat as she sent her character racing across the game.

"I'll flip the sand timer," one of the other volunteers said. "Ready, Heidi?"

"I'm ready." Heidi leaned forward and her wings spread behind her, forming a golden screen that gave a glorious glow to her face.

"Now!" Fran said.

Suddenly, all the players were frantically tapping on the buttons of their controllers while something chaotic happened in the game area.

Bart was getting too old to follow these convoluted modern games, so instead, he watched the crowd. Most of them were cheering, some leaping up and down in excitement. There were phones out, taking pictures and videos. Several people held up signs telling Heidi how much they loved her or her TV character. Even the store's staff seemed to be enjoying themselves, despite the awkward task of managing the crowd.

Only one person didn't look like they were having fun. Near the front of the stage was a witch with a scowl on her face. Her hand was up her baggy sleeve, and she was toying with something there.

"Is that woman all right?" Bart tugged on Elethin's elbow to get her attention.

Elethin gave the witch a brief, dismissive look, then turned back to watching the game. "Probably annoyed that she didn't get to play. Or maybe her boyfriend's up there and looking too fondly at Heidi."

"I'm not so sure."

Bart started working around the front of the crowd, squeezing himself between spectators and the platform, trying to reach the witch. If something was upsetting her, as a representative of the company throwing this event, he felt like he should ask what it was.

He'd almost reached the witch when the players leaped to their feet, hammering their buttons harder than ever, and the crowd began to roar. It was hard to make progress with all these bodies pushing forward.

"We did it!" Heidi shouted and waved her controller in the air.

Above the table, the FDS projected fireworks and the words "YOU WIN!" The players high-fived each other. The crowd took more photos.

The witch drew a knife from her sleeve and shouted something that got lost in the bedlam. Alarmed, Bart pulled himself up onto the edge of the stage as the witch planted her foot there. She lunged at Heidi, knife outstretched.

Bart flung himself at the witch. Someone screamed. The two of them crashed into the table, which broke beneath the impact. They landed on the platform, and the FDS landed on Bart's head.

The witch kicked and slapped Bart. He flinched, expecting the knife to stab him any moment, but she'd lost it in the fall. Store staff dove in to restrain her.

"This is for Jason!" the witch screeched madly, staring up at Heidi. "I'll get you for what you did to him. I'll get you, I swear."

Security guards dragged her away while Heidi knelt by Bart and helped him to his feet.

"My hero." She hugged him tight. Then she took his hand, held it up high, and turned to face the crowd. "I might have played the hero today, but Bart here was a real hero, saving me from that attack."

A lot of phones were pointing their way and a couple of TV cameras. Bart looked around in bewilderment. Everything had happened so fast that he wasn't completely sure what had occurred. The fact that Heidi remembered his name was a bit of a surprise, given how briefly they'd met before, but acting did involve remembering lots of words and names.

She let go of his hand and knelt again, making it easier for the cameras to photograph them together. "Are you all right? You aren't hurt, are you?"

"I don't think so." Bart patted himself to make sure. "Can I ask a question?"

"Anything for my hero."

Bart blushed. "I'm sure I'm showing my ignorance here, but who is Jason?"

Now it was Heidi's turn to blush.

"My character's ex-lover on the show. She had him framed for fraud after they broke up, and he ended up dead. None of it's real, the actor moved on to play the detective in a prime time crime drama, but some of our fans, they can get a little, um..."

"Overinvested?"

"That's a nice way of putting it, yes."

"So I saved you from being murdered for something you didn't do to someone who doesn't exist?"

"Essentially, yes."

Bart laughed. "Well, I did join Fran's business for a more exciting life."

Lots of the waiting fans wanted autographs from Heidi, and some wanted them from the gnome who'd saved her. It took a good hour before the Mana Wave team could start packing away and getting ready to leave. Bart was helping disassemble the stage when Elethin strode over.

"Look at this." She held out her phone.

The screen was showing the front page of an entertainment site. It carried a story about Bart saving Heidi from a crazed stalker.

"They got my name wrong," he said as he scrolled down. "And my age. And my job."

"But they got the company name right." Elethin grabbed hold of his hand. "Don't you see, Bart? This is even better. Thanks to you, we're all over the news tonight. Ten times as many people will hear about today's events, the game, and Mana Wave.

"I've been calling some of the morning shows. Tomorrow, I'm taking you on TV, and Heidi with you. You can talk about risking your life to save a famous actress. Of course, you'll have to explain why we were here, which means explaining the company, while Heidi talks about how much she loves us and our game. This may be the best thing you've ever done for Mana Wave."

"I run all our finances! I make sure we turn a profit and pay the bills."

"Yes, and that's nice, but this gets us attention. One last push before the IPO." Elethin was smiling wider than he'd ever seen. "Well done, you little bean-counting hero."

CHAPTER THIRTY-THREE

Handar looked around the basement room. Something was wrong. Not only the fact that Julia was late for one of their regular sessions going through the prophecies. Something about the room. It took him a moment, with all those papers hanging on the walls, but when he realized what it was, his whole body tensed.

Some of the documents were missing—a selection of the older prophecies that Julia had set aside in a box near the end of the table. Some of her notes too, ones that he hadn't understood, but that seemed to be about magical theory. Had Julia taken them? If so, she should've talked to him first. After all, they'd agreed that nothing left the room, that this was too important to risk. If she hadn't, that was a whole other problem.

He stepped out into the corridor, the door thudding shut behind him, and pulled out his phone. There was no answer from Julia.

"Call me when you get this," he growled into her voice mail. "Something's up. I'll be looking for you."

He stalked down the corridor and up a stairwell to one of the company's security offices. A pair of uniformed guards sat watching a bank of monitors. One of them took his feet off the desk as Handar came in, and the other jumped to his feet.

"Mr. Ennis, we were just—"

"Where's Julia Lacy?" Handar snapped. "I need to talk to her."

One of the guards turned to a computer.

"According to the logs, she last used her pass on the ninth floor half an hour ago."

"Show me."

On one of the monitors, footage of a corridor wound back to the point where Julia walked into view with a box of documents under her arm, opened the door to a meeting room, and walked in. She was followed a moment later by another witch.

"Show me inside that room," Handar said.

One of the screens filled with dark static. The guards frowned.

"Sorry, sir," one of them said. "There seems to be a fault with that camera."

Handar frowned too. Julia was on his side, wasn't she? So why had this raised his fighting instincts?

"Do you want us to go up there and fix the camera?" the guard who'd had his feet up asked.

"I'll deal with it," Handar said. "You stay here."

He rode the elevator up to the floor they'd been watching and walked toward the meeting room. Despite his bulk, he could be quiet when he needed to. You didn't survive long in some war zones without that skill, and Handar had seen all sorts of war zones back in the day.

The door handle was cold as he took hold of it and turned. The door wouldn't budge. Locked. One of the advantages of running security was that no door stayed locked to you for long. He took out his master key card and swiped the security pad. With a soft *click*, the door opened, and Handar stepped through.

A dozen witches sat around a meeting table with runes carved into its top. Candles flickered in the center, letting out a smell like pine forests and summer rain. Most of the women had their hands outstretched, palms down against the table, fingertips touching those next to them.

Julia sat at one end of the table, her missing notes stuck to the wall behind her. At the opposite end sat Josie Bullworth, the young manager Julia was so fond of, reciting lines from one of the books he'd worked so hard to obtain. The air was full of magic and power swirling around the witches.

"What is this?" Handar closed the door behind him. He brought his hand around slowly toward the opening of his jacket.

The witches looked up, but at a signal from Julia, they kept their seats and kept chanting. Handar recognized all their faces from around the office.

"What's she doing here?" he added, pointing at Sylvia Dodd. "She was fired."

Julia brought her hands together, carefully tying off two strands of power, then got to her feet. "I'm sorry we didn't wait for you, Handar, but we needed to act quickly. Time is of the essence."

"What is this?" he repeated.

"The spell I've been working on, of course. The magic that all those prophecies were working toward."

"What's it do?"

"It channels magical power, redirects it so we can use it."

"What power?"

"Power that's about to flow through this building. That's why we needed to act now."

"Power the boss is summoning?"

"Exactly. His plans are coming to a head. He's about to carry out the key ritual, so if we're going to help him, it has to happen now."

"Help him…"

Handar slid his hand inside his jacket. Did Julia flinch at that? His fingers brushed over the grip of his gun, but he took out his phone instead. "Just gonna call the boss and check this fits his plan."

"I don't think that's a good idea," Julia said. "You could interrupt him at a critical moment. You wouldn't want to disturb his plans, would you?"

"His plans."

Handar looked around the room. He didn't know much about magic, couldn't have described what was going on here if he'd tried, but he had a good eye for when he was being lied to.

"Maybe you're right." He slid his hand back into his jacket to put the phone away. At the same time, his other hand brushed his forearm, activating the magic-repelling bracer he sometimes wore under his suit. Good thing he'd felt paranoid today. "Or maybe you're full of shit."

His hand emerged, gripping his gun, which he pointed at Julia's head.

"All of you, stop what you're doing right now."

"Don't stop," Julia snapped as the witches looked around in alarm. "No matter what, keep the ritual going."

Dodd started to get out of her seat, but another of the witches grabbed her wrist, and she sat. They all kept chanting, the sound rising, power flowing between them.

"You stop right now, or I will fire," Handar growled.

"No, you won't." Julia looked him in the eye. "We're friends."

Handar snorted. "I've killed people I'd called friends before when the job called for it. After pulling this, you ain't no friend of mine no more."

"I don't want to hurt you." She held her hands wide, palms open, no sign of her wand.

"That won't be a problem."

"Handar, you're making a mistake. Howard is going to be very angry when he finds out."

"Maybe. Or maybe you've been lying to me all along. Maybe you're stabbing our boss in the back. That's what this looks like to me."

"That's because you don't understand magic."

"Maybe. Or maybe it's because you're a liar. Now, I'm giving you until three, and—"

A suddenly flaring of light drew Handar's attention. The witches were glowing, all different colors as power streamed through them toward the end of the table. He only looked that way for a moment, but when he looked back, Julia had a wand in her hand.

Handar should've shot right then, but despite everything he'd said, he had a soft spot for Julia. In the second's delay before he pulled the trigger, she snapped a word he didn't know. The gun barked, and the air rippled in front of her as a magical shield deflected the bullet.

"I wish you hadn't done that," she said.

She waved her wand again. A spell shot at Handar, but he flung up his arm, and his bracer deflected the power.

"I forgot you had that," Julia said. "Do you really think you can win with it?"

"I'm gonna win with this." He leveled the gun and fired again. The bullets bounced off her protective field and punched through the wall at the side of the room.

Those bullets weren't the main point. As the field in front of Julia rippled, Handar charged. She got off another spell, which he dodged, then he slammed through the force field into her.

Julia was so light that it was like lifting a child. He bore her off her feet and into a wall. The room shook, and she grunted beneath the impact.

"Keep going," she groaned. "Don't break the spell."

"Break the spell, or I break her neck." Handar got his hand against Julia's throat and held her up, choking off her air supply. Her eyes bulged, and her face started to turn red. "I said stop."

Julia wheezed something, a fragment of a word. It was so little, but it was enough. Magic flowed from her wand where it was pressed against his belly, too close this time for the bracer to save him. Cold flowed across his body, so bitter and intense that it hurt. He pushed away from her and staggered back, ice falling from his legs as he struggled to keep them moving.

"Really, I didn't want to hurt you." Julia rubbed her neck as she stepped toward him, wand outstretched. "You're not the problem. Howard is. But if you can't see that, we'll have to take you out of the mix."

"You..." The ice was spreading across his body, frost forming on his suit. Despite the waves of numbness and pain, his grimace turned into a grin. She was so busy gloating that she'd come too close.

With half-numbed fingers, Handar grabbed Julia's wrist. The ice flowing through his hand froze it hard and tight in place as he twisted. The wand fell from her hand as he wrenched her arm up and pulled her close.

"Got you," he hissed.

A chair scraped back. Josie got to her feet, power still flowing through her. She continued her chant, but she'd passed the book in front of her to Sylvia Dodd. The other witches were chanting too, all different words, hands waving in different ways, but the noises, movements, and sounds made a pattern, one that felt like a wave bearing down on Handar.

"Stop that, or I'll break her arm." His breath frosted as the cold crept up his chest.

Josie held out her hands. Power flowed from her, a green glow heading for Julia.

"No, you don't." Handar turned and raised his empty hand, about to grab at Josie.

"Poor Handar," Julia said. "Always looking the wrong way."

Something jabbed his stomach. He looked down to see her wand, caught in her off-hand. Then there was another burst of icy magic, and words froze on his lips as the magic overwhelmed him.

Although he couldn't move, he could see and hear everything happening around him. Josie, still chanting, reached for his arm.

"No," Julia said. "Back to the circle. Don't waste that power."

She touched his hand with her wand and warmth ran through it. For a moment, his fingers defrosted, and she pulled her hand free. Then she tapped him again and the fingers re-froze.

Julia returned to the table, as Josie had done. Handar didn't know much about magic, but even he could tell that this was building toward a climax. Strands of power ran from the glowing witches down the table to where Julia sat. She closed her eyes and gasped as it ran across her and into her. Her body shone in every color of the rainbow, glittering sparks cascading from her every movement.

She opened her eyes and cupped her hands in front of her. It looked like she was catching something out of the air, a trickle as black and thick as oil. It flowed into her glowing hands and sat there, its surface rippling like water in the wind.

"We're ready," Julia said. "So is he."

Her voice joined the witches chanting, their voices soaring toward a note that would've made Handar groan in awe if he could've made a single sound. Then the magic settled and silence fell.

Still glowing, Julia got to her feet. The other witches were glowing too, but none as brightly as her. "Time to go before it's too late."

She stood in front of Handar for a moment, fingering her silver necklace and looking at him.

"I really am sorry. Maybe you can work with us when this is all done? The company still needs a head of security, but not for the next hour."

Then she headed out of the door, and her coven followed, leaving Handar alone, icy cold, staring at the aftermath of his defeat.

CHAPTER THIRTY-FOUR

Howard Phillips stood on the roof of Philgard's head office in the middle of a ritual circle. He'd had it marked out when the building was built, the shapes he would need embedded in the concrete along with crystals to help the power flow. It was all part of a plan years in the making. Now, at last, he stood in the center of the circle, ready to bring that plan to fruition.

It seemed strange to carry out the magic while still dressed as a human, still wearing his disguise of skin and cloth. That was part of the magic too, the lies he'd woven around himself. Like all the best nightmares, he was the grotesque hidden beneath the mundane.

When he burst through that skin at the height of his power, the magic would be complete. The thin skin between worlds would also split, and his nightmare realm would pour forth, first into Mana Valley, then through it, using all its magical technology as a conduit, into the world he really wanted: Earth.

He raised his hands, tentacles wriggling beneath the

skin, and called upon the magic he'd prepared. Across Mana Valley, it responded. From Watchmakers' Hall, from the riverside cemetery, from a hundred other places where he'd set devices and spells, power flowed. Stolen power, leached from the people there, their hopes and dreams, their darkest fears, the magic they used every day. Across the city, people shivered as unseen forces drew off part of their spirits.

Phillips grinned as the power came. Invisible to the people below, it poured across the rooftops, dark streams of magic flowing together into rivers, waves, then a tide of magic that poured over him and into him. It filled the grooves in the roof, turning the concrete circle into one of pure darkness, so deep that it sucked the light from the air. The runes around it filled with darkness, then shifted like snakes so the roof squirmed like a living thing. Crystals that had glittered in the sunlight turned as dark as night.

He spread his hands wide and sketched shapes in the air on either side. Each one was a circle of its own, a reflection of the dark shape on the floor. They were hazy for now, no more than a trickle of smoke tugged at by the breeze. Their power would come, forming the portals, one into this world and one out, two portals that would eventually become one, a tunnel straight from the nightmare realm to Earth. All his followers, all his pets, all his power would be unleashed.

Faint as they were, he felt the forces on either side of those circles—the strength of the nightmares, rich and dark. The weakness of Earth, its magic faltering. He hadn't made that happen, didn't know who was behind it, but it could hardly be better timed. The people there stood no chance.

Antennae on the roof helped him direct the power, weaving a network of magic that would hold up the portals, empower them, and guide the power he was drawing in. Why run a magitech firm if you weren't going to use the technology too?

Now came his masterstroke, the one he'd been dreaming of all this time. Magic no one could ever have carried out in any previous age. Magic that he'd waited centuries to perform, patiently anticipating the arrival of the right tool at the right time, for these foolish magicals to embrace their destruction.

He stepped out of the circle and placed his hands on the building's towering cellphone mast. Its gleaming girders turned black as the magic flowed.

In the back of her car, Mother Harball was on the phone. It was a Manaphone with the latest black market encryption software. Some of her competitors in other criminal gangs claimed Philgard itself made the software and illicitly released it to encourage people like them to use the phones. If that was true, it was a great scam. Even if it wasn't, this was great software, and the authorities hadn't yet managed to listen in on anyone using it.

"I don't care who's been watching you," she hissed. "You promised me that he'd be dead by yesterday, and I saw him this morning, still swaggering around the streets. You've got until tomorrow to…to…to…"

She felt strange all of a sudden. Terrible images flashed through her mind, visions of being grabbed by the Silver Griffins, of being gunned down by another gang, of her precious boys betraying her. The blackest of thoughts that usually only came in nightmares.

She felt weaker too, like something was being drawn from her, but she couldn't tell what. She clung to the phone, clutched it to the side of her head, and slid down her seat.

"Ma?" one of her burly guards said, looking at her in alarm. "Ma, what's wrong?"

"…all that, after these messages from our sponsors." Don Karelsky kept his grin up a moment longer, then let it slide as the light above the TV camera went from red to green. He pressed his hand against his eyes and drew a deep breath. He needed a drink, but he'd been dry for six days now. One more and he'd make it a week. Maybe this time he'd make it a month, and if he kept that up, maybe his producer would stop making him go to the meetings.

Maybe. Always maybe. He knew exactly how good a drink would taste.

He needed some distraction to get him through the ad break. For no reason that he was aware of, his Manaphone came to mind. He took it out of his pocket and unlocked the screen.

"You know you've only got two minutes, Don," his producer called from behind the cameras. "Don't get sucked into a game or another of your social media feuds."

"I know, I know," Don replied, waving dismissively. "I'm only checking my investments."

As he opened the app, a thought raced into his mind. A stock market crash, his wealth wiped out, his apartment repossessed, the house in the hills too, reducing him to a life like the little people. He shuddered at the thought.

Then came another. The thought of screwing up live on TV, humiliating himself in some way that the world could never forget or forgive. A career in tatters. Becoming an object of mockery for everyone.

These nightmare thoughts had never been far from Don's mind, but he'd always had the bottle to comfort him. Forgetting where he was, he pulled out his wand and cast a spell, trying to summon a drink, but his magic failed him. He waved his wand, but nothing came, and he stared at it, incredulous.

"Don?" his producer cried in alarm as Don's muscles went limp and he slid down his seat.

Gail Ortiz didn't use her Manaphone much. She wouldn't have got one for herself, but Fran had insisted on buying them for Gail and Raulo as a thank you for letting her start her business under Worn Threads. Raulo played with his occasionally, but Gail mostly kept hers in a drawer under the cash register, along with her knitting. She took the knitting out far more often.

For some reason, today, she felt an urge to see the phone. She took it out of the drawer and on her second attempt, remembered the password she'd used to lock it. The screen lit up, and she tapped an icon.

From nowhere, an image floated into her mind, the worst she could imagine: Raulo leaving her for another woman. She let out a wail of panic and looked up, but Raulo was still there, standing on the other side of the store, looking at his Manaphone. The sight of him, usually so reassuring, didn't help her now.

Other images flashed through her mind. Raulo hit by a car. Raulo crushed by a roll of carpet. Raulo becoming cruel and bitter, mocking her like the other kids used to on the playground all those decades ago. Tears rolled down her cheeks.

Gail didn't notice the magic being drawn out of her as she sagged into her seat, the Manaphone still open in her lap. Its screen had turned a deep black, like a hole in the world.

Howard Phillips let go of the signal tower. He didn't need the contact anymore. The stolen power flowed effortlessly through the airwaves, down the antenna, into him. Power from all across the city, magic and dread tangled into something dark and delicious. He laughed, barely able to contain it all. The whole thing was so potent, so tasty, so perfect, even better than he'd imagined.

He placed his hands in the center of the ritual circle and let the magic flow. It filled the circle and the air around him, flowing up into those outlines of portals he'd sketched. They became darker, more solid. Soon, the moment would come.

He looked down and frowned. Something was wrong. Around the edges of the runes, a thread of light surrounded the darkness. It glowed and glittered in a hundred different colors. There was a thread like it around the circle as well, and another around the portal to Earth.

"What is this?" he muttered, and touched the shining thread, then jerked back as it sent a jolt through him.

"This is me." Julia stood across the roof from him with a dozen other witches behind her. They all shone with a light like the power surrounding his darkness, but Julia glowed brightest. She almost seemed to be made of magic, and the air shimmered as she lifted her wand to point at him. "This is me taking control."

"You? Ha!" He laughed cruelly. "You can't control this. You couldn't even control the pitiful powers you were playing with before I found you. If you could, your brother wouldn't be dead."

A glimpse of darkness appeared in the light shining from her face, a single black tear running down her cheek. Julia's worst nightmare, and it was already real. The power that Phillips needed to control her.

Julia wiped that dark magic from her cheek and held it cupped in the palm of her hand.

"You think I can be so easily controlled?" she asked. "I've learned from you, Howard, for better and worse."

She chanted, and her hand glowed. The black power turned gray, then white, then into different colors as she absorbed it.

Phillips stared down at the black pool of power around

him. Strands of it were peeling away at the edges, being swallowed up by the witches' magic, his power turning from nightmares into something else.

"How are you doing this?" he snapped. "You don't have the power to do it."

"Oh, but we do." She gestured at the women behind her, chanting and waving their wands through the air. "Together, we are stronger. Together, we've taken control of the tools you set up here, these conduits you created. Your building. Your business. Your intricate web of lies and illusions. It's ours now."

"Not yet it isn't."

Phillips saw the moment teetering on the brink, the glorious power he'd summoned getting leached away. He wasn't done yet. He still controlled so much of it.

He raised his hand. Tentacles burst through the skin there, snatched up the nightmare power around him, and poured it into one of the portals. The stronger portal. The one he'd used so many times before. The one connecting him to his true home, his origins, and the things that gave him strength.

The shining strands around the portal shattered. It became deeper, blacker, a void in the air. He hadn't wanted to do this yet. It was a waste of strength, expending magic on a brief, small opening instead of saving it to make the great rip in reality, but it was his best chance.

Within that void, the boundary between worlds parted.

"Come to me," Phillips called.

A nightmare hound stepped out of the portal. Its claws scratched the surface of the roof. Fangs like broken glass gleamed as it stared at the witches and licked its lips. Another hound emerged behind it, then more.

"You're not the only one with help." Phillips relished the looks of dread on the witches' faces. "Let's see who's in control now." He pointed. "Kill them."

The bell above the door of Worn Threads rang as Fran skated into the carpet shop.

"Hi, guys," Fran called brightly. "I brought coffee and cake. It's time to talk about…"

Her words trailed off as she saw how Gail slumped in her chair, then noticed Raulo lying on the floor, his Manaphone close to his hand.

"Guys?"

The darkness of the phone's screen expanded, and something stepped out of it: a monstrous hound, midnight black, with eyes that shone like fire. It growled at Fran.

"Good doggy." She dropped her backpack and raised her hands. "I don't suppose you're here for a pat on the head?"

The nightmare hound bared its teeth and charged.

CHAPTER THIRTY-FIVE

Josie stared past Julia at the black hounds standing behind Howard Phillips. The very sight made her heart hammer like it was trying to burst out of her chest and run away. Howard had his hand outstretched, black magic flowing from it, so thick that it seemed like tendrils of night had replaced his fingers.

"What is this?" She wanted to ask something more eloquent, more pointed, but her mind couldn't wrap itself around the challenge.

"Fuuuuuck," Sylvia drawled. "This is…"

"Worse than anything you ever imagined was happening here?"

"Yes, and I imagined some awful things after he fired me."

"So now what?"

"Now we fight," Sylvia said. "What else can we do?"

"Hold them off," Julia said firmly and clearly. "Keep them busy as long as you can. I'll drain his power, bring this nonsense to an end."

Raw power throbbed from her as she spread her arms wide, and Josie felt the tides of magic flowing across the rooftop, the light and the darkness, horror and hope. The animal part of her brain wanted to run, even if that meant flinging herself off the rooftop and begging the ground to save her. Still, she was made of better stuff than that.

Josie walked past Julia, and the others followed. Already, they were casting spells, flinging up shields and wards, building their defenses. The hounds charged at them, and they flung magic at the creatures. Josie knocked one back with a spell she normally used to move dishes around the apartment, then used the same spell to spin another hound around. She'd taken some magical self-defense classes, but nothing had prepared her for this.

"Go for the legs," Sylvia said. "If they can't move, they can't get to us."

"Agglutino," Josie chanted, and a thick clump of glue appeared around the forward feet of one of the beasts, sticking it to the roof. Its momentum carried it forward, and its face slammed into the concrete, smashing those terrible teeth.

She was about to turn her attention to the next hound, but the first one wasn't contained yet. With a ripping sound, it pulled itself free, leaving behind fur and skin. It howled as it planted its tender feet on the rough rooftop and bared those broken teeth, dribbling acid that hissed as it splashed down around its claws.

"Oh, no," Josie whispered, taking a trembling step back. "That is really not good."

Fran lurched sideways as the hound charged. She still had her skates on and managed to keep her feet under her. She pushed off as hard as she could, racing down the aisle between piles of carpets, wheels whirring beneath her.

"Good doggy," she called as the hound ran after her, smashing carpet rolls aside. "Do you want to play a game?"

She knew how insane this was, drawing the beast on, but she wanted to keep its attention off Gail and Raulo and to keep it from spotting the door down to where her employees were. Who knew what carnage it could cause in the basement, which was packed full of people with only one way out.

She grabbed the end of a shelf and used her momentum to carry her around the corner. The jolt of her weight pulling on it shook the shelf, and rolls of carpet fell onto the hound. It shredded one, leaped over another, and kept coming after her.

There was a sturdy craft table with a tape measure and a yardstick on it for when Raulo was cutting pieces of carpet into special shapes. Fran grabbed the stick and waved it.

"Want to play fetch?" she called and flung it.

The hound leaped and caught the stick between its teeth, chomping it to pieces. The creature swallowed splinters without any sign of pain or distress.

"How about this one?"

Fran snatched a carpet sample as she passed and skimmed it across the room. This time the hound ignored it, intent on pursuing her.

"All right then, let's have another lap." Fran rounded a corner, heading back down the first aisle. She turned and skated backward, watching where she'd come. "How about a little magic this time?"

As the hound rounded the corner, Fran unleashed a blast of light straight into the darkness of its face. The power was the brightest she'd ever summoned, and it left the creature howling, flailing, blinded, and raging.

Skating around the corner and past the table again, Fran snatched up a craft knife.

"I hate to do this, but…"

She skated around the corner and launched herself into the air at the back of the blinded beast. The knife blade sank into its neck. The hound writhed and squirmed, driving the blade deeper, then dropped to the floor.

Fran stood and wiped her hands on a carpet sample. "Urgh, I'm glad that's over."

A moment later, something howled out in the street. "Or not."

One of the hounds lunged at Josie. She twisted aside, its teeth missing her by millimeters. Light burst from her wand, making the beast blink, and she brought her knee up under its chin. There was a crunch, and the beast took a stumbling step sideways, but it was still on its feet.

Josie twisted her wand through the air as she cast another spell. Colored ribbons appeared, wrapping themselves around the hound. It wasn't much, but they might tangle the creature for a moment, and she had to work with the spells she knew.

"Use the power the ritual gave you," Sylvia called as she

used a club of pure magic to fight off a hound.

"What if Julia needs it?" Josie replied.

"She's not going to get anything from us if we wind up dead."

She was right. Josie looked at her hands, which were pulsing with magical energy. She raised them, channeled the power, and pointed it straight at the hound. The creature ripped itself free of the ribbons and stalked toward her, claws clicking on the concrete.

"Eat this," Josie exclaimed.

A bolt of pure magic shot from the end of her wand. It hit the beast in the head, knocking it back. Smoke billowed from the wound as she followed it with another and another, each making the hound growl in pain as she drove it across the rooftop. She aimed one last blast low, catching it on the belly and flinging it off the side. The hound howled as it fell.

Josie stared in disbelief at her wand. Had she really done that? She felt like a hero out of an action movie. This was amazing!

A mess of fur and claws slammed into her, knocking her over. It pinned her to the roof, her body pressed beneath the weight of a hound, except for her head, which hung over the edge. Her wand, knocked from her hand, tumbled through the air, becoming a speck as it headed for the street far below.

The hound opened its mouth wide. Teeth torn from her deepest nightmares split into two uneven rows, like the edges of broken bottles, then lowered toward her neck. Caught between having her throat torn out or falling to her death, Josie screamed at the top of her lungs.

"Help!"

The shop bell rang as Fran shot out into the street. Across the road, magicals were clustered around a bus stop. Several of them lay on the ground, a pool of darkness forming in the space between their fallen Manaphones. Another nightmarish hound stood nearby, a mad glint in its eyes.

The traffic in the street had stopped with some vehicles bumper-to-bumper or dent-to-dent. Drivers cowered in their footwells or leaped out and ran for their lives.

"Hey!" Fran shouted, trying to get the hound's attention away from the magicals at the bus stop. "Over here!"

The creature didn't look her way. It had plenty of options right in front of it.

Fran pulled out her dummy wand and waved it around her head. High shrieking like an alarm sounded from her. Now the hound looked around.

"That's it," Fran bellowed through the piercing noise. "Over here."

The hound advanced on her, trampling over the hoods and trunks of steam wagons, which buckled under its weight.

"I've got something to show you," Fran said. "Ready?"

The hound had almost reached her. It growled.

Fran raised the wand and fired a bright light beam as she'd done in the store. The hound howled and leaped forward into a blind attack. Fran sidestepped and held out her hand, fingers spread, calling for whatever weapon lay nearby. There was a crash as a baseball bat hurtled through the windscreen of a car and into her hand.

"That'll do nicely." Fran tossed aside the dummy wand, and the clatter of its landing drew the hound. It turned away from Fran, who gripped the bat with both hands and slammed it into the back of the creature's head once, twice, three times. Her strength grew with each blow and the thrill of battle.

Was this how it felt to be her father? What drew him to hunting grounds and war zones?

One last blow and the beast lay still.

"Phew." Fran bent to pick up her dummy wand. She might still need that.

A howl sounded from around the corner, and another hound charged into the street. It looked at her and licked its lips.

"Just try it." Fran hefted the bat.

Then a mass of chains shot out from another side street, wrapping themselves around the hound and bringing it to the ground. A group of Silver Griffins appeared, flinging more spells at the hound to keep it down.

The lead Griffin looked at Fran with her wand and her borrowed baseball bat, then at the hound she'd already dealt with.

"You did that?" the Griffin asked.

"Yep." Fran beamed. "Not bad for an amateur, right?"

"Come with us," the Griffin said. "We need every wand we can get."

Josie pressed her hands against the hound's throat, desperately trying to hold it back, to keep those terrible teeth away from her throat. As she pushed, her head tipped back, and her view filled with the dizzying drop below her, the people like ants in the street so far away. The hound's body and her wriggling pushed her further, shoulders hanging over the edge.

There was a flash, and the hound fell, knocked past Josie over the edge. Its claw caught her as it passed and dragged her over the edge. She opened her mouth to scream, but a cushion of air caught her. She could've cried in relief as gentle magic pulled her onto the rooftop and set her down on her knees.

Julia was standing over her, bright with the magic that flowed from every inch of her skin.

"Thank you," Josie croaked, "but shouldn't you be fighting him?"

"I couldn't let you die." Julia sounded so sincere it hurt. "And I need your power. What I have isn't enough."

Josie looked around. There were still plenty of hounds on the rooftop and tendrils of magic shooting out from Howard Phillips, whipping at the witches. Several of the coven had been knocked out or were being pushed back toward the roof's edge. Giving up any power now meant leaving herself vulnerable, exposed to a terrible attack. Not helping meant they might never win.

"Here." She raised her hands and let the power of the ritual flow out of her into Julia. "I trust you. Protect us. Stop this."

"Thank you."

Julia whirled, glowing brighter than ever, and strode to

the center of the roof. Bright magic flowed around her, waves of it that crashed against the darkness Phillips had summoned. With each new surge of her power, more of his was carved off, dark magic turning into light. Julia was absorbing it, her presence growing, and with each moment, Phillips looked smaller, weaker.

"No," he screamed, sinking to his knees. "You can't do this. I'm in charge. Do you hear me? This is my company. This is my power."

"It was." Julia stood over him, an avatar of light, and laid a hand on his head. A cage flowed down around him, light and dark wound together, trapping him in place. "Now it's ours."

The cage bars touched the roof in the pool of oily black magic Phillips had summoned. That power drew inward, flowing up into Julia, rippling across her. With one last howl, the remaining hounds fell to the concrete, then vanished. Julia snapped her fingers and the two portals that hung in the air, one substantial and one still hazy, disappeared. Calm and quiet finally fell.

The witches gathered around Phillips, the injured held up by their friends.

"Did we do it?" Josie asked. "This isn't how I imagined it would end."

"We did it," Julia said. "Thanks to all of you. And now..."

She sank to one knee and touched the rooftop. The power flowed from her, and Josie felt it running into the building. The others did the same. Their bright glow faded, but Josie felt something below, powerful and hopeful.

"Hold on to a little of that power," Julia said. "You'll all need it for what comes next. Josie?"

"Here."

Julia touched Josie's shoulder, and some of the magic that Josie held before returned. Not as much as she'd carried out here onto the roof, but more than she'd ever known in the past.

"You've earned it," Julia said. "Now use it well."

"What was this all about?" Josie looked around at the rooftop that had been a battlefield. "What was he doing here?"

"It doesn't matter," Julia said. "What matters is what we do next."

Sylvia Dodd kicked the cage holding Howard Phillips. "This is what I call a hostile takeover."

Fran stood in the middle of the street, a dented baseball bat in one hand and her dummy wand in the other. She'd lost a wheel off one of her skates, and there was a long scratch down her arm. Her clothes had torn, her muscles ached, and she had no idea where in the city she was.

She'd never felt more alive.

"Where did those hounds go?" she asked one of her new Silver Griffin friends.

"No idea," the Griffin admitted. "I'm just glad they're gone."

Fran looked around. The streets were a mess, full of injured people, damaged vehicles, and the glass of broken store windows. She should be glad that it was over, but she had to admit, she would've liked a little more of the fighting.

CHAPTER THIRTY-SIX

There was a *pop* as the cork flew from the bottle and a cheer from the crowd. Standing on a table in the middle of the new Mana Wave office, still missing half its furniture and even a couple of walls, Fran looked around her with a broad smile while champagne ran down her fingers and dripped onto her bright yellow shoes. She took a sip from the bottle and giggled as bubbles got up her nose, then giggled again as the champagne fizzed over and dribbled across her chin.

"Okay, Okay." She wiped her face and handed the bottle down to Elethin. "Enough laughing at me. There's more champagne to come, so you can all make yourselves look silly."

That raised more cheers. Almost everybody in the company was there—workers from the old office who hadn't moved over yet, ones who'd started in the new place, staff from the factories. Even some of the moving team she'd invited to join them in a fit of enthusiasm.

Of course, the original team was all there. Elethin

looked as elegant as ever. Gruffbar searched for a drink that wasn't champagne. Singar and Smokey dismantled a smart printer to see how its control system worked. Bart made sure that everyone was comfortable and had refreshments.

There were guests as well. Her mom, Cam, Gail and Raulo, some of Smokey's political pals, even Heidi Trill and a couple of her colleagues from *Orchard of* Stars were here. It was quite a crowd and quite an excited one.

"As you've all heard, the IPO was a huge success," Fran called, and the hubbub subsided as people strained to hear what she was saying. "We have the funding we need to take this company forward into the next year of operations and beyond, to keep building better, more exciting gadgets, developing cool new software, and generally doing the most awesome, creative work we can. I am so proud of you guys. Give yourselves a big cheer."

That applause went on a while longer, with whooping and hollering and glasses *chinking*.

"Don't make me use this to make myself heard." Fran waved her wand. There was laughter, and the noise subsided again. "Thank you! I have some more good news. It's now official. We've sold our millionth copy of the Fun Delivery System, which is, like, staggering to me. Given how young this company is, how new that product is, to have reached this point is just, I mean, wow!

"This company started as a dream I had, when I wanted out of my crummy office job, working for a boss I didn't respect. Now I'm providing you with crummy office jobs, and I'm the boss you don't respect. Isn't it amazing how the world comes around?"

The laughter was good-natured, mixed in with people shouting about how wrong she was. Fran blushed.

"Anyway, that's why we're celebrating tonight, to mark two big milestones for the company. None of it would be possible without you. You're helping me live my dream, which is the most awesome thing a magical could want. So thank you again, from the bottom of my heart. Here's to you and the next big step for Mana Wave."

"To Mana Wave!" Everybody raised their glasses and cheered.

Fran climbed off the table. Around her, the party was starting as a DJ spun up his decks, and the disco lights came on. Caterers emerged from the elevators, pushing trolleys of food.

"Do you think that was okay?" Fran asked.

"It was perfect," Cam said. "Right, Elethin?"

"I told you that you didn't need me to write it," Elethin said. "Of course, I was right."

"It seemed a bit rambling in places, like I could maybe have—"

"Fran, sweetheart, it was a delight." Elethin took a sip of champagne. She looked pleasantly surprised. "Gosh, we didn't go for the cheap stuff, did we?"

"That wouldn't be a great way to celebrate," Fran said.

"I couldn't agree more." Elethin glanced around. "Now excuse me, there are some actors here somewhere, and the glamor of spending time with celebrities never wears off."

Fran turned her attention to Cam. "Was I good?" she asked. "You're not just saying that?"

"You were. Everything you've done here is amazing."

"Thanks. I couldn't have done it without your support."

"I haven't been much support lately."

"No, but I knew you'd be back, which was support in itself." She kissed him. "I wish that Josie could've made it."

"She did. Look."

The caterers parted, and Josie emerged from the elevators. She was dressed almost as well as Elethin, in a matching skirt and jacket with a shimmery blouse and delicate gold jewelry.

"You're here!" Fran rushed over to her. "Yay!"

"I wouldn't have missed it for the world." Josie hugged her roommate.

"You almost missed it for work."

"I will admit, I was starting to wonder if I would get stuck, but when the others realized that I was missing something important to a friend, they insisted that I should go."

"It sounds like things are getting better at Philgard."

"They are."

"Thanks to having you near the top, I bet."

Josie laughed. "The others do more than me, but I feel immensely privileged to be there. I'm learning so much and taking on a senior management role at my age, it's..."

"It's like me selling a million game systems. It proves that we can do anything we set our minds to."

"Yes, it does." Josie grabbed a glass of champagne from a passing waiter. "Here's to us."

Fran never got tired of toasting, especially when she could enjoy the bubbles of sparkling wine.

"Is everybody at your company okay?" she asked. "I mean, after the incident."

Josie looked down at her glass. "A few people were hurt, but we didn't lose anyone."

"That's great! I heard from the Silver Griffins that the attacks by those big scary dogs were most intense around your office, so I worried that they might have gotten someone."

"Not that I know of."

"There's this conspiracy theory online that the hounds ate Howard Phillips, and that's why he hasn't appeared in public since."

Josie laughed, but it wasn't a very convincing one. Fran started to wonder if talking about this might be a bad idea. She'd relished fighting off the hounds, but from what little Josie had said, her friend had been through a more troubling experience—troubling enough that she wouldn't tell Fran the details.

"I'm sorry, I'll shut up about this," Fran said.

"No, it's okay. We can't pretend it didn't happen, can we?"

"No. Crazy that no one knows what caused it, as well."

"Yeah, crazy." Josie downed her drink, then waved her glass. "I'm going to find another of these. Catch you on the dance floor later?"

"Of course!"

"Fran, seriously, congratulations. I'm so proud of you."

Beaming wider than ever, Fran worked through the crowd, accepting congratulations, thanks, and handshakes. She grabbed a tray of mini pizzas from the caterers and skipped over to where Singar and Smokey were still playing with the dismantled printer while Bart looked sternly at them, his arms folded.

"You understand that this isn't ours, don't you?" Bart said. "We have it on rental. If you damage it, that will cost us extra."

"We're not going to damage it." Smokey poked his head into the compartment where the ink cartridges went. "If anything, we'll make improvements."

"That's not how the suppliers will see it."

"Then take the cost out of my budget." Singar pried open another panel. "Figuring out how other people's machines work is part of research and development, right Fran?"

"Don't drag me into this," she said. "I only came to deliver treats."

She set the tray on the floor so Smokey could easily reach, and took one of the mini pizzas for herself. It turned out to be almost as tasty as the champagne, but she was willing to admit that might have been the alcohol and her empty stomach talking.

"We've come a long way, haven't we?" she said to Bart. "I mean, from whizzing around the skate park, you encouraging me in my business while I helped you stay on your wheels."

"We have. I can almost do a salchow jump now."

"Really?"

"Almost. On a good day."

"That's fantastic, Bart."

"Thank you."

Elethin and Gruffbar approached, caught up in their familiar bickering.

"…not saying you should shave it all off. Just cut it into a new shape. Something smarter."

"I like my beard how it is, and I'm not going to let you talk me into some style that makes me look like an idiot."

"You don't need me to make you look like an idiot. Those awful biker leathers do the job all on their own."

"I love my leathers."

"That's why you need fashion advice."

"You guys!" Fran waved them closer. "Look at this, the old gang together. Isn't it great?"

"It could be worse," Elethin admitted.

"You mean you could be back in prison?" Gruffbar asked.

"Your words, not mine. I've made peace with my past."

"You mean you've scared it off."

"How better to keep things peaceful?"

"While you're here," Fran said before they could find a new thread to their banter. "I wanted to say a personal thanks to you all. We've done great things together, and I'm sure we'll do more."

"We are pretty awesome," Smokey said.

"And awesomely pretty." Elethin tugged Gruffbar's beard. "Despite all this."

"I love you guys." Fran flung her arms wide. "Come on, group hug."

Elethin rolled her eyes, and Gruffbar snorted, but no one resisted as Fran and Bart brought them in together.

"This is the best," Fran said, choking with emotion.

Gruffbar's phone buzzed. "Thank the deep mines." He withdrew from the group.

Pulling the phone from his pocket, he walked away from the others and around the corner into a quiet corridor where the party music was less intrusive. All alone, he answered the call. "What's up, Vander? Busy evening at the courthouse?"

"Thought you'd like to know, we've had a new case come in that relates to Mana Wave."

The tone of the court clerk's voice sobered Gruffbar up faster than any amount of coffee.

"What sort of case?" he asked.

"Civil. Someone's suing you guys. I've only seen the initial documents, but this thing looks well-funded. Someone's taking a proper run at you."

"To the deep with them. We've got a great team. We can fight it."

"I hope you're right. I wouldn't want anything to delay the release of that ax crafting game. Anyway, it's not official yet, paperwork won't reach you for a few days, but I wanted to give you a heads-up."

"It's appreciated, thanks. I'd better go tell the boss."

Gruffbar put his phone away and headed back to the party. To his relief, the group hug was over, but the team was still standing around chatting while Bart refilled their glasses.

"Anything exciting?" Fran asked. "It must be an important call to drag you away from this."

Gruffbar looked at her, then around at the festivities. He ought to tell them, but he didn't want to spoil the big evening. Besides, it wasn't like he knew any details yet.

"Just a friend from the courthouse phoning with gossip," he said. "Nothing to worry about."

Elethin looked at him with one eyebrow raised. He gave her the smallest nod. They could talk later and start planning the PR to get ahead of this, whatever it was. For now, what mattered was the party.

Across the room, bright lights were flashing.

"Dancing time!" Fran exclaimed, flinging her hands up. "Who's with me?"

"Always," Singar said. "They'd better play some rock this time."

"It's our party. We can have whatever music we want." Fran ran across the room, waving her glass of champagne. "It's time to celebrate the best magitech company in two worlds."

Get sneak peeks, exclusive giveaways, behind the scenes content, and more. PLUS you'll be notified of special **one day only fan pricing** on new releases.

Sign up today to get free stories.

Visit: https://marthacarr.com/read-free-stories/

AUTHOR NOTES - MARTHA CARR

APRIL 6, 2022

These past few years have been tricky. I'll hold here for a moment for the guffawing and eye rolling. I know, it's an understatement. Our moorings were ripped out from under us as a collective.

And, just when we think we know what's coming next – there's a plot twist. Never ending plot twists. Have aliens invaded yet? (Anyone remember that the DoD said they have evidence of something strange – and we barely blinked? That's how much weirdness there has been.)

It's all wearing me out, and this time a nap is not going to do it.

But there is something to be gained from having the world upend itself repeatedly.

We become willing to change. It's the motivation behind the phenomenon in this country of people quitting to get a better job or at least something they love to do. It's happening en masse across lots of different types of jobs. Why now? Why so many?

Sure, there are a lot of reasons to want to do it but at

some point – the tipping point – there has to be a primary reason. Here's my stab at it.

If everything I counted on is shifting then letting go of what is, what I have and thought I could rely on, is not as much of a sacrifice. I become willing.

Willing is the key factor in all change. Without it, I'll stop at the first roadblock and tell you why it can't work. I'll come up with what appear to be very reasonable arguments and go back to what I already have. But with it, I will plow on through to see what happens next. With a snout full of willingness, I will let go of having to know the future and keep going.

And often, in the middle of an endless storm is where a lot of us discover that magic deep inside of us and we become willing.

But how do we navigate what comes next?

I have two simple tools to get you through whatever comes next. It's two questions, actually and you can use them for the rest of your life.

First one is, What do I want? It's the most important question there is. Not what you want for someone else and not what you should or ought to be doing. What do I want?

It's not easy to answer at first but keep asking it. The answers will start coming. Try out a few, figure out what you liked and what you didn't and refine your answers.

Okay, second one is, Do I like the consequences? This takes everyone else's opinion out of it – the subjective good and bad of it all – and replaces it with the outcome. Did I like the outcome?

No, then make some changes. Yes, then keep heading down that road.

It takes learning to trust in myself to pull it off and some days that can seem like a tall order, but it's worth it. The more I can follow these two simple questions and bring along my willingness, the more I can build a life that is uniquely suited to me. My personal definition of happiness is to find that life. I'll be in my garden writing if someone needs me. More adventures to follow.

AUTHOR NOTES - MICHAEL ANDERLE

APRIL 5, 2022

London, England

Thank you for not only reading this book but these author notes as well! Before I go into any of my personal… issues, I want to thank you for following us w/ the Evermore series!

Dammit – Jetlag made Mike its Bitch…

So, I'm in London getting ready for the London Book Fair. The second major book event (not including 20Booksto50k™) I'll have spoken at since the COVID restrictions eased.

I had to attend an 8:00 AM breakfast meeting downstairs. That we didn't need to go to another location was a nice change of pace.

It meant I could sleep late, right? No.

I couldn't sleep at all. I'm used to Pacific Standard Time, and I'm presently about eight hours ahead of where my body WANTS to be. So, I think I might have gotten about one and a half hours of sleep last night, all told, and I just called it quits about 6:30 this morning and got up to get ready.

Judith and I met our contact (sounds so clandestine to say it that way) and talked shop until 9:15 AM. We went on over to the Olympia Center (a block and a half from where we are staying) and dealt with getting in line, getting our badges, etc.

By the time we figured out where I needed to be for the panel I was sitting in on, we had an hour to kill.

It was SUCH a hard hour! I was sleepwalking, trying my best not to randomly bump into other conference attendees like marbles on a Hungry Hungry Hippo game. We waited in a huge line for a can of Coke™ (yeah!) and made our way back to the Author HQ and the ALLi (Alliance of Independent Authors) event with Joanna Penn as the host, Orna Ross (Founder of ALLi), and me talking about the new Creator Economy and the importance and still-vibrant opportunities for self-published authors.

It was a fun hour. I had NO problem staying awake for the panel or most of the business lunch right after… Until 1:45. We went back to the room, and ANY horizontal surface started to look good.

Scrunchy small couch? I can hang my legs over the edges, I'm sure.

Hard-as-hell floor with no carpet padding? All good. I figure I won't fall off the furniture that way.

Stay awake for the next meeting at 3:00? *I hate my life.*

I did make it to the meeting, and I finished like the brave soul I am. I would say Hell Week has nothing on me, but that's BS. I'd wash out of the military effort by midnight the first night.

Military Instructor: "You will tell us EVERYTHING you know, or we will not let you sleep!"

Me: "So, I tell you what I know, and I can sleep…right?"

Military Instructor: <blink…blink> "Uh, yeah."

Me: "Ok, on Monday…"

I finally have figured out my issue with all of the jet lag.

I'm just too old for this shit...

I hope you have a fantastic week or weekend. Talk to you in the next story!

Michael

BOOKS BY MARTHA CARR

Other Series in the Oriceran Universe:

THE LEIRA CHRONICLES
CASE FILES OF AN URBAN WITCH
SOUL STONE MAGE
THE KACY CHRONICLES
MIDWEST MAGIC CHRONICLES
THE FAIRHAVEN CHRONICLES
I FEAR NO EVIL
THE DANIEL CODEX SERIES
SCHOOL OF NECESSARY MAGIC
SCHOOL OF NECESSARY MAGIC: RAINE CAMPBELL
ALISON BROWNSTONE
FEDERAL AGENTS OF MAGIC
SCIONS OF MAGIC
THE UNBELIEVABLE MR. BROWNSTONE
DWARF BOUNTY HUNTER
ACADEMY OF NECESSARY MAGIC
MAGIC CITY CHRONICLES
ROGUE AGENTS OF MAGIC

OTHER BOOKS BY JUDITH BERENS

OTHER BOOKS BY MARTHA CARR

<u>JOIN THE ORICERAN UNIVERSE FAN GROUP ON FACEBOOK!</u>

BOOKS BY MICHAEL ANDERLE

Sign up for the LMBPN email list to be notified of new releases and special deals!

https://lmbpn.com/email/

For a complete list of books by Michael Anderle, please visit:

www.lmbpn.com/ma-books/

CONNECT WITH THE AUTHORS

Martha Carr Social

Website: http://www.marthacarr.com

Facebook: https://www.facebook.com/groups/MarthaCarrFans/

Michael Anderle Social

Website: http://lmbpn.com

Email List: http://lmbpn.com/email/

https://www.facebook.com/LMBPNPublishing

https://twitter.com/MichaelAnderle

https://www.instagram.com/lmbpn_publishing/

https://www.bookbub.com/authors/michael-anderle

Made in the USA
Middletown, DE
02 November 2022

13961939R00210